THE VAMPIRE INSIDE Me

LIZ HSU

The Vampire Inside Me. Copyright © 2021 by Liz Hsu.

Edited by Katherine Locke and Rachel Lynn Solomon. Cover by Sumo Design. Interior Book Design by Break Through Author.

Published by Li-Mei Publishing, 2886 12 Mile Road, P.O. Box 721414, Berkley, MI 48072-9998. For information, visit www.lizhsu-books.com.

ISBN: 978-1-7365434-0-5

LI-MEI PUBLISHING

To my lupies (and all those chronically sick), you are not alone! We deserve to love and be loved—and have our love stories told.

To my mom and dad, who supported me emotionally and financially during the most difficult period of my life.

To my Matty, ti voglio benissimo!

To my husband, writing this made me cry so much. How did I get so lucky to find someone who loves me as I am and still wants to be my best friend, travel buddy, and forever wedding date? Wo ai ni!

AUTHOR'S NOTE...

The romance and story are fictional. Liz has five diagnosed autoimmune diseases, Raynaud's, Sjogren's, Systemic Lupus Erythematosus (SLE), Pulmonary Arterial Hypertension (PAH), and Primary Biliary Cholangitis (PBC). The flashbacks and medical issues all reflect real medical experiences of hers. Please note autoimmune diseases presentations, symptoms, and long-term prognosis vary widely. She was diagnosed with most between 2008-2009. Luckily, medicine, treatments, and long-term prospects are always improving. All names of characters, medical professionals, and locations have been changed and/or are fictional.

One

January 5

I shifted uncomfortably on the exam table. Without warning, my barking cough came barreling out of my chest again. The deep, wet sound finally stopped, and I struggled to catch my breath for several minutes. Even after I was done coughing, I was still panting.

I'd been sick a lot in the past three years, from strep throat to bronchitis, and had even dislocated my ribs twice due to coughing just last year, but I'd never had a cough like this before. It sounded just like a seal—*bark, bark, bark*—not at all like my normal cough, which was why I was here instead of in class for my first day of graduate school.

I frowned at the cream-colored wall, struggling and failing to find relief. I didn't even want to be *here*, in Atlanta, for graduate school. I'd been accepted into The George Washington University, my dream school, for a Master's in Economics. It would have given me easy access to an internship at the International Monetary Fund (IMF), my dream job. I'd been lucky to live in Europe for the past several years, but there was so much of the world I wanted to see—no, not just see but explore, understand, and interact with.

The cough ripped through me again, my breath coming out in raspy gasps. *This* was why I was fucking here. This was why my ex, Alessandro, had cheated on me. I couldn't stay healthy for two weeks in a row. I couldn't even start graduate school on the scheduled start date. No—of course I'd be sick. I didn't want to go to grad school at Georgia State or to live at home, but I needed help. Something was wrong with me. There had to be. No one should be sick this much.

I shifted again against the wall, my breath still heavy, as comfort eluded me. Holding my body upright was a struggle, but if I lay down, I couldn't breathe. I hadn't been this exhausted in a long time, if ever.

My ears perked up as the exam room door opened.

"Lucia," Dr. Steinberg said softly. His gray eyes traveled over me, slowly cataloging everything. He had an analytical brain and had studied medicine at Harvard. He was the smartest and most considerate person I knew. Maybe it was also because he pronounced my name correctly, *Lu-chi-ah*. I was half-Italian, not Spanish, so most people said it wrong.

I smiled despite it all. I had a deep affection for Dr. Steinberg, who'd seen me off and on since I was fifteen. He'd even had me tested for Sjogren's last year when I thought I was losing my mind over how dry my mouth was and the fact that my eyes couldn't open in the morning without eye drops, or that they'd get painful scratches due to dryness. I'd tested positive and had started medicine for it that week. I wished *he* was my rheumatologist.

Julia, his PA, entered behind him and my shift to acknowledge her started the barking cough again. When I finished, I was more aware of Dr. Steinberg's concerned gaze and wondered why Julia was in the room too. Normally, I just saw him.

"Is it pneumonia?" I tried to joke. My trip to the chest X-ray had just about killed me. It was just down the elevator and through a hallway maybe three hundred feet long, but I'd had to stop about every ten feet to catch my breath.

Julia and Dr. Steinberg shared a look. "Lucia, it's not pneumonia," he said gently. "We need to do a few more tests, but I am going to be admitting you to the hospital. Can I see your ankles?" He stopped to feel them. "Do you have any other symptoms besides the fever, fatigue, and shortness of breath?"

I nodded weakly. "My shoulder is killing me. It feels like someone is stabbing me in the right shoulder blade." He and Julia shared another look as I started coughing again. Usually, I just got my antibiotics and was sent home, then came back in a few days depending on how sick I was, but I'd never been this tired. "What is it?"

"Well, the reason you are short of breath is you have a large amount of fluid around your heart, and also some in your lungs, which is why you can't lie down and why your coughing sounds the way it does. It's probably why your shoulder hurts. Lucia, your heart is stressed. What we don't know is why. A few things can cause it, but we need to do a few more tests. We need to start the admission process. It's four now, so you'll be admitted through the ER." He paused and added, "Do you want us to call your parents?"

"Yes." I nodded again, more numbly this time. "What could cause it?" My words weren't fearful—just confused. My heart? I was twenty-one. Wasn't that too young for heart problems?

Dr. Steinberg motioned to Julia, who left, presumably to call my mom, who was working nearby in her faculty office at Emory. "Lucia, have you taken any drugs? I need you to be honest with me."

"No." I shook my head vigorously.

I'd been as sick as I ever had been my last semester of college; drugs were the last thing on my mind. Not that I'd ever wanted to try them anyway—I took my dream of working for the IMF too seriously to ever have jeopardized it by doing drugs. I wanted more than just to see the world, but to be involved in the lending policies between nations that allowed infrastructure to improve lives. I dreamed of seeing bridges, schools, water purification systems—so much—built with funding I'd helped approve. I'd promised myself this time in Atlanta was just a stopover until I started my Ph.D. at GW.

"I've never done any drugs," I repeated firmly. "I swear."

"The pericardial effusion, this fluid around your heart, is most often caused by a virus," Dr. Steinberg said. "But we have also called Dr. Ramsey. Sometimes lupus can cause this, or a few other things."

I frowned. My rheumatologist, Dr. Ramsey, hadn't endeared himself to me in the past. He'd dismissed me at nineteen, telling me I didn't have any autoimmune diseases, despite positive blood work, joint swelling, and a history of sun rashes. I hadn't been back until my tongue got so dry it split in two places, bleeding, and Dr. Steinberg did my Sjogren's testing. I still had the scar on my tongue.

"We also need to do a CT scan to get a clearer picture of your heart and to rule out a pulmonary embolism. That's a blood clot in your lungs," he said. "From your cough and X-ray, we believe you also have a pleural effusion, or fluid in your lungs. That too can be caused by lupus or a blood clot, or it is possible something else. That's why we need to do more tests—so we can treat you properly."

The terms I hadn't understood swirled around my head, and suddenly I was almost as afraid as I was tired. A frightening thought struck me. "Am I going to die?" I asked hesitantly.

He looked at me with years of warmth in his gray eyes and put his hand on my shoulder. "I am going to do everything in my power to take care of you, but Lucia, I cannot lie: you are much sicker than I realized," he said in his calm voice. "You shouldn't be walking—"

He was interrupted by a knock, and the door bumped open. Julia pushed a wheelchair into the room with a smile. "I have your chariot. Your mom is on the way."

My breath was once again coming in short pants as I struggled to breathe. Dr. Steinberg's voice steadied me, though. "Lucia, Julia is going to take you to the ER and help you start your workup. I have one more patient to see here, and then I am coming to make sure everything is okay. Do you have any questions?"

I started up that seal bark again until finally I was able to say, "Not right now."

"Then let me help you off the table." He reached out his hand, and I was grateful for his steady support. Julia gave me another comforting look as I settled into the chair. "I am going to take good care of you, Lucia," Dr. Steinberg said in his reassuring voice.

We whipped through the hospital hallways much faster than when I'd had to stop every few feet to catch my breath. In no time at all, we were at the ER admission desk.

"Hi, I am Julia, Dr. Steinberg's PA," Julia told the woman at the front desk. "This is Lucia Farris. We called about getting her fast-tracked."

The woman looked down at her computer screen. "Take her to triage two. No traumas in the bay."

"Thank you," Julia said, and we pushed into the ER and into a tiny room. "Lucia, Mark will take good care of you. I need to help Dr. Steinberg wrap up clinic, but we'll be back soon."

"Thank you," I mumbled.

A young man I assumed was Mark held out a large plastic bag for me and closed the curtains. With unsteady legs, I changed into the hospital gown before sitting on the plastic chair, shivering and alone in the cold ER.

"Dressed?" he called through the curtain.

"Yes."

He hurried back in and hooked me up to a pulse ox, the machine that monitored your blood oxygen level, and his eyes quickly became enlarged.

"I have Raynaud's," I said. Stress or cold made my fingers

and toes have a vasospasm, which meant the blood vessels constricted and turned white. It made the pulse ox read wonky sometimes, because it decreased blood flow from my fingers.

"Thanks," Mark said with a smile, looking slightly more relieved. It must have been bad when it read that I had no blood oxygen, so I was glad I'd remembered to tell him.

As he hooked up the heart leads, the machine beeped in a way I didn't think was normal. Just then, two people in different colored scrubs came in with a stretcher.

"Is this the patient for the CT scan?"

"Yes, Lucia Farris."

"Hi, Lucia. Let me see your wrist, please." Neither of them pronounced my name right, *Lu-chi-ah*, but few people did. I held out my wrist for him to read my admission band as the transport man asked, "Date of birth?"

"May twenty-sixth."

"Thank you. Let's get you on this bed, okay? Have you had a CT scan before?"

"No," I said as I sat down. "Can you raise the bed? I can't breathe when I'm flat."

"Sure."

The transport team started telling me about the CT scan, and I tried to process their words as the walls of the ER and hospital sped past. I still couldn't believe this was happening—I was supposed to start graduate school today, not go to the hospital. After waiting all day to see Dr. Steinberg, since he only did clinic in the afternoon, suddenly everything seemed to be happening dizzyingly fast. Into and out of the CT. The techs were grim-faced, no longer joking as I was rushed back to the ER. They kept casting me looks with brows drawn together and lips turned down.

When we entered my room, my mom was there. "Lucia!" she exclaimed before switching to rapid Italian. She kissed my forehead and I answered as best I could before I was interrupted by a nurse.

"I'm sorry, ma'am. I'm Carol, Lucia's nurse. I need to take some of her blood."

My mom backed away and paced as Carol made good use of the IV the CT tech had started. When I glanced over, I saw she had drawn about ten vials of blood. She left as Dr. Steinberg, Julia, Dr. Ramsey, two other doctors in long white coats, and a small woman with a large machine entered the room.

"Lucia." Dr. Steinberg smiled warmly at me and nodded to my mom. "Mrs. Farris, this is Dr. Manson. He is an expert in pulmonary hypertension. And this is Dr. Carson; he is a cardiologist. Gloria"—he pointed to the woman—"she is going to do an echo. It's an ultrasound of your heart. This is going to give us an idea of what is happening." Despite the warmth in his expression, I could tell he was worried. "The good news is it is not a pulmonary embolism, meaning no clot that we can see." He drew a breath before continuing. "The bad news is the right side of your heart is enlarged. The left side of your heart is supposed to be larger, but your right side is twice as big."

The room suddenly seemed crowded, and I guessed my mom sensed this too. "I'll wait outside and call your father again," she said, kissing my cheek quickly. "You know how traffic can be in Atlanta this time of day."

I nodded, and Gloria got me geared up and spoke softly to me as the doctors twisted to look at her screen. The swooshing of my heartbeat was the only sound that echoed through the room. Worry darted across all the doctors' faces. I knew almost nothing about the heart, but I could see my heart rate was 140. That didn't seem normal when I was at rest.

Finally, Dr. Manson turned to the cardiologist. "Have you ever seen anything like that before?"

"No," Dr. Carson said, rubbing his jaw, then nodding to himself. "She needs a window. I'm calling Dr. Major before he leaves."

Dr. Manson sighed. "I agree, please." He motioned for Dr. Carson, and he stepped outside and shut the door.

My mom reentered, but I strained to see Dr. Steinberg's face as Gloria undid my echo leads and left. I didn't understand what had just been said, but my doctors looked stoic.

Dr. Steinberg sat on my bed and took my hand. "Lucia, you are in decompensated heart failure. That's why it hurts in your shoulder. Your heart is not able to adequately do its job. Your pulmonary artery pressure should be under 25, and it is reading 137. Your heart is having what's called tricuspid regurgitation, and most of what is entering your right heart is being pushed back out, which is part of the reason you are so short of breath. If left untreated, even overnight, you have a high risk of dying." My mom gasped. "Your doctors want you to have what's called a cardiac window. It will drain the fluid off your heart, and this could ease the strain on it significantly."

I didn't understand why he and Dr. Manson, the other attractive younger doctor in the room, had seemed so worried. Frankly, I hadn't understood much of what was happening. "There's a treatment. That's good, isn't it?"

"Your heart is already in failure," Dr. Manson cut in gently, with an accent that gave me the impression he was from the Islands. "There is a chance you might not survive the surgery. The shock might be too much for your heart. However, your body is fighting hard. But we need to do this surgery. If we don't do anything, I don't think you'll survive the night. Even without fluid on your heart, it's not functional and will need strong medications to keep it working."

His voice was so calm that it took a moment before the impact of his words sunk in. I nodded numbly.

He glanced at Dr. Steinberg before continuing. "Lucia, the fluid isn't the only thing causing the pulmonary artery pressure. With the testing we've seen so far, I can confirm you have pulmonary arterial hypertension, PAH. We'll need to find the underlying cause and start you on medications for it as soon as the surgery is over. That's why I'm here, and Dr. Steinberg and I will take good care of you."

I closed my eyes a moment. I had never been this tired in my life. *Pain* wasn't the word I would use, not exactly. The past two days, I'd had stabbing pain in my right shoulder blade, yes, but more bone-weary exhaustion. I couldn't continue to live how I felt. It'd been a struggle just to dress or brush my teeth.

But I didn't want to die.

There were so many places I wanted to see. When I worked for the IMF someday, I would be able to travel. They'd have to fix me—I had too many things I wanted to do first.

Just then, an older man with a head of gray hair entered, disrupting my swirling thoughts. "Lucia, hello. I'm Dr. Major, chief of cardiac surgery. I've been briefed on your case and am going to be operating on you. Do you have any questions?"

"Will you break my breastbone?" Vain, but I had to ask. I used to volunteer in the hospital, and I knew cardiac surgeons left a brutally long scar from your belly to your neck.

Dr. Major smiled broadly at me. "No, actually, we enter under the heart, and it will drain into the lung cavity. You'll have two smaller scars, but we don't break the breastbone." His face turned serious, his gray eyes sympathetic as he said softly, "Lucia, your heart is in bad shape, and I cannot guarantee the outcome of this surgery. I need to be honest with you: there is less than a fifty percent chance you'll survive the night. They will be taking you back in a few minutes if you need to call anyone not here."

"My dad's not here yet," I said. I'd walked into the hospital this afternoon, but wouldn't walk out tonight, or possibly at all. My breath sped up again and I coughed, the ferocity of it shaking the bed.

Dr. Major's face stiffened as the noise barreling out of me continued, and he looked ready to push me into the OR that second. But when he spoke, his words were gentle. "I'm sorry. We need to do the surgery as quickly as possible because your heart could give out at any moment. You'll need to talk to him on the phone. We cannot risk waiting to remove the fluid. Anesthesiology will be in soon. I need to go get prepped for your surgery. I'm going to take good care of you." With a pat on my shoulder, he left with Dr. Manson, the two of them talking as they walked away.

A noise drew my attention to my mom—she was crying.

I thought about my life. This wasn't what was supposed to happen. I was supposed to start graduate school today. I had graduated from university just two weeks before. I was only twenty-one and felt way too young to die. At the same time, it hadn't been a bad life. I'd spent the last three years attending college in Rome and had traveled extensively in Europe. I wasn't ready to go, but realized I was proud of the life I'd lived.

When I opened my eyes, Carol, the nurse, started prepping me to go to surgery. My mom stepped out, I presumed to call my dad again, and a young anesthesiologist came in, but I was past comprehending anything else.

As he left, mom walked back in and hugged me. "*Ti voglio bene, carina,*" she whispered.

"I love you too, Mom," I whispered back in English. "Dad?"

Tears ran down her cheeks. "He parked, but it's time for you to go. He didn't want to delay your surgery."

My dad suddenly came into view, panting as my bed was pushed into the hallway. "I made it." He kissed my forehead and wrapped an arm around my mom. "We'll be here when your surgery finishes, baby."

The OR rolled closer as I risked one more backward glance at my parents' somber faces. Dr. Major's words burned in my ears as I righted myself and closed my eyes.

"Lucia. Lucia, can you hear me?"

Words sounded all around me, and I opened my eyes. My

blurry vision opened to blinding lights.

My tongue stuck thickly to the roof of my mouth. "Can I have some water?" I managed. Words were hard to form, and my mouth was horribly dry. Where was I?

"No, it's too soon. You've just come out of heart surgery. In a few minutes, we are going to be taking you to your room in the cardiac ICU. Are you in any pain?"

At her words, I recalled pieces of the day. I shook my head but instantly regretted it as it made me nauseous. Before my mind cleared, I was whisked through the hospital corridors yet again to be buzzed in to the CICU.

My eyes landed immediately on my mom and dad.

"Baby," my dad cooed. "How are you feeling?" His eyes gleamed as they ran the length of me.

Before I could answer, Dr. Steinberg entered. "Lucia," he said warmly. "I am not on your case, as it wasn't an infection that caused this." Dr. Steinberg was an infectious disease doctor, so that made sense. I'd had a history of complex skin infections, so he'd become my primary care physician. "But I will be here with Julia twice a day to check on you."

I loved his smiling face at that moment. He had always made me feel safe. I reached out, and he took my hand in his warm, dry one.

"The fluid will be draining for several days. Dr. Manson will explain further, but your heart will not recover from decompensated failure overnight or, honestly, after many nights," he continued. "Let us know immediately if you feel increased shortness of breath, or especially if your shoulder starts hurting more. We aren't quite out of the woods yet, so don't hesitate to call Ken, your nurse, if anything feels different—if you need anything."

"Thank you for everything, Dr. Steinberg. Thank you for taking such good care of Lucia," my mom said in a strained voice.

"Of course," he said mildly, squeezing my hand once before dropping it. He could have left likely hours ago when it turned out not to be an infection, but I was glad he hadn't. "I'll see everyone in the morning."

As he left, my dad leaned over and kissed my forehead. "Baby, I can't stay tonight. Only one person can spend the night in the cardiac ICU, and I'm going to let your mother. There's a priest outside. He, um—" He stopped and looked at my mom.

"Lucia, he offered to give you your last rites," she said softly.

I looked at her for a moment—"decompensated heart failure" and "we aren't quite out of the woods yet" ringing in my ears—and then down to the tangle of tubes connected to me. "Yes, please send him in."

"Okay, I'll be just outside."

I took a deep breath. I was raised Catholic, and the last rites were an important part of the seven sacraments, although I hadn't gone much to church in the last few years. Dr. Major told me I might have died in surgery, but I didn't realize my chance of dying was still so high I'd need my last rites. I'd survived the surgery, but was still in heart failure.

I'd never seen the last rites performed. I tried to take a steadying breath as the priest and a nun entered my room.

"Hello, Lucia," the priest said. "I'm Father Luke and this is Sister Anna. We know you've been really sick and came to say a prayer with you and offer you the Holy Eucharist."

Two

Three and a half years later, Present Day, July 28

Something was stalking me. My heart thudded, warning me it approached—closer, closer. Steps pounded loudly, not hiding its advance—not anymore. It knew I was trapped in the dark cabinet. It would find me; somehow, I knew it would find me. My own breath seemed a scream in the silence. It was getting closer—hunting me.

Suddenly, the door to my cupboard was ripped open and strong arms yanked me hard flush against a cold chest. I threw all my weight against it, fighting, although I knew struggling was useless—I was dead. The vampire's teeth shone piercing white just before it sank its fangs into the artery and tore open my neck.

I woke with a gasp and fumbled around to turn on the bedside light. I felt my heart thump, thump, thump in my chest, my breath coming in rapid bursts. I tore off the sweat-drenched covers, trying to calm myself. My long, thick chestnut hair was a sweaty tangle, and my tongue stuck dryly to the roof of my mouth. I freaking hated that recurring vampire nightmare.

I sat up and took a sip of water and then my morning medicine. I was still shaken. I petted my furry Pomeranian, Bea, a few minutes before letting her go back to sleep.

Stretching up and out of bed, I moved to turn on the overhead lights and blast away the darkness of the nightmare. Bea looked at me with reproach and snuggled back into the covers. I plucked at my baggy T-shirt, my sweat starting to cool, but still, it was gross.

I *knew* there were no vampires. I might have had a lot of illnesses, but delirium wasn't one. Yet I'd had night terrors since I started taking Plaquenil three and a half years ago to control my lupus. They'd become less frequent, thank god, but I'd quickly learned the difference between nightmare and night terror. They felt so real, and I didn't know how to make this recurring one stop. Always vampires. Always hunting me. Always finding me—killing me.

I shuffled into the bathroom and turned the shower to preheat, then started the coffee maker before I scrubbed my skin to burn away the horrors I'd felt as much as seen. It had been a few weeks since I'd had some variation of that nightmare, but with the new school year pending and my graduate papers just having been submitted from my summer classes, it wasn't really a surprise.

I enjoyed teaching high school, I really did, but the job was taxing, and a new year also brought on the jitters. If I lost my job, I'd be out of insurance. Last year I'd been sick so much—the stress of the job, the germs, and my shitty fucking ex-boyfriend always vexing me about something. *This second year will be better,* I willed as I rinsed quickly.

I rubbed my sternum absentmindedly as anxiety pinched my chest—as if it'd help. I turned off the water and threw my hair in a towel before grabbing coffee. Today was supposed to be for a relaxing hike. It had taken more than three years to get where I was. Every mountain I climbed reminded me of that. The cool, shady mountains and quiet of the woods always helped calm me down. Although unease always spiked through me when I went with new people, like I would be doing today. Would they talk about my breathing? Would they notice?

I laughed, piercing the silence of the apartment. Of course they would notice. I drank more coffee before taking Bea on a walk to distract myself from the dread of explaining pulmonary hypertension—again. Then, because it was still just five in the morning on a Saturday, I plopped down on the loveseat and I decided to chat with my best friend. Sometimes it was good she was in China.

I opened WhatsApp and called Ru, who'd been mainly based in Shanghai for almost two years. I'd been hoarding every penny to visit her. My dream of working at the IMF might be lost, but I still had wanderlust—unrequited, so far.

As the video opened, she said, "Lucia, don't tell me you are still having those vampire dreams. You have got to stop binge-watching *True Blood*."

I laughed as I took in my best friend. She was gorgeous, with high cheekbones and long black hair that showed her Taiwanese American heritage.

"All right," I said. "Guilty on both counts."

She giggled and her boyfriend, Edward, popped onscreen. I'd given up trying to say his Chinese name a year ago when I still couldn't get it right and after countless assurances being called his English name didn't bother him.

"Hi Lucia," he said. "When are you visiting?"

"Hopefully next summer." I hadn't been able to do so many things I'd dreamed of, but visit Ru in China? I hoped for at least that.

Edward nodded. "We will take good care of you. Don't worry if you get sick."

"Thank you," I said as he exited the frame to let us chat, whispering in Chinese to Ru. I caught the words "seven" and "eating." I held back my grin. She wasn't always—or, ever—punctual.

Ru waved him away and exclaimed, "So you'll really come next summer?"

"Yes," I answered. "I've been saving up and I should be finished with graduate school."

She clapped. "Second master's—congrats! We're going to take over Shanghai! It will be an eat-a-thon. I cannot wait!"

We talked for a while before Ru and Edward needed to go to dinner. We exchanged our *love you*s, and I told her I couldn't wait to see her in a month when she visited home in Atlanta. Before I knew it, it was time to head out to my hiking group.

The Mansell Park and Ride was deserted at seven in the morning on a Saturday, save one car with the windows down. I was early, but my nerves always demanded it. I got out my backpack and waved, approaching the car with a ready smile.

A large guy with short brown hair and warm melting brown eyes got out of the car. I couldn't pinpoint what it was about him—his lopsided grin, his left dimple, or those alluring eyes—but my pulse quickened. He was yummy looking. Suddenly, my body, traitor it was, wanted to remind me just how long it had been since I had dated someone or gotten laid. Six months—or more?

"Hi," I said, trying not to ogle his broad chest as I craned my neck up and up to meet this tall cutie's gaze.

"Are you here for the trekking?" he asked with a German accent I immediately recognized.

A second thrill ran through me, and I bounced on the pads of my feet. "Are you German?"

With a hint of tension in his voice, he said, "No, Austrian."

I switched to German. "I'm here for the hike. Where in Austria are you from?" My parents had made me go to an international school because they wanted me fluent in Italian and German as a tribute to my mother's heritage. I'd taken half my courses in German and enjoyed keeping up with it.

"Innsbruck."

Man of few words, but my mom always joked I could talk to anyone, or at least I could have before I got sick. So I continued undaunted, happy to speak in my grandparents' native tongue. "It's so pretty there! I went a long time ago. My grandparents live in South Tyrol, so once my cousin and I drove up there for an art festival after visiting them. I liked the city. I'm *Lu-chi-ah*, pronounced the Italian way." I held out my hand.

At my words, his whole face brightened, making him even more handsome. He flashed me his dimply grin again as he took my hand in his larger, firmer ones—god, the man had beautiful hands, and suddenly I wondered how they'd feel on me.

My cheeks heated as he said, "I'm Oskar, spelled the German way, with a K." We both glanced up as another two cars pulled in. "So, do you do this a lot?"

"Speak in German, talk to strangers, or hike?"

He chuckled, and I immediately knew I would try my best to make him produce *that* sound again. It was a rich, full laugh that made me smile. "All?"

"I don't have any German-speaking friends here, but I talk to my grandparents in German a few times a month. I'm pretty friendly and have been told I could speak to a brick wall, so I do talk to strangers. I like to hike, but don't get to do it too much. I'm wrapping up graduate school and I teach fulltime, so it's pretty busy. Summer is a lighter workload, but only briefly." I finished with a shrug, realizing I'd rambled a little. "You?"

He laughed again. Help me, that sound even made my lady parts want to smile. "Clearly, I speak German, but now that I live here, it's harder. None of my Atlanta friends or colleagues speak it. I haven't done a Sierra Club meetup before, but I used to trek a lot back home, so I wanted to try it. I'm in graduate school, so I wanted to get some fresh air while I could." He grimaced. "Even with the heat."

Atlanta was super muggy in July. It wasn't called Hotlanta for nothing.

We were interrupted by a few other people introducing themselves, including the hike leader, Lee. We were seven so far, and Lee said we were waiting on three more. Two were meeting us at the trailhead. I hadn't hiked with this particular group before, so everyone was a stranger. My anxiety spiked again.

As we signed in, Lee pulled me to the side.

Here it comes, I thought.

"So, I read your notes."

He looked me over, like every person did when they learned about my medical history. I didn't look sick.

"You're okay to do this hike?"

I felt my cheeks burn as I fiddled with my backpack straps but I forced a smile and said, "It should be fine. I just have to break occasionally to catch my breath when the trail gets too steep, but I haven't had trouble keeping up with a group in the past. I've done the Coosa Trail to Blood Mountain twice with no issue." It was a nine-mile hike considered a little more strenuous than this.

"Okay, then just let me know if you have trouble. This is a hard hike," he warned before moving back to the sign-in process and release of liability forms.

I nodded and tried to hold my smile in place. I understood I had to fill out a waiver and no one wanted to be slowed down or held liable in a free hiking group. My PAH embarrassed me often, even though I was unable to control it. It made me look lazy, out of shape. My regular hiking friends understood, but I'd wanted to do this hike for so long. School would start soon, so I'd signed up with this new group. Hopefully they'd understand too.

I risked a glance and was relieved to see Oskar was tinkering with something in his car, an older gray compact, and had missed the whole ordeal.

When the full group had assembled and carpools broke off, I went with Oskar, as did Marcia, a petite middle-aged woman. He drove, claiming he had to sit in the front because of his legs. It was about an hour and a half drive to the Arkaquah Trailhead, rumored to be one of the prettiest hikes in metro Atlanta. Once we passed the highway, the scenery was pleasant as we headed into the bucolic rural mountainside, a mist hanging low on some of the fields and rolling hills. Marcia was friendly and had recently gotten into hiking, much like me. Most people didn't hike to make friends, although that benefit happened sometimes, but on the longer, more remote trails, it could be dangerous to hike alone, without cell service. Oskar was fairly quiet, but even so, the ride passed quickly, and we were at the trailhead before I knew it.

"The first two miles have really steep switchbacks," Lee said as we all stretched our stiff legs, "and watch for poison ivy."

As we fell in line, I was half-distressed and half-joyous, the strange feeling I got before every hike. If I pushed too much, I could re-damage my heart. That fear never fully left me, and cardio would always carry some trepidation. I was behind Lee and in front of Oskar. I prayed I wouldn't embarrass myself with my labored breathing, but I was eager to talk to him more. He cut a striking figure—tall, broad-shouldered, muscular, and it was a rare delight to speak German with someone other than my grandparents.

Suddenly and surprisingly, my whole body tingled to my core as I imagined intimacy with Oskar *in German*. I'd always adored dirty talk, and the idea of it in German was shockingly arousing. I cut off that train of thought as quickly as it started. I was in a self-imposed dry spell, which might explain my wayward thoughts. I needed to buy a vibrator, not daydream about a stranger—it just wasn't polite.

I'd intentionally not dated since March, but talking to Oskar didn't seem like too big a risk, even if my body thrummed in awareness in a way that was far from friendly. If we chatted, it would halt my mind from drifting to other things—things I warned myself away from.

"Oskar, where did you go to university?" I asked.

"I went to the Technical University in Munich, TUM, for

undergraduate and for my master's in biochemical engineering," he answered, a little stiffly.

"So, now you must be doing your doctorate?" I continued to press before resigning myself to an introverted hike with just me, myself, and the tree roots.

"Yes, at Georgia Tech."

"Why Tech of all places?" My curiosity was piqued.

"It's a good program," he said casually. "They offered me a stipend and a scholarship." The words hung in the air; he wasn't giving me much to converse with. Then he added, "It was something different—somewhere different."

He didn't ask me anything, so I reluctantly fell silent. I didn't want to annoy him, since some people liked to hike in silence. I tried to concentrate on the trail—the tangled roots I was stepping over, on anything but him, not wanting more unsolicited sensual thoughts about his firm hands or German voice. *Lucia, stop!*

"Lucia." The sound of my name from his mouth sent a spark of heat through me I'd been trying to contain. "You didn't tell me where you went to school or what you studied."

"Oh, when you didn't ask, I thought maybe I was bothering you," I teased.

"No," he said seriously. "Please, tell me."

"I went to La Sapienza, in Rome—"

"Wow." He cut me off, shock deepening his voice. "You went to college in Rome?"

I laughed. I'd gotten that reaction before—many, many times. "Yes, I'm half Italian."

"Oh." He sounded disappointed. "You must have family there, then?"

"No, they all live in northern Italy—hence me speaking German—but I thought Rome would be more fun." I couldn't keep my lips from curving upward—Rome, the eternal city, so vibrant, romantic, and magical.

He chuckled again. "Most certainly, but bold. What did you study?"

I flushed at his praise. "International affairs and economics. Then I came back here and worked on a master's in teaching and economics. I received my MAT, Master's in the Art of Teaching, last May and took a position teaching high school while still doing the economics master's part-time."

"Very impressive," he said quietly. I itched to turn around and try to read his face because I couldn't read his voice, but I resisted the urge.

We stopped talking as we hit the switchbacks. It was dense in this part of the low forest, the humidity and heat hanging heavy in the air. I knew from experience hiking in North Georgia it would cool off considerably as we climbed and gained a little breeze. I had my Buff-headband keeping my hair and sweat out of my eyes until then, but nothing could control the increasing rapidness of my breathing as my body geared uphill into cardio mode—or the fear. There was no more room for conversation or daydreams.

After a few more turns, the feeling of my swiftly beating heart and staccato breathing made me halt. It was the worst feeling in the world—like the hospital was closing in on me. *Just breathe, you can walk now—just a short breather,* I told myself as I braced myself on my backpack straps. I stepped to the side for a moment to let Oskar pass as I tried to slow my breathing, overworked heart, and nagging fears.

He surveyed me before passing, brows crinkling with confusion. "All good?" I nodded, and he stopped. "I thought you hiked a lot?" he asked with a raised eyebrow.

I didn't like the accusation I felt like I'd heard in his voice or the surprise I saw in his face. "I do," I panted out. My breath was already starting to normalize. "I have a lung disease." Then I started walking uphill again, totally ignoring him. I didn't care to hear his response.

Oskar muttered something that might have been an apology, but I couldn't hear it over my labored breathing. The next hour of the hike was difficult for me, emotionally and physically. I hated the feeling of my heart speeding up and the horrible dyspnea that happened when my pulmonary artery went past its capacity. It always reminded me of the days leading up to my heart failure and the feeling of literally suffocating.

I hated the looks from people who clearly thought I was terribly out of shape—lazy. People who knew me understood, but none of those people were here.

Finally, the brutally steep first two miles ended, and as the trail evened out, my emotions did too. I allowed myself to smile in the tranquil quiet of the woods, save the chirping of birds and the rustling wind. We were higher up and had begun the granite phase the Arkaquah Trail was famous for. The air was a bearable temperature again, too. This was the part of hiking I loved—the beauty and pride in pushing myself. I was *alive*.

At a small cluster of large granite boulders along the ridgeline with glimpses of mountains just visible, Lee gave us a break. I thumped down onto one and rustled inside my pack. I felt body heat and swiveled my head to see Oskar sitting on the boulder too, nearly rubbing his thigh against mine. His words still rang in my ears, but my body didn't have the same reservation as my stinging pride, now re-humming to life.

"I didn't mean to offend you earlier," Oskar said in a low voice.

Glancing up, his mahogany eyes seemed concerned, not judgmental. I did breathe pretty freaking loudly—it always shocked new people.

"It's okay," I said with a shrug, and it was. "I just get embarrassed about it. I don't like it when people point it out, but I've heard that was the worst—well, until the very top, which is steep too. I shouldn't get that short of breath again. And I *do* hike often."

"Do you mind if I ask your lung condition?" He continued to hold my gaze. "I think medicine is really fascinating, and I mentioned I'm studying biochemical engineering with a biomedical focus."

"It's just, you may have to walk next to me to hear about it," I tried to joke. "It's not a simple answer."

While I was self-conscious when people pointed out my shortness of breath, I didn't truly mind discussing it, not with friends. Plus, hearing I had autoimmune diseases—plural, four— had made some guys run for the hills. I found him attractive but wanted to be honest, brutally honest. If he looked at me differently, it would cool my body faster than swimming in a glacier-fed stream.

He beamed at my response, showing me the cutest dimple that made my heart flutter, but in a good way. "I think we have time."

I laughed too. "A little bit."

We'd only gone about three miles of eleven. Lee motioned us to restart the hike, and Oskar stood, grinning. "Plus, it's kind of nice to hear your accented German."

He held out his warm, firm hand and I took it, letting him help me stand with a jolt of awareness. His eyes held mine a moment before he released my hand and we restarted up the trail. The flutters in my heart and the hitch in my breath had nothing to do with pulmonary hypertension. I felt a pull toward him I hadn't felt in a long time, but I wasn't sure if that was something to be excited about or something to run from.

Three

Three years earlier, January 7

Dr. Manson sat silently, hands on his knees, examining me. His ebony skin contrasted with the crispness of his white coat where it met his wrists. He'd said he had some questions to ask me by myself, but he hadn't spoken yet.

"Please tell me the number of sexual partners you've had and if you've been tested for HIV."

My eyes darted to his and I opened my mouth, unable to speak. His cheeks reddened, clearly as embarrassed as I was. He was a pulmonologist, not a gynecologist.

"Two," I stuttered, thinking about Raúl, my first. The Brazilian consulate's son who'd gone to my international high school—it was a sweet first love before his family had moved away. Then Alessandro, or Ali as I'd called him, my longest and most recent boyfriend. "I was tested in September, and everything was negative. I haven't slept with anyone since."

Ali had cheated on me, so I'd gone to the doctors for an STD panel. I'd been far too sick those last months in Rome to date anyone else.

He nodded and dropped my eyes. "Good. It's still negative. Sometimes HIV takes a while to show up and it can also cause this, so I wanted to be sure."

Breath hissed out of me. Everything going on was bad enough. I did not want HIV on top of it all.

He smiled then, reminding me he was human, even handsome, before he continued in a studious, doctorly tone. "Some good news, I just wanted to confirm it. I want to explain a little more about your disease. You have what is called pulmonary arterial hypertension, group one, stage four, secondary to lupus, SLE. Its short name is PAH. It only affects two in a million people, and there is no cure. Most people with pulmonary hypertension have it due to underlying heart disease, lung disease, or a blood clot. In your case, pulmonary hypertension *is* the underlying cause."

He stopped to make sure I was following. "What happens is your pulmonary artery develops an excess of cells, called endothelin, that overtime clog the pulmonary artery," he continued.

"Like cancer?" I asked hesitantly. That sounded bad too.

"A little, but the cell growth is limited to your pulmonary artery. Also, the pulmonary artery loses elasticity, which makes it have difficulty expanding. You noticed this when you had trouble breathing. Even simple tasks, such as brushing your hair and teeth, can be a challenge. As a result, your blood cannot properly pump to your lungs. Your heart doesn't like that, so it tries harder and harder to pump the blood through your small pulmonary artery. It grows dangerously large with excess muscle, and eventually it becomes too hard for it to do its job." His brown eyes were warm and sympathetic as he said, "You were in decompensated heart failure last night and still are, so we need to get your heart in good shape before you're discharged. We need to get you from decompensated to compensated by getting you on the right medications. Do you have any questions so far?"

"No," I said weakly. He'd explained it clearly; it was just

a lot to take in. Too much to take in. I was glad for his accent because at least his voice was reassuring and pleasant, which made this slightly more bearable to listen to.

"So, one medicine you will take will help make your pulmonary artery nice and open. That one, you might have heard of—sildenafil, or better known as Viagra." He smiled at my shocked face. "Bosentan is a little less known. It works to break up the excess endothelin and keep it from reforming. And the prostacyclin, you will be starting tomorrow. Hopefully that will help decrease your right heart muscle—it's too big and needs to renormalize. We just wanted to get you stable. It will be an IV directly into your heart. You'll have a permanent line called a Hickman catheter installed."

The morphine and surreality of it all clogged my brain. He continued speaking, but I'd lost my focus. My mind and my body were a mess, but I attempted to keep a serene face. My belly already had four huge black bruises from the heparin shots I'd been getting to thin my blood. The testing had revealed I had a lupus indicator, which made me more likely to have a blood clot. With everything else going on, a clot would be deadly.

So much medicine, and for how long, he hadn't said. I could only hope—dream—that it wouldn't be forever. I glanced up to ask and realized he'd left. I must have zoned out. The dry scratchiness of my nose burned from the six liters of oxygen being pumped into it. Tubes, so many tubes. The pink liquid still drip-drip-dripped into the box collecting fluid from my heart. I'd heard Ken say in an amazed tone that they'd collected two liters so far. I looked at the pink fluid still leaking out of me—that had been this morning.

I twisted my head, but it was slowed and tangled by the line in my neck artery called a Swan-Ganz catheter monitoring my heart. I also had two IVs running fluids into me. Heart monitors and the pulse ox jingled and beeped. I felt like I was part plastic and not wholly me.

"Here you go, Lucia." Dr. Manson's voice interrupted my

own bodily examination. Relief filled me—I hadn't missed him leave entirely.

"Thank you," I said, taking the paper. "What is it?"

He cleared his throat. "That is the flyer on PAH I just mentioned." His eyes met mine with understanding; he knew I was only half here—which was the truth.

"How long will I have the IV in my heart?" I blurted out before he left, or the morphine distracted me again.

He clasped his hands and tilted his head down to peer at me. "I don't know. Some people are on it a few years, and some patients take it forever. People with PAH secondary to autoimmune diseases seem to do better, but we are going to take it day by day. Okay?"

"Thank you," I managed to get out.

I waited until he left to inspect the flyer. My pulse shot up—I knew because Ken came rushing in to look at the monitor, so I had, too. He scrutinized me before leaving again. Then I googled PAH on my phone. I found people with Stage Four—that was me—had a life expectancy of six months or less after being diagnosed. PAH was incurable; and fewer than a thousand people in the US were diagnosed with it each year.

My phone dinged with unread and unresponded to messages, but I put it on my bedside table, face down. I hadn't told anyone I'd been hospitalized besides my parents. I could barely think and handle my own emotions. I certainly didn't want to talk to anyone else and deal with theirs.

And who would visit? I had no friends in Atlanta. My best friends were in Rome and NYC. I was alone, and Mom hadn't been handling it well. She might have thought I hadn't seen her crying, but any time her friends or our family had called, she'd left the room. I'd seen her tears. I had to be strong.

Suddenly, my face was wet. I was crying. Quickly, I scrubbed the tears away just before my mom entered the room. *I'm alive and I can get through this,* I told myself.

Mom chattered nervously, evidently not liking the silence.

"So, I hear you are going to be having surgery tomorrow to start taking this medicine called something-cyclin. It's supposed to help remodel your heart. Dr. Manson said a nurse will be by later, and the medicine is so rare the hospital can't even order it! The pharmacy ships it here specifically to you."

I managed a smile for her. "Yeah, I heard I'm one in a million. Well, two in a million, but still, I'm pretty special."

Her eyes watered, but she tried to maintain my dry humor. "I always knew you were."

When her gaze held mine, I could tell we were both trying to be brave for each other, but I didn't feel brave. This was the most scared I'd ever felt in my life. I'd been slowly realizing that even if I survived, life might be very different for me. No, not might—*would* be different. I inhaled, then smiled. I held in the tears.

When she left for the night, I could cry. Then I could let it out.

Four

Present day, July 28
OSKAR

Fuck, was all I could think as I listened to Lucia's story. She'd given the most cursory summary of her conditions and their effects on her body. I'd bet my Ph.D. there was more to it. I could tell from how she spoke she was cautious about what she said, almost like she didn't want to overwhelm me with information. Or scare me away.

Normally, I was reserved. I liked my privacy, maybe too much. Yet she'd been so open with me, so I admitted, "My dad has type one diabetes, so I know a little bit about medicine from him."

She turned around and nearly blinded me with her gorgeous smile. Damn, she'd certainly had braces, unlike me.

"Thanks for telling me. You know it's autoimmune too, right?"

"Um, yeah, I think my dad's mentioned it." I rubbed the back of my neck, embarrassed I *didn't* know that. I changed the subject because I'd gotten the strong sense she was waiting for me to judge her and she wasn't enjoying this conversation—at all. "My mom has worked for years at a big medical company in Innsbruck that creates hearing aids. My dad wears a pump. I'm studying biochemical engineering because medical equipment has interested me since I was a kid. It's amazing how medicine helps you. How it can help so many different people. That's why I want to do what I'm doing, even if the hours and time in the program have been beyond intense."

She nodded, her braid bobbing in front of me. "We need more innovation and that sounds really, well, amazing." I could hear in the change in her voice; she sounded more relaxed. I fucking sure as hell wouldn't want to talk about my health with strangers. I felt a little embarrassed and intrusive I'd asked at all. It was just that she looked like a perfectly healthy girl; it was hard to imagine she was dealing with everything she casually mentioned.

She perked up when the topic changed to travel, regaling me with stories of trips with her cousins and friend Paola, from Istanbul to Krakow and everywhere in between. Fascinated, I hung on her words, picturing the places I had and hadn't seen.

And that mouth—sarcastic, witty, and sensual. My stomach hurt from laughing so much. Her stories drew me in and surprisingly made me want to share my own. Her figure in her tight pants in front of me had made intelligent conversation difficult at times, but she'd talked when my words had faltered. To each man his own, but I agreed with Queen on fat-bottomed girls. God, yes, her ass was spectacular—full and round. I'd had plenty of views of it on the five-and-a-half-mile trek up here, tempting me like I hadn't felt in months.

When we reached the Brasstown Bald parking area after hours, I couldn't help catching her arm and saying, "I think it's really amazing you are still doing all this." I motioned to the trail behind us. I quickly withdrew my hand before the urge to caress her skin became too powerful. Fuck, maybe my roommate was right: I needed to get laid.

She tilted her chin up to catch my eyes. Her smile was warm, genuine. Something sizzled through me. The hints of green-gold in her hazel eyes in the sunlight were stunning. They'd seemed amber-brown in the woods, but they were so much more dynamic now. Her hair, too: auburn with golden highlights, not light brown. Something flared inside me as I looked down into her beautiful face. She had a spectacular personality to match, and I wanted more than to look.

"Thanks," she said. When we held eye contact a moment longer than we should have, a tint of pink hit her cheeks I didn't think had to do with the heat. Finally, she broke the spell. "Yes, the switchback part of the hike was a challenge"—her nose crinkled—"but I'm here. And I feel really proud every time I go hiking."

Her words impressed me and reminded me I'd been staring. God, she was brave. I couldn't imagine hiking with a serious lung condition. I hoped this budding feeling I had wasn't one-sided.

"You should be," I said. She flashed me a blinding smile before we turned to the restrooms. I added quietly, "My dad is the same. I'm constantly impressed with him."

"I'm just trying to be alive and not just stay alive," she said, almost too soft to hear.

Her eyes flashed in surprise when she saw me still outside. "You could have gone ahead and saved me the embarrassment of you having to listen to me panting again." She almost looked like she wished I had gone.

"I don't mind hearing you panting."

Even though the comment was innocent, I found myself suddenly imagining her panting in other ways. Would she bring that passion for life to the bedroom? Would she be adventurous like in her travels? I glanced at her. She didn't seem to have noticed my slip-up or growing hard-on I attempted to halt. She chewed on her lip, looking pensive, which didn't help my condition at all. Shit, it had been too long since I've gotten laid.

I hadn't tried to date in months because my course load had kept me too busy. But if there was ever a girl who was worth a little effort, it was her, with her bright hazel eyes and curvy figure. I felt my cheeks heat with more than Georgia summer as I imagined that ass again, now unable to stop thinking about how it might feel in my hands with Lucia pressed against me. I'd bet it was firm from how much hiking she did.

I forced my thoughts to lunch before I embarrassed myself with something I wouldn't be able to conceal.

The commotion of the masses after hours of quiet hiking jarred my senses and nerves. After two breather breaks for her, we finally made it to the lookout tower. Leaning side by side over the top railing, me crowding her space as much as I dared, we lingered on the view of the rolling blue-green mountains of North Georgia. I'd grown up in the Alps and had missed them. At 4,784 feet, this was the tallest point in Georgia. It wasn't home, but still, it was something. If it felt like that to me, I could only imagine how it felt for her. I couldn't resist squinting down at her pensive profile as she chewed her lip.

"It isn't the Alps," she said softly, as if reading my mind, "but I enjoy hiking here."

I felt her about to pull away for our short lunch, so I blurted out, "No, it's not, but you can't do trekking in the Alps year-round either." It gave us a few minutes more alone with the view. For the first time in months, I wanted more than my hand in the shower—I wanted her.

"True," she said with a laugh. "But you can ski."

"And you ski often?" Excitement jolted my movements as I turned to face her. I loved skiing.

"Not here, but once a year. I think I mentioned my grandparents live in South Tyrol? They own a small hotel in Alta Badia. We go visit them there and ski every Christmas. As a child, I spent a month with them every summer."

"Your accent gives you away." I couldn't resist teasing her. "My sister and her husband own a small hotel too, but in Tyrol, not South Tyrol. I try to visit at least once a year for skiing. When I lived in Munich, more often. Are you a good skier?"

She laughed again and moved away from the overlook with one last wistful sigh. "Not as great as anyone in my family, but yes. I've been skiing my whole life."

We walked down the steps to where our group was sitting. "I haven't been to the Dolomites, but I've heard they are even prettier than the Austrian Alps."

"They are." She gave me a playful wink and bumped my shoulder.

The region her mom had been born into was German-speaking Italy. Tyrol, where I was from, was in Austria. South Tyrol was just south in Italy, but the regions shared a rich history, and most Italians there spoke German before Italian. Her grandparents were surprisingly only two hours from my home by car, but I'd never been there.

I took out my lunch and she did the same. We didn't have too much time left to eat, but I still wanted to know more about her. "You went back to Italy for university?"

"Yes, my parents sent me to a school growing up that taught classes in a few languages; mine were Italian and German. I heard them arguing once about the cost, but it was really important to my dad I not lose my mom's first languages. I knew they'd want to help me pay for college, and I wanted to live in Europe anyway. I'm sure you know how much better the rates are in Europe. I'm a dual citizen, so my tuition was only two thousand euros a year. I shared an apartment outside the center, led some tours, and did some tutoring in English and German to supplement my income. I'm lucky to have no debt."

"Yes," I agreed wholeheartedly. "Europeans are lucky in that sense. I too paid very little."

"And Munich was near home. I bet that was nice?" Her face was so happy saying that that she had to be close with her family. Something softened in her expression when she said "home."

I couldn't help laughing. Sometimes it had felt too close. I'd leaped at the opportunity to move far away—far, far away. Yet, now that there was so much distance between us, I missed my family and friends and couldn't wait to get back. Atlanta had been a disappointment so far, although I liked my courses at Tech. I'd been introverted and boring, watching cricket with my roommate Sujit and dodging invites from Ryan to "pick up chicks" since I'd moved here. Or in the labs—I was always in the labs.

"Yes, it's hard to be so far away and in a different time zone." My eyes dropped to my food, suddenly painfully homesick. "I'm sure you understand. I haven't been home since Christmas." When I pivoted to see her face, her brow was furrowed, and she looked a thousand miles away.

"Yes, it's worse when you're sick." I could barely hear her whispered words. "That's what brought me back. I have family in Italy, but none in the south where I was. It still felt far, so far, those last few months. Those days—weeks, sometimes—I'd been too sick to leave our tiny flat."

"Why did you pick Italy, not Austria or Germany?" I couldn't help wondering. I wanted to break that melancholy expression as she gazed vacantly toward the forest. Austria was closer culturally and physically to where her grandparents lived. How daring to move to another country at eighteen. I still felt I'd been only half ready last year at twenty-five.

She shrugged, but her eyes lost some of the dullness that had just clouded them. "Well, I guess Italian's more natural to me. I studied German in high school and talk to my grandparents often, but I talk to my parents in Italian. My dad doesn't know German."

"Sometimes your accent is strong, but typical of your region. You haven't said anything I don't understand. You haven't seemed confused by me yet." Her German was very good, and I didn't want her to think she didn't sound native.

She grinned impishly at me, her eyes once again cheerful. "I guess I *feel* more Italian. Plus, with so many universities, Rome sounded exciting. La Sapienza is one of the largest in the world, and Roma Tre and Cattolica are there too. Plus, with so many study-abroad programs, it's crawling with university students."

"And did you like it, living in Rome?" I needn't really ask. Her face glowed when she talked about it—she'd loved living in Rome. I wasn't good at small talk and wanted her to keep going.

She laughed again. Her eyes seemed to glitter bronze-emerald as she turned to me. "It was *la dolce vita*." Her face changed, and her expression fell for a minute. Her look held an almost raw anguish she tried to hide by standing to throw away her trash. I almost wasn't able to hear her say, "Well, until I started getting sick."

I couldn't help feeling slightly awed by her. I found myself willing—no, wanting—to go on a date for the first time in months. I wanted her for damn sure, but she also intrigued me.

When she returned, I stood as we prepared for the return trek downhill. "Do you think I could have your number?" I said nervously. "It's really nice to speak in German again, and we might grab some beers or hike sometime."

It came out awkward. I didn't ask for numbers often, and she was gorgeous, smart, and well-traveled—exactly the type of girl I'd always wanted to date. Well, when I wasn't too busy with work to think about dating. She might be out of my league, but it'd been so nice talking to someone in German again, someone with a similar family as mine, someone whose smile I felt all the way to my cock. I couldn't resist.

She paused a moment, and my breath caught. *Don't say no, don't say no, don't say no.* She'd been friendly, but not flirtatious so far.

Finally, she said, "Sure, I'd like more German-speaking *friends*."

I understood what she was implying. Still, I decided to consider it a victory if it meant I could spend more time like today. I handed her my phone, and she entered her contact information. *Lucia Farris.* I couldn't resist noticing her long slim fingers as they circled the phone. They were as gorgeous as the rest of her.

I could almost swear I saw the same heat in her gaze as I felt in mine.

"Text me your full name, Oskar with a K," she demanded playfully.

Oskar Reidl, I typed. "Plus, you know where Innsbruck is." Teasing her was too fun. She smiled, but it was funnier to me. *Duh,* I told myself. *Of course, she doesn't get that dumb-ass joke you share with Gunter.*

As we hiked down, I continued to watch Lucia's gorgeous backside in front of me. I was very glad I'd decided to sign up for this hike.

After a while, Lucia turned around and looked at me. I realized guiltily I'd been so distracted by her generous round ass and hips I'd lost track of the conversation. The girl could talk—a lot. She had a kind of frantic energy to her, a zest for life. I'd always been even-keeled, but it intrigued me.

Her hazel eyes mesmerized me, but I managed to say, "Sorry, I zoned out."

Her smile faltered a moment. "Oh, sorry," she said as she turned around, resuming her fast strides. "I talk too much. You probably want to enjoy the quiet of the woods for a little bit."

For the second time today, I'd seriously put my foot in my mouth. *Great, Oskar,* I chided myself. *This is what happens when you spend more time with books than people.* She'd been vulnerable when she talked about her lung disease, and I didn't blame her.

"No, no, it's okay," I said, trying to reassure her. "I really miss talking in German, even with your funny accent." She laughed like I'd hoped she would. "It's part proper High German and part a little accented from your grandparents in South Tyrol. It's nice to hear the two contrast."

I talked with my friends back home occasionally and my family frequently, but speaking in German again had been amazing. Her accent was damn cute.

She flashed me a quick smile. "What I said was, have you

been to Monday Night Brewing?"

"What?" I hadn't even heard of it.

"It's a brewery. It's not Augustiner or anything, but it's local and I really like their wheat beer," she said. "It's not too far from Tech."

"I haven't been, but I like beer."

"Living in Munich, I'm sure you do."

"I want to try it, but maybe I need a local guide," I joked. At least, I hoped the joke was obvious this time. "You know, to make sure I try the right beers."

"They don't have *that* many."

"Would you take me?" I tried being more direct. I couldn't tell if she didn't know I was fishing to ask her out or if she wasn't interested.

She paused a moment and adjusted her backpack. My heart hammered faster.

"I'd like that."

We ended up talking most of the way down and the car ride back, too. I wasn't bored at all. Plus, my body was thrummed every time I looked at her. There had been a lot to look at in her spandex pants and tank top, and all of it was fantastic. When her head tilted back as the laughter spilled from her full lips—Jesus, it killed me.

Too soon we were back to where we'd left the cars. I tried to keep cool when I told her I'd text her sometime this week to grab dinner or beers, but I was beyond charged up. We needed that date soon.

Five

Three years earlier January 9
LUCIA

"It's freezing in here! The thermostat says fifty-nine," my dad said. "Lucia, do you want me to turn it up?"

"No, *amore*," my mom said. "The medicine makes Lucia warm. She'll need a few days to adjust to it." She wore a ThermoBall for the outside winter weather. After a brief glance at her, my dad followed suit and put his jacket back on.

In my hospital gown with no covers, I was hot and battling the worst headache I'd ever had. I'd had three migraines in my life, but this was worse. Dr. Manson had said I would get used to the Hickman catheter in my heart they'd inserted yesterday. The medicine was a type of drug called a vasodilator and worked to remodel my heart and expand my pulmonary artery. The problem was it expanded *every* blood vessel in my body, including my brain, and damn, did it hurt. *And* I was almost sweating.

Just then, Dr. Steinberg strolled in. Julia had already been by before seven. True to his word, even though I had nothing ID related, my faithful doctor-friend had stopped by my room every day.

"Lucia," he said softly. "I hear you have a bad headache from Julia."

"Yes," I said, inwardly groaning. Even talking made me wince.

"But everything else going okay? Is the new anti-nausea medicine working?"

Like a magician, Dr. Steinberg had been coordinating with Dr. Manson to adjust my medicines and make everything better for me. He'd asked Dr. Manson to order me an IV anti-nausea medicine that stopped me from throwing up and had made several other small fixes to make my stay more comfortable.

"Yes." I smiled, looking at the little teddy bear his wife had brought me. "Everything else is better."

He clinically scanned my neck where I had the Swan-Ganz catheter before he put on gloves and peeked at my IV site for any sign of infection. "No site pain or swelling anywhere?"

"No, they all feel all right."

He nodded and gave me a small smile. "Good, I'm going to work on getting an okay for you to try this headache medicine I recommend. Does that sound good?"

"Yes," I said, shoulders sagging with relief. "Thank you, Dr. Steinberg."

He smiled affectionately at me as he left, his phone to his ear. I heard him saying hello to Dr. Manson.

As he left, a nurse from the drug company that would be supplying my IV medicine came in. I shuddered when I saw the model pump. How was I supposed to carry that thing around? It was the size of my foot!

Something must have shown on my face because my mom said, "We may need to buy you some new purses." Yeah, seriously. No clutches for me.

The nurse spoke for almost an hour about the medicine and briefly explained how to use it. I would be getting two because my heart would get used to the medicine and if it stopped suddenly, my heart could spasm and fail—*scary*. In the CICU, I'd use their equipment, but the nurse would come the day I was released from the hospital to help me set it up.

I paid attention the best I could, but all the medicines I was on made me loopy. I had to take four pills a day for Sjogren's, like I had for eight months, three different medicines for lupus, and now four for PAH. Plus, the constant IV fluid and pain meds.

I masked a yawn before we were interrupted by my daily echo tech coming to monitor my heart. After she left, the nebulizer team came for my twice-daily nose hydration therapy. The six liters of oxygen has been drying out my nose so bad it started bleeding, so Dr. Steinberg had asked Dr. Manson if I could use this hydration therapy.

By the time lunch arrived, I was worn out from the stream of visiting techs and doctors. My phone rang, glaringly loud, flashing Ru's name. I felt a twinge of guilt I hadn't told her what happened and had ignored her and Paola's calls. I didn't want to tell them about this, especially when I felt this exhausted and my head hurt so much. Telling them made it real. If they didn't know, then I could almost imagine it was a bad dream—and you woke up from dreams. Instead of graduating, I'd be flying back to Rome soon and dancing with Paola until the sun came out.

Mom observed me as I turned the phone face down until I broke our gaze. She sighed, but she didn't say anything. After a few minutes, Ken asked my parents to leave for me to rest. I flinched when my mom opened her mouth. Her shoulder wilted and she kissed my forehead, but thankfully her only words were, "Ti voglio bene, carina."

With everyone gone, I said softly, "Ken? Can you help me stand so I can go pee?"

With a smile, he nodded and hurried to start the laborious process. They'd finally patched my heart drain after it dripped out two full liters, so at least that was gone, but it still took about ten minutes for me to get attached to the portable IV pole with all my IVs and equipment latched on and another five for me to slowly waddle to my toilet, holding Ken's muscular arm for support.

Ken walked to the front of the room as I prepared to pee in my little bucket over the seat. The kidney was normally the first organ affected by SLE, not the heart and lungs. They measured every drop of my urine and tested it like they kept coming for my blood. Always testing and more testing.

"Ken?"

He rushed to my side to help me huff back to bed and then reset my lines. I watched him lethargically, barely able to stay awake. The bathroom excursion had used up my remaining energy.

A few weeks ago, I was living abroad independently; for the last few days, I'd needed help to stand and breathe. Without drugs and oxygen, my heart would have already stopped working.

When Ken exited my room, the tears I'd held in around the doctors and my family fell as I grabbed my teddy bear and turned my face to the pillow to muffle my sobs. I couldn't call Ru or Paola back, not yet. I was glad to be alive, but was this what the rest of my life would be like?

Six

My phone chimed and flashed Mom's WhatsApp contact. Surprise and then worry rippled through me. It was near midnight in Innsbruck and late for a call from my parents. She'd sent me several messages I hadn't gotten until it was too late to call back.

"Mom?" I asked as her face popped up.

"Oskar, all is good, but I wanted to tell you your dad is back in the hospital. It's his kidneys."

"Is he okay?" I asked, taking in her tired eyes on the screen.

"Yes, he's stable. I just came home. I needed a shower, and he wanted me to sleep at home. I was wondering, can you change your flight?"

"Is he that sick?"

Changing a ticket would be outrageously expensive, especially on my graduate student budget. My dad had had episodes with his diabetes most of my life, but he always seemed to pull through.

"No. No, he's fine. I'm sure he's fine." She didn't look sure.

"I'll call, but it's last minute—I'm mean it might be a thousand dollars. Should I change it?"

"No. No, no," she repeated. "I'm sorry I called. I'm sure I'm just tired."

"Hey, no worries. I'll call. If it is reasonable, I can change it."

"No, don't change it. I know your money is tight. I'm going to bed. I'm just tired."

"Okay. I love you, Mom. But I will call and see what I can do."

"Love you and goodnight."

The screen clicked off, and I logged in to my ticket reservation. After a little digging and a long phone call, I found the type of ticket I'd bought didn't allow changes. Last minute like this, a new one would cost two grand. I emailed Mom, explaining the situation. Guilt swamped me; I couldn't go see my dad right now. Georgia Tech was one of the best biochemical engineering programs in the world and with a Ph.D. from an English program, I'd have so many more doors open to me for jobs. Yet suddenly I questioned my decision for the thousandth time. I couldn't even see my fucking dad in the hospital. If I were in Munich, I'd be there in two hours.

Scents of my roommate's curried northern Indian food from the shared kitchen made my stomach rumble, reminding me how much I'd exercised today and pulling me from my brooding.

I wandered into the cramped kitchen with its bright white florescent lights and tacky lime green countertops. I was paid as a Ph.D. student but the stipend was small, and this shared place was all I could reasonably afford. Sujit and Ryan, my roommates and also Ph.D. students, were in the same boat.

Sujit smiled when he saw me. "Hey, you hungry?"

We'd become friends, despite having very different upbringings. Or at least we'd become as good of friends as you could be with our schedules. He was a super roommate—quiet, clean, and didn't mind sharing his cooking. But he wasn't one of my friends from home.

"Sure," I said, trying to return his smile. "How spicy is it this time?"

He laughed and shook his head. After living together for a year, he'd toughened up my stomach and I'd come to crave his spicy cuisine.

"Me too," Ryan, our other roommate, said and scraped a chair out loudly before plunking down. Everything about him was loud and slightly abrasive. He turned to me. "Oskar, you want to go out tonight? I need to meet some girls, and I know you haven't been on a date in a while." He cackled like a hyena. "Months!"

He was one of the most socially awkward people I'd ever met. I tried not to laugh as I took in his plaid shorts and baby blue polo shirt. Men in the American South dressed strangely in the summer. Ryan had a hard time getting dates, which was why he liked taking me or Sujit. He was smart and actually fairly nice, but the desperation leaked off him and girls seemed to sense it.

Sujit was engaged to a girl from Delhi he'd met while studying at the Indian Institutes of Technology (IIT) Delhi campus, India's premier technical school. She was planning on moving out here after they got married and he graduated. He didn't like going out too much. I honestly didn't either, despite being single. I was always so busy with school and hated dating. I knew I might not stay long, if at all, in America after graduation. Talking to my mom cemented that. It had been better just to watch cricket with Sujit than waste my time and money dating.

Even as I thought that, I visualized Lucia and that vibrant smile and curvaceous body. Heat electrified me, as if I was actually looking at her, not just imagining. For her, I'd put in some effort.

Even though Ryan tried to persuade me all throughout dinner, I managed to avoid going out with him by claiming genuine exhaustion. Sujit and I watched cricket after dinner instead in the folding chairs we had in the living room since no one wanted to waste money on a sofa. I glanced between the screen and my cup of water, feeling restless since meeting Lucia and worse since talking to my mom.

By ten I couldn't handle any more cricket, and I left Sujit still avidly watching. As I got in bed and drifted closer to sleep, I thought of Lucia again. Was tomorrow too soon to contact her? She was off work and school and so was I. I'd much rather spend a week getting to know her in any way she'd let me than watching cricket and fighting Ryan about going out to the bars.

Seven

I felt my gut tighten with nerves as the pharmaceutical nurse lectured us. Mom had a little notebook and pen held with almost white knuckles. Today, instead of learning about international politics, I was learning how to do my heart pump medication myself. Step after step, I watched. Plastic sanitary pieces and biohazardous waste collected on the bedside table as the process neared the end.

So much mess. So many steps. The knot in my gut tightened. I'd need all that to survive each day—the medicine, sterile water, IV tubes, sterile prep pads—just for one drug. This was not how I imagined my life. But I was alive and feeling better and better, so I tried to stay grateful.

As we wrapped up and I stared at my pump in my hand with a mixture of love and loathing, my mom handed me a little gift bag.

I raised an eyebrow, but she just said, "Open it."

I unveiled a tiny one-shoulder backpack.

"Well, you have to wear the pump all the time," my mom said. "I thought this might be comfortable for around the house and as a place to store it when you're sleeping."

The pump, the IV, and me: tangled, intertwined, and inseparable for an unknowable amount of time.

"Thank you," I said, although the thought scared the crap out of me. My mom had barely left my bedside during my recovery. I wouldn't be able to get through this without my parents' support, both emotional and financial. Terror almost choked me as I consider my mounting medications and lifestyle alterations. And their costs, which I had no way to pay for.

I still needed to call Ru and Paola. I'd finally been texting them back, but just said I'd been busy. It'd been becoming clearer and clearer that I might not go back to a normal life. This hadn't been a nightmare. I needed to call them, but where to start? I slid the pump in the shoulder backpack, and it fit well. That was something I could do—carry my pump.

Ken entered, flashing his white teeth in a grin. "Sweetie, you get to go home today."

"Yes," I said with a genuine smile.

"We will miss you, kiddo."

"I'll miss you too, Ken, but I'm glad to go home."

"I bet! Well, if it's okay with you, I'm here to remove your IV and then your mom can help you dress. Afterward, you can sit in the chair and Dr. Manson will be by to discharge you."

I held up my wrist guard, as apparently, I only had one good IV site in my entire body and said, "Yay!"

Ken worked fast, and I hugged him firmly when he finished.

"Thank you, Ken." He'd been a cheery constant, never far from my side during my long weeks in the CICU.

Mom helped me dress, careful not to tangle the tubing. The neckline of the shirt she'd brought revealed the heart IV site, a visible white disk and tape. It wasn't even low cut.

Mom followed my gaze and said, "Don't worry, carina. We can buy you some new shirts."

I nodded numbly. *Everything* in my life had changed. I'd slowly been processing my life will would be what it was, and I might never be the person I'd been before this lupus flare. Maybe that was why I hadn't spoken to my friends. I wasn't sure who I was anymore. I didn't feel like the girl who'd lived with Paola for three and a half years, or who'd been best friends with Ru for decades. I didn't know who I felt like, but that carefree girl seemed gone. I didn't know what to say to them or even if they'd like this subdued version of me.

Before I could dwell on it more, Dr. Manson strode in, looking as happy as I'd ever seen him. "Hi Lucia, you're getting out of here! I'll see you on Friday in my office to check in with you. I've heard you're still having issues with your blood thinner, so you'll be going every day to have it monitored until it regulates." He looked at my mom. "You know where it is?"

"Yes, I have the directions here." She slid a ginormous packet of papers into her large purse. That was what I would be studying instead of trade embargos and microlending strategies. I'd been weak and on morphine in the hospital, but now I needed to learn about my drugs and diseases. I'd always been fiercely independent—at eighteen, I'd moved to Rome, where I knew no one—and I wanted to understand what the hell was happening and what drugs were going into me.

"Good. And I hear the headaches are improving?"

"Yes," I said. They were better, but still occasionally terrible.

"Wonderful, so you'll be discharged with the script for the headache pain medicine. Call me if you need more, but I'm glad it's getting better. I know you've been walking with help around here, but I really recommend a walker for the first few weeks as you build up your heart. You have one?"

"Yes," my mom answered again.

"Good." He turned to me, face softening and voice lowering, "Lucia, do you have any questions before you go home?" I shook my head, and he put his hand on my shoulder. "You are doing really well. You don't realize how well." He squeezed my shoulder and dropped his hand. "Keep it up. We'll talk soon."

After that, everything seemed to rush by. Before I knew it, my mom was standing next to the transport person who'd wheeled me to the curb to wait for Dad. When he pulled up and of course I needed help, it really struck me, yet again, how weak I was. Mom would have to go to the DMV this week to get my handicap tag because even walking just a few feet from the wheelchair to the backseat had caused dyspnea. No one had told me when—if—my strength would return. This couldn't be the way I'd live forever. I'd take every drug they'd give me, no matter how much my stomach hurt or how much it made my head want to explode. I set my jaw—I'd wear this pump because I wanted a reset.

As all the doors shut, panic gripped me. "How am I going to be able to get up to my bedroom?" God, why hadn't I thought about that before?

Mom and Dad exchanged a quick look before Mom said, "Well, I thought you could use my office. I don't mind doing some grading down on the kitchen table, and it has a pull-out twin bed. We know you can't walk up the stairs right now, Lucia. You can use it as long as you want. And we converted the downstairs bathroom to a full just two years ago, so it's perfect."

"Thank you," I whispered. The scenery raced past, like my feelings—blurred and dizzying.

"Of course, baby," Dad said in his deep baritone. "We'd do anything for you."

And they had. I was so grateful to be going home, so lucky I had my parents who loved me and would help me through this. It was impossible to imagine navigating this alone. I couldn't have. I'd have gone to extended care.

Suddenly, misery threatened to overwhelm me. I was going home, but I still couldn't even walk up the stairs.

I'm going home and I'm alive, I repeated to myself. If I didn't repeat this mantra all the people who had asked about my mental state and if I felt depressed over the last few weeks would get a different answer.

Eight

My pulse sped up as I glanced at my dinging phone. I hated to admit it, even to myself, but I was looking forward to seeing Oskar again way too much. I hated dating, but there was something compelling enough about how he'd awkwardly asked me out— not to mention his broad chest and dimples—that'd made me throw caution to the wind. I'd seen his expression when I said "friends." He clearly was not looking for a friend.

It could be hard for me to put myself out there. My last boyfriend had left me, telling me my health issues were just too much for him, and I hadn't tried to date seriously since. I'd thought he'd loved me. Before that, my long-term Italian boyfriend had started cheating on me because I'd been sick so often. I'd gone on a few halfhearted dates, but school and work had been busy. Plus, heartbreak hurt, and I'd felt it both physically and emotionally— they both sucked. Dating scared me, and the fact that Oskar made my heart race and skin flush made it all the more frightening, not less so.

I took a deep breath. *You're looking for a friend—do not get attached*, I told myself before reading his text. *I'm on my way*.

My heart skidded in a way it didn't do for friends, making my jaw clench, and I forced myself to repeat the word "friends" out loud.

My long-sleeved shirt slipped on easily over my now-dried sunscreen-covered arms. Lupus was always in the back of my brain. The sun caused lupus flares, so I'd planned to meet in the late morning, which would reduce my sun risk. My left arm and face were the most sensitive. As long as I wore a light long-sleeved shirt, carried extra sunscreen, and we took the shady route, my sun exposure shouldn't be too bad.

I bent down and gathered up little Bea, who would be joining me, and strolled out the door. I was glad Oskar had said he liked dogs. Bea loved walking as much as I did. The MARTA station parking was shady as Oskar's car pulled in and then finally his tall figure rolled out of the compact that seemed too small for him.

We stared, and the greeting became awkward for a moment as we both seemed to wonder how to greet each other. He was a handsome biochemical engineer with no need to be anxious. I was sure he had his pick of dates. Me, I was just a girl with a lot of diseases. Of course, I'd *like* to date him, even if I wasn't really sure I wanted to put myself out there. My eyes raked over his sculpted shoulders—he was even better looking in normal shorts and a t-shirt than in his hiking gear.

"Excited to walk to Decatur?" I finally asked.

"Yes, very." His lips curved upward at me before he squatted to pet Bea. Diva that she was, she was up on her hind legs waving her paws at him.

"Ah, this is your little friend!" He reached out to her. We'd chatted on the phone twice since our hike and I'd mentioned Bea.

"Bea, meet Oskar. Oskar, meet Bea." I smiled as Bea licked his hand.

"Hey there, you're so soft!"

Bea was loving all his pets, and now her big tail was sashaying her body around. What a freaking flirt. She made me smile.

"It is really pretty here. You live here?" Surprise tinted his voice as he glanced around the beautiful historic Inman Park neighborhood, full of towering oaks, small parks, and vibrantly painted homes.

"Yep, that big Victorian mansion over there," I said, pointing to a massive white and green one with three visible balconies and a paint job that looked like it would cost the same as my teaching salary. A giggle escaped as I took in his slacked jaw. "Kidding. I live in a dinky one-bedroom, but I love this area."

"I can see why," he said with a grin.

"Let's go this way." I gestured toward the PATH trail.

We ambled along, chatting and sharing grins and glances that made my resolve to say the word "friend" more urgent. His adorable dimple nearly made me trip each time he flashed it. Between my favorite walk and his company, I was nearly bouncing with excitement. The route I'd chosen was mainly through parks with hundred-year-old oak trees or Victorian and Craftsman-style homes.

As we passed near the Carter Center, I pointed it out. "I've been to several lectures there," I said with glee. "They have really cool free lectures and book talks."

"It sounds interesting. Maybe we could go together sometime?" He flashed his dimple again. That thing was dangerous—it made me go completely melty inside. Oskar had a nice smile, even if you could tell he'd never had braces. He was doing his best to make my body fight the word "friend."

"Sure," I said, a little surprised. My obsession with the Carter Center's discussions was too nerdy for some of my friends.

The conversation turned to the courses he was taking and teaching in the fall. He really wanted to work with medical equipment. His voice lightened and sped up when he talked about it, making me beam. His passion for helping others was clear.

"I have just to complete my final course, for better or worse, and will be starting my thesis in the spring," I said. "I did the international economics concentration, and my thesis is called *The Cost of Unpaid Internships: Implications on Diversity in the United Nations Workforce*. It's long been a complaint that developing countries and interns from moderate- to low-income economic households are underrepresented as interns in branches of the UN because the intern labor is largely unpaid, and the headquarters are in some of the most expensive cities on the planet. UN headquarters are in NYC and Geneva, the Food and Agricultural Organization, FAO, is in Rome, the IMF and World Bank are in DC, UNESCO is in Paris, and the list goes—"

"Wow." Oskar stopped me with a chuckle. "You're super passionate about this."

I laughed, embarrassed I must have been rambling. My thesis was ever my bleeding-heart cause. I couldn't join the UN branches, but I could examine and write about them.

"I guess it's a good thing, as I'm knee-deep in stats and research and have to craft a massive paper on it," I joked bumping his shoulder. "It's just a big complaint that I would like to see highlighted."

He laughed again. "You're right, but why so much interest?"

I stumbled slightly. It was still so hard to talk about, even years later. "I thought about working for the IMF at one point." Then I pushed that thought far from my mind and in a cheerier tone, I rattled off the facts. "It's an amazing institution, and so is everything the UN does, but it's also hard to help developing countries when they are underrepresented as staff."

He stopped suddenly, making me halt and twist toward him. His gaze on me was intense enough to make me blush.

"What?" I asked, suddenly self-conscious.

"You're pretty incredible," he said, his voice slightly husky.

My whole body flushed with pride and embarrassment at his words. "Why do you say that?"

The look on his face told me it might have unintentionally slipped out. He paused, as if unsure what to say, before responding. "You're just so smart and enthusiastic—about everything, your studies, the walk, the restaurants we've passed—it's refreshing. Your perspective is dynamic, and I enjoy it."

He rubbed his hand compulsively on his pocket as if that had been difficult to admit or he was flustered. Something loosened in my chest. He was a little awkward and shy. I'd always been a sucker for nerdy guys who loved intelligent conversations as much as I did. Since I didn't know how to respond to that, I shook my head and laughed before I started walking again. His words made me feel like a million dollars.

I tried to think of something to say, then decided to make my PAH joke because I'd always liked dry humor. "I'm one in a million."

I peeked at him from my peripheral vision, expecting him to laugh, but instead, he said, "You are," and gently threaded our fingers together as we walked.

Nine

Three years ago, End of January
LUCIA

"I bet you want a shower first thing," Mom said as Dad stopped the car and they both helped me into the house.

"Yes, so much," I said, fiddling with my bag strap.

She'd been a saint while I was in the hospital, coming every day with clean underwear for me and taking my old pairs away. She'd bought me tons of cleaning wipes and would hand me a hot wet washcloth each night. She'd even found these bizarre showerless hair wash packets and helped me "wash my hair" every few days. But a real shower sounded like heaven. Still, I also was apprehensive about how this would work with my IV and pump. I was again reminded how *everything* in my life had changed.

"Come on, I'll help you," she said cheerfully as we entered the house and headed excruciatingly slowly toward the downstairs bath. "Your dad made a pouch for your pump."

My mom led me to the shower and turned on the hot water.

We both drew a deep breath as she helped me strip. I was still so weak. I suddenly felt like a child again, needing my mom to help me wash.

I caught sight of my pale, gaunt figure as the clothing came off. My stomach had been hurting from all the new medicines, and the multiple surgeries had taken their toll with scars, bandages, bruises, and weight loss. Twenty pounds, Ken had told me, and it was obvious in my ribs and lack of usual curvature in my butt. I glanced away, not wanting Mom to notice the pain in my eyes. *Is this really what I look like?*

A loud intake of breath told me she saw what I did. "Now I'm turning into Oma, but we need to fatten you up, carina."

"I think the steroids will do that for you," I retorted as she stepped away and brought the AquaGuard for the IV site and helped me cover it—it should never, ever get wet. Both Dr. Manson and Dr. Steinberg stressed to me the importance of keeping my right breast area as sterile as possible. Any infection would go directly to my heart, which apparently would be very bad—like, I could get an infection in my heart.

Without a hospital gown or shirt, the circular foam and short white IV lead were glaring before they attached to the clear IV tubing. Before I could dwell too much on my right breast, Mom took my pump from me. I watched as she looped the pump to hang in the plastic Ziploc bag-slash-coat hanger contraption my dad had assembled for me outside the shower curtain, since the pump was absolutely not waterproof. To my extreme embarrassment, I sat in the waiting shower chair while my mom helped me wash my hair and held onto me as I stood to wash the parts I needed to stand for. It took everything I had in me not to let my tears run with the water. It felt like a little bit of my dignity and independence was scrubbed away with each swipe of her hand.

I was a twenty-one-year-old college graduate who couldn't even shower herself. I focused on feeling clean and pushed the emotions away—I would not break down in front of my mom.

Huge clumps of my hair fell out as mom rinsed it. With my

IV tether, I couldn't even reach down and grab them from the drain. We both eyed them wearily. I'd gotten a bald spot the size of a quarter twice before, which I now knew was from lupus, but that looked like a lot of hair.

Mom said gently, "It might just be because it hasn't been washed in a while."

I gripped the sides of the shower chair, unable to speak. I was trying to be strong.

After the shower, peeling off the AquaGuard sucked. There was no way around it. It tore the tape covering my surgery/IV site, and my skin was red and angry underneath it. With a sigh, I sat on the small stool my mom had brought into the bathroom for me while she ran out to get the items I needed to replace it.

The stool was because stage four PAH was marked by an inability to do simple tasks, such as brushing your teeth without being short of breath. It was really important, Dr. Manson had stressed, not to strain my heart at all as it was recovering. The unsaid implication on everyone's mind was if I did, it would simply give out and I would die. I was starting to wonder more and more if that would even be a bad thing. Was *this* life all I had to look forward to? Some part of me wished I hadn't survived the surgery.

Mom reentered with the supplies, and I put on some gloves before I applied the alcohol prep pad to my upper breast and around the IV hole. It stung, but I tried to keep a stoic face as I covered it and braided my hair before slipping into some PJs.

Mom left me with Dad in the living room after that, and I napped in a chair while she went to the pharmacy and cooked dinner. When I took my walker back to "my room" that night, wearing the small backpack storing my pump, medicine container, and phone inside, my parents followed me with a glass of water. Mom's office, which had always been small, felt crowded with the three of us and with the twin bed out.

A cry choked me when I looked at it because my parents had bought me a pillow wedge. God, they were so sweet. They'd thought of everything I should have thought about, but it was scary that my brain wasn't working quite as well as it used to. My mom had told me not to worry, it was just the medicines I was on, but I couldn't help it. I felt like I couldn't think. My degree in international affairs was worth nothing without strong cognitive thinking skills.

My mom misunderstood my noise and said, "I hope it's enough. I brought you two big pillows, too."

I hugged her. "It's perfect, Mom."

My lupus attack had apparently affected not only my pericardial sac but also my lungs, which was why my cough had sounded so strange—it was coming through water. The cardiac window, which irrevocably severed that sac and saved my life, created a permanent hole, so my heart would forever drain into my lungs. I'd been sleeping and sitting in the hospital bed at a sixty-degree angle. If I lay down flat, within a minute I was coughing and felt like I was suffocating. I imagined it was what drowning felt like. I was taking a ton of steroids, sixty milligrams of prednisone and 2,000 milligrams of immunosuppressants, four times the dose of an organ transplant patient, but my lupus blood tests, C3s and C4s, were still coming back as active. Who knew how long this fluid would sit in my lungs? But some part of me thought, even once it was gone, I'd be afraid to lie flat.

"Are you sure you don't want me to sleep in here your first night back, Lucia?" Mom asked, wringing her hands together.

I shook my head and let my mom tuck me in like a child. "No. Thank you, Mom. I have my cell phone and my walker is there. I'll be okay. I promise I'll call you if I need anything."

Worry clouded her eyes. "Are you sure, carina?"

I felt so much guilt already for everything they'd been doing. Mom had taken family medical leave and had been with me every day. She'd given up her home office, and they'd been so gracious. No one had mentioned my stacking bills, or what would happen if I couldn't resume grad school in the summer like my deferment and insurance allowed.

"I'll be fine. Goodnight, Mom. Goodnight, Dad. I love you."

They both kissed my forehead and said they loved me before they went upstairs. When I heard the click of their bedroom door, I turned my face to my pillow, and ragged sobs shook me. The tears I'd been containing all day fell like Victoria Falls now that I was finally alone with my anguish.

I thought about *Twilight*, which I'd rewatched in the hospital. Bella had said, "Death is peaceful...easy. Life is harder." It wasn't the first time I'd recalled that quote. Some part of me wondered why they'd worked so diligently to save me to live like this. Fighting to improve was harder than letting go.

Ten

Present day, July 31
OSKAR

My gaze was constantly drawn to Lucia as she practically skipped with her overly happy and very vocal dog. They say dogs are like their owners, and I saw the resemblance. Both seemed to have a sense of boundless energy and buzz about them. Both were adorable, too. It was clear she'd been trying to keep her walls up, but I'd caught her eyes on me more than once. I'd swear they were as hungry as my own. And you didn't usually hold hands with friends.

Lucia had chattered practically nonstop about the neighborhoods we'd been passing and her favorite places to walk, or eat, or go to lectures, and I was honestly mesmerized by her. Her zest for life was contagious. I was eager to see and do everything she talked about. Between the hike and today, I'd had longer conversations with her than I'd had with anyone in months—maybe the whole time I've been in Atlanta. I was glad for it; I'd been beside myself worrying about Dad, even though he and Mom said he was doing fine.

Before meeting up with Lucia, I'd read up on SLE and PAH. Both were shockingly serious conditions, or at least they could be. SLE was in the top twenty causes of death for all women and PAH sounded grimmer than that. I'd caught her taking pills once on the hike and once around eleven this morning. I was interested in what they were and how often she took them, but I felt it was too early to ask.

As if taunting me, the sunlight highlighted her silky auburn hair just then, and my gaze drifted lower to her flat stomach, ass, and toned legs. Fuck, she was hot. It was hard to believe she was sick at all. She just seemed so vibrant, almost pulsing with energy, and the hike had been difficult. Even I'd been sore the next day. But her panting was real, and the website had nicknamed lupus an "invisible illness."

My eyes roamed her hungrily once more. I still wanted her. She didn't seem to notice how many people glanced her way. Her ass was fantastic in the shorts she was wearing today. I had to think about something else or I'd get another boner. "Oh, there's the water fountain! Let's get some for Bea."

She dropped my hand and picked up her little dog. With one hand, she turned on the water fountain and with the other, she held the dog to drink, which it did. Clearly, this wasn't the first time she'd done this.

"I don't let her tongue touch the faucet," she said as if to reassure me.

I just laughed and shook my head. "So, you guys do this often?"

"We take this walk a few times a week, but only occasionally do I walk to Decatur. It's a little far. Where do you want to eat lunch?"

Her quick topic change had me grinning as much as her rapid-fire talking.

I smiled as she lowered the dog back down with a kiss on its forehead—lucky dog. I wanted those lush lips on me.

Instead, I coughed out, "I've heard from some friends that this one place is really good. Aperitivo?"

She laughed so hard her dog started barking. I just gaped at her.

"Sorry," she finally got out. "We can't go there. My dad owns that restaurant—I basically grew up working there. Maybe one day or you can go with your friends, but, um…" She dissolved into laughter again.

"Seriously?"

Her cheeks were tomato red. "Yes, he's the owner-chef. He was studying at a culinary school in Bologna when he met my mom. She always jokes that cooking is his first love. He started Aperitivo when I was a little girl."

"Well, maybe one day," I said. "I've heard it's amazing."

"Yeah, but not on our first date."

I couldn't help a happy laugh that escaped. "Oh, first date? I thought we were just hanging out as friends. Isn't that what you said?"

Her eyes widened as she rushed to talk even faster than usual, which was some feat. "I didn't—"

I laughed again, cutting her off. "Lucia, I'm joking. I hope you consider it a date. I kind of do."

She glanced at me from the corner of her eye. A charming blush lit her heart-shaped face, then her lips turned up in a quirk of a grin. "Well, I guess I won't argue with you. I don't want to hurt your ego."

I took her hand in mine again. "So, not Aperitivo. I guess I'll just have to look around."

We kept walking for another thirty minutes until we hit the main strip of Decatur and started checking menus as we went along, but nothing was really catching my eye. Except her, of course. She was pretty damn distracting, and I was doing my best to control my reaction to her.

"Do you want a beer?" Lucia asked, gesturing ahead. She talked as much with her hands and body as with her words.

"There is a place here with good beer and they even have quite a few bottled German beers. That's why I ask—the food is okay, but the beer selection is great."

"I can always have one. You?"

"Oh, absolutely," she responded enthusiastically. "Although it's really far to walk back and we don't pass any bathrooms, so maybe it's better if I don't. You know what they say about beer."

"We could take the train." We'd met up at the MARTA station, and that was where my car was parked.

She smiled sheepishly. "I think Bea needs a carrier. I didn't really think about it. Sorry. Go ahead, have a beer. Come on, I'll show you the place I mentioned, and they have a patio, so it's fine for Bea."

As I followed her, I frowned, suddenly embarrassed. She had a lot of health issues, so maybe she didn't drink, despite what she'd said. Did I want to drink if she wasn't?

She turned to me with a smile but must have read my face because she said, "I'll have one. I do drink, but we have to walk around downtown Decatur before we walk the four miles back. Actually"—she cocked her head—"maybe someone at Dad's restaurant will give us a ride back. I still work some weekend shifts, so I can probably negotiate a favor."

"Weekend shifts? Are you always working?" I asked lightly, bumping her shoulder, glad to have an excuse to touch her.

"It's good money!" She whacked my arm back.

"And teaching isn't?" I asked in mock surprise.

"No, not really, but I actually like it more than I thought I would. I do enjoy it." Her eyes glinted with humor. "In case you missed it, I like to talk. And I actually like creating projects and things like that. I love seeing the kiddos get all passionate and creating videos and drawing conclusions, but it is a lot of work."

"But what happened to the UN branches?" I blurted out, remembering the way she'd talked about her thesis. "You seemed really interested in working with them."

Whatever I said was the wrong thing. For a moment, she

lost her sparkle. She looked devastated—gutted. *Fuck*, I had to get my foot out of my mouth yet again.

Before I could do anything, her lips curved into a big smile. "Here we are!" she said. But I could see it was forced. She greeted the hostess and indicated her dog before I could apologize for being too nosy.

When the waitress seated us on the patio with some menus and finally left, I said, "I didn't mean anything by mentioning working at the IMF. Being a teacher is a great job—very respectable." The words stumbled out.

"Thanks, I like teaching too." She drew in a deep breath and then surprised me by answering my original question. "The IMF and World Bank do pay some of their interns, but the time period is longer than my school's summer. Technically, I could apply, but I'd have to leave my job. I can't risk it, Oskar." She was looking down as she spoke, fiddling with a small water container for the dog. "I would need to take out a private loan, if I could get one, to afford my medicine and health insurance. I don't really want to risk that type of debt, and even if I could get insurance, it might not be the same. Some pay for barely anything." She petted the dog once and sighed. "Some other reasons, too. Can we change the topic? Teaching is fine."

I regretted my careless comment because despite her obvious excitement about teaching, she still had some lingering desire to work for the IMF or she wouldn't look so upset. I'd worked tirelessly toward my biochem Ph.D., and I couldn't imagine that being ripped away.

She placed her hand on my arm and in that moment, I wanted to pull her to me and hold her, telling her I was sorry for mentioning it, sorry it was no longer a possibility. The emotion shocked the fucking hell out of me.

"Maybe one day, though," I said.

She shook her head. "It's okay, Oskar. I am who I am. I would never say I'm glad this happened to me or that I want to be chronically ill, but *it is who I am*. I've always been me, but dealing with all this has made me more empathetic and mature. I like who I am now better than who I was four years ago. I'd like to hope I was always a nice person, but I was spoiled and carefree. I like who I am now better," she repeated. "We can't change the cards we're dealt—we just have to make the best of it."

Before I could tell her that I thought she was courageous, that she had an amazing outlook, the waitress plopped down some waters and took our drink order. We shared a warm smile when we both ordered two German-style Helles beers.

Lunch went again too fast for my liking after that, and we both opted to walk back. As we strolled the four miles back, the heat of the day was a little more brutal than before. Lucia offered me some of her sunscreen and put on her hat. The shade wasn't as consistent as it had been earlier, but talking with her more than made up for getting a little sweaty.

As we approached my car, she took off her hat. She seemed a little tired, and I hoped I wasn't boring her. I wasn't nearly as interesting as she was. I couldn't remember the last time I'd spent so many hours in a row with someone I liked so early on. Surprisingly, it didn't make Lucia stale. I was greedy for more— and for more than talking.

I cleared my throat awkwardly. "I don't know if it's too soon, but I know we are both going to be super busy once the school year picks up. Would you want to do something again on Thursday?"

The brilliant smile she gave me made her whole face come alive. "That would be awesome. Have you been to the High?" I must have had a funny look on my face because she laughed. "The High Museum. I'll take that as a no."

"What is it like?"

She looked embarrassed for a moment. "Well, it's not the same scale as many European museums, but at least they didn't steal any art."

Her words made me grin. I was reminded she'd lived

in Rome, which had many of the best museums in the world. And the Romans had been stealing artwork since before Julius Caesar and the Egyptian Obelisks. They hadn't let up between the Crusades and the present, either.

"They have this cool exhibit right now," she continued. "Something Woodruff—historic murals about a slave revolt, and it's open till nine on Thursdays. There's a cool bar there…" Her voice trailed off.

Fuck, I loved that she took initiative and had ideas about what to do. It was so freaking sexy she wasn't afraid to tell me something she liked to do. I hoped she'd be as decisive and bossy in the bedroom. My last serious girlfriend had wanted me to plan everything, and it had been exhausting.

"That would be great," I said, edging closer. Nerves fluttered in my belly, but still, I charged forward the question I'd been wanting to ask for hours. "Can I kiss you?"

Her eyes widened momentarily, but then she leaned forward and up to touch her lips to mine. Her scent surrounded me, a heady mixture of her shampoo—grapefruit—and sunscreen, yet it wasn't unpleasant. When her mouth opened, my hand almost of its own accord found its way to her lower back and pulled her and her curves, closer. She sucked my tongue deep into her mouth, tangling it frantically with hers, making me wonder how that would feel on other parts of my body—the part which seemed to come alive at that thought. Her firm body molded against mine, making me eager for more, to be closer, to grasp that fantastic ass and pull her core to mine.

I barely controlled my desire, knowing it would be much too much, too soon. I had to break the kiss because I didn't know how she felt about my friend rubbing against her in public. I was trying to be a gentleman. I'd planned to just test the waters, but the kiss ended up only igniting my passion for her.

Hands still tangled in my hair and face inches from mine, she whispered, "I had fun today," before she stepped back.

My heart beat faster as I rubbed a soft caress against her

long-sleeved arm. "Me too. I'll text you, and we can work out the details for Thursday."

I bent to pet Bea as Lucia waved a last goodbye and turned, allowing me to leave without revealing my rigid attraction to her.

Eleven

"Are you ready, Lucia?" my mom asked me.

No, I wanted to scream, but didn't. This was my first time changing the medicine in the pump myself, and I was totally freaking out.

"Yes, I think so." I glanced across the table. "I have the IV tubing, the medicine, the sterile water, alcohol prep pads, pump, pump medicine box, syringes, bio haz box, directions. Yep, I think I'm good to go."

"Okay, well, I'm here if you need me," she said in her calm mom voice.

I nodded but said, "I need to be able to do this myself, but thanks."

I reread the direction quickly. There were a lot of steps. Too many. The complicated process started with mixing the sterile water and my medicine dosing.

Once the medicine was in the box, I gently turned it upside

down a few times to mix the medicines. It was important because if you shot straight prostacyclin in your heart, you'd die. Next, I cleaned a new IV tubing and attached it to the pump. Finally, I double-checked the instructions and started the new pump, holding the end up and free so it stayed sterile. The pump made its strange squashy noises, and after a minute or two, the medicine finally reached the end. I stared, mesmerized by the fine droplet at the end of the IV.

I looked at my mom. "Okay, I guess here it goes."

The nurse had told me to never stop the pump, so without anything with my original pump, I held the new IV tubing in one hand and started disconnecting the existing tubing with the other. Within seconds of disconnecting the original tubing, bright red blood squirted out of my heart and everywhere.

"Oh, my god!" I screamed at the same time my mom yelled, "*Mio dio!*"

Adrenaline surged through me as I frantically tried to attach the new tubing. In less than a minute, my new pump had started and the IV line attached to my heart shifted from blood-red to pink to clear as the pump made those squashy sounds again, pushing the medicine into my right atrium. My heart thump-thump-thumped, beating a hundred miles a minute. Blood had soaked my chest and shirt. My mom appeared as pale as a ghost.

"I think I did something wrong." Understatement of the year.

I shut the other pump off, which had slowly been leaking medicine onto the floor. Using the nearby alcohol pads, I began scrubbing my chest as my mom whipped out her phone and called the pharmacy nurse.

After a short conversation on speakerphone, I understood the issue. The pump should never be turned off, which was correct, but since I had a continuous IV and not a port, I should have clamped the white IV attached to my body shut every time I changed the pump, or the blood would come pouring out. I'd unclamp it again when the new pump was attached.

Medical trash was scattered across the table and my bloody shirt filled my vision. Now I needed to clean up. Since I wanted to be as independent as possible, I refused my mom's offers to help as I put everything away. For better or worse, this was my life. If I wanted to live, I needed to start taking charge of it.

Twelve

I checked my reflection in the mirror one more time to be sure I hadn't smeared my mascara or eyeliner. With my dry-eye issue from the Sjogren's, it seemed like I always did, but my face was currently okay. Then I continued to run around wildly in my apartment, making sure everything was in order while listening to Spotify through the speakers.

Despite not wanting to date, not wanting to like Oskar, I felt my nipples and core tighten at the memory of his powerful arms locked around me and his hungry lips against mine. My skin felt overly sensitive.

Great job staying friends.

Oskar had texted me yesterday to work out the details of our plan. When he said he would pick me up, I suggested we take the train. Parking at the High was expensive, and it was one of the few places in Atlanta where taking public transport made sense, at least from my house. He was on a budget, I was sure, since graduate student pay was notoriously low. Being the good European he was, of course he agreed. He was due at any minute, so I used a Clorox wipe on my counters one more time. Bea barked steadily, always knowing by my frantic energy when company was expected.

I glared at her and said firmly, "Be quiet," even if it did no good.

I glanced around, painfully aware my place was nothing to write home about; in fact, it was a little blah. Well, artsy-blah. But it was mine and gave me a sense of independence I'd desperately needed. It was an old apartment building with wood floors and dated kitchens. The black-and-white checkerboard floors in mine had slowly grown on me. The dishwasher didn't fully open because the kitchen was so narrow, and in the hallway the washer and dryer were simply closed off by a fabric curtain, but it felt like home. And my rent hadn't increased in the three-plus years I'd lived here. It also meant I could afford the things I really needed, like medicine, while trying to save up for a trip to China.

A loud knock sounded on the door. Even if I should have been expecting it, it had me stumbling, and Bea running to the door barking more furiously.

"Coming!" I yelled as I grabbed little Bea so she wouldn't run away. I kissed her head, despite her being annoying—she was lucky she was cute—because I couldn't resist her. I peeked out my peephole to confirm it was Oskar.

"My humble abode," I said as I welcomed him in and then stepped to the side.

Grinning, he petted Bea, who was thumping her tail wildly against me. "Hello, Bea."

He smiled, shifting to me as I closed the door and put Bea down. His eyes roved over me, and my skin tingled under his perusal, wanting more than his eyes on me. Good lord, this dry spell had me horny.

His smile widened as he took in my olive-green dress. "Wow, you look better and better each time I see you."

THE VAMPIRE INSIDE Me

"Thanks," I said.

It *should* be true. First, I'd been in sweaty hiking gear, then walking clothing. Now I wore one of my favorite casual cotton dresses, which was the best because I could get away with not wearing a bra—always a plus in the summer.

"Do you want to see my place? Have a beer before we go or leave right away?"

He stepped closer, and I took in his scent, something little like DAX Wax and sandalwood soap that left my skin feeling even more heated. I leaned toward him, breathing him in.

"Yes, I'd like to see it, but first..." He paused, seeming unsure of himself.

I laughed lightly at his nervousness. I closed the distance between us.

With that, one of his hands found the back of my head, and the other caressed my bare back, making me shiver as he pulled me closer. Every inch of my body thrummed with awareness. Then our lips touched, and I felt my skin vibrating with need. My nipples tightened almost painfully in response to his touch and kiss. His groan against my lips told me he'd felt it where our chests met.

He had more than a half-foot on me, so I wrapped my arms around his neck to pull us closer, inching me higher. It brought our hips closer and pressed me tighter to him in a way my body wholly approved of. His hardness now torturously ground against my lady parts, making me want to keep going, while also warning me to slow down.

With one lingering swirl of my tongue, I released him and took a step back. Slowly, he withdrew his arms, his fingers lingering on the bare skin of my back in leisurely circular caresses before falling to his sides. When he opened his eyes, they held a passionate intensity. Butterflies fluttered in my gut, but I shushed them away. Instead, I focused on the tour.

"All right, this is my living room and office." I gestured to my cheap futon, which was helpful for overnight visitors, loveseat, and the desk I'd found on the side of the road. I loved that desk despite it having been someone's trash. It was great for stacking papers.

"This is my kitchen," I said as he followed me in. I whirled to face him. "Do you want a beer?"

I caught him checking out my butt, and couldn't help grinning. Only ass guys dated me. I'd always had a prominent one, and hiking had made it even bigger—but at least also firmer.

His cheeks turned a little pink. "Yes, thank you."

"I have Monday Night Brewery. You want to try it?"

"Yes, that'd be great."

He looked nervous again as I moved around the small kitchen to my bottle opener. I handed him the beer and said, "*Prost*," before walking back toward my bathroom, laundry area, and kitchen. "The bathroom." I pointed vaguely farther. "My bedroom, which you can see sometime *if* you're really good."

He laughed, like I hoped he would, and said, "I'll be on my best behavior, then."

The flash of his dimple killed me, and my nipples pebbled again at that—likely obvious in this dress. Maybe not the best choice.

"Come." I grabbed his hand. "We can drink this on the patio then walk Bea and get out of here. Do you mind taking my beer?"

He took it from me and asked, "Do you need any help?"

"No, no," I said with a wave, grabbing Bea and buckling her into her harness and leash. "I just need Bea and the fan; otherwise the mosquitos are terrible."

I juggled Bea and got the outdoor fan. I attempted to be graceful as I looped her leash around the chair, plugged in the fan, and turned it on. I adored my back patio. It might have been my favorite thing about this place, well, that or my neighbors. Luckily, I had the end unit, so it was more intimate.

"I like this beer," Oskar said, and we fell into an easy conversation about the exhibit we were seeing.

I'd looked it up on the website and found some articles

about it, since I had access to academic journals through my grad program. I briefly—ha, well, attempted to be brief—explaining to Oskar what I'd found. The murals were by Hale Woodruff and depicted important events in African American history. I told Oskar what I'd learned about Hale Woodruff, too, from a cultural history standpoint. Woodruff himself was an interesting person who'd studied with avant-garde artists in France, Diego Rivera in Mexico, and started an art program at one of Atlanta's historically Black colleges—in the twenties and thirties, no less. The High was part of a team that'd funded the restoration of these murals, so it was kind of a big deal, and I loved seeing history in more than just written annuals.

As I spoke, Oskar hung on my every word. He mentioned the Pinakothek der Moderne in Munich and how he'd been a few times on one-euro Sundays. I'd always been a sucker for a man with a brain, which Oskar proved he unequivocally had. And he liked culture.

I warned myself not to get too excited. If I just wanted to bone him, I wouldn't be too worried, but I liked more than his warm brown eyes, dimple, and hard body. I knew myself—I was a passionate, emotional person.

When my heart had been broken in the past, it had been weeks of crying myself to sleep—weeks of pain. I'd tried to hide it from my friends and family, but when Frank hadn't been able to handle lupus after Ali had cheated on me for basically the same reason, I'd been devastated.

Despite what I'd heard from fellow lupies, I seriously doubted any guy could truly handle me. In the past, love had been one of the most beautiful and painful things in my life. As excited as I felt about Oskar, I felt more trepidation. I was content with my life, and while being in a good relationship would make it better, I'd forgotten what it felt like. If someone left me for lupus again, the wound would be fresh and the loneliness that inevitably followed only more intense.

"Hello, Lucia?"

I shook my head, embarrassed I'd zoned out. "Sorry, sorry, I thought I saw a spider."

As Oskar repeated himself, realized it might already be too late. I was starting to like him, and even if I went back to being single now, his warm body and grin were a reminder of all I'd give up. Giving him my number had been a big mistake.

By the time we finished our beers, we were both eager to see the exhibit in person. We walked up to the MARTA station and crowded onto the narrow train bench. Oskar's leg brushed against mine the whole ride in the small train seats, and the friction made me very aware of him beside me. The seats couldn't contain his long legs and broad shoulders, so Oskar draped his arm around me to give himself more room. His calloused fingers prickled my arms, and he put his hand on the small of my back as we left the station. Both our bodies seemed to gravitate toward each other.

As we started moving through the exhibits at the High, I was drawn in, as I always was. Socially informative art always gave me goosebumps—thinking about what people did to promote change and how different things were now. And I loved discussing it. I was so enthralled with one piece I hardly noticed when Oskar threaded his fingers through mine. I glanced up at him, but he was studying the mural too. A bead of warmth expanded in my chest as I turned back to the art.

Oskar enjoyed this too, or so it seemed. As we walked hand in hand, I found myself grateful he hadn't been too slow or too fast for me; he gave me time to read the information before we discussed aspects of the painting or social history.

I couldn't help but smile shyly at him as he stared at a piece, deep in thought. I recalled Ali, my ex-boyfriend in Italy, my attempts to take him to anything cultural, and how horrible it had been. We'd lived in Rome, and he hadn't even visited the Vatican Museum.

Frank, my other ex, had been pompous, trying too hard at everything. That hadn't been fun either. Being with Oskar was easy and natural.

Oskar caught me staring at him and flashed his dimple, then leaned in close to my ear. "What is it?" he whispered.

His breath was hot against my neck, making me shiver. "It's nice to see you like this—that's all. I'm happy I suggested something you like."

He squeezed my hand and licked his lips before responding. "I like that you suggested it," he said with some hesitation. "My ex-girlfriend never planned anything for us; she always wanted me to plan something. I'm not always creative, and it's stressful always being in charge."

I beamed at his compliment, and that bead of warmth spread a little further. "I'd be a backseat driver, even if I was just a passenger. I get too excited about things not to have an opinion. But you can suggest things too."

Just then, my stomach growled loudly, and I laughed as he said, "Maybe dinner?"

We drank beer and ate at one of my favorite places, tension simmering between us. Throughout dinner, our bodies kept accidentally bumping into each other. And it was remarkable how well we got along, the conversation never lagging. When we finally took the train back, we did it with our fingers twined.

The back of the MARTA wasn't full, and the air was on full blast. I used it as a full excuse to snuggle into Oskar, and he didn't seem to mind at all.

"Do you want to come in?" I asked as we left the station.

"Yes," he answered immediately.

With a look that might have dampened my panties, we walked down the hill toward my apartment. I chewed my lip, suddenly nervous. I liked to set expectations before I let someone in. I'd never gone further than I'd wanted. Even with the few guys I'd dated who were jerks, I'd found guys appreciated knowing what to expect.

Before we entered my building, I said quietly, but firmly, "I don't want to have sex."

"Of course, Lucia," he said. "You set the pace. I don't ever want you to feel like you did something you regret."

He held my gaze a moment, and I nodded. Anticipation surged through me as we entered the hallway. His expression had been earnest.

"Thanks. I just don't like to sleep with someone unless we're exclusive."

We paused in front of my door. "I'm not seeing anyone else," Oskar said in a low voice. "Lucia, it's kind of early, but you're—that is, I don't think I've ever met anyone quite like you. I'm okay with being exclusive."

I paused with my hand on the door, wondering if I should change my mind about letting him in. I hoped he wasn't just saying that to get in my pants. Had I read his face wrong? I lifted my eyes to his beautiful mahogany ones. It was way too early to be exclusive. Maybe this was all a bad idea.

He must have noticed my hesitation. "Lucia, I swear to you I'm not saying that to have sex," he said in a low voice, aware we were in the hallway even though we were speaking in German. "I like you too much to blow it on one night of sex."

I nodded and opened the door. Bea, of course, was there, wagging her little tail so hard her whole body was swaying.

"Hi, Bea!" I said to her in my high voice. I rushed to the loveseat and Bea ran up and kissed me. "I have to take her outside. Why don't you turn on the music and make yourself at home?"

Once outside, Bea went potty as fast as I'd trained her. Nerves hit me as I approached my door. I hadn't thought he'd agree to be exclusive. It had just kind of slipped out. I knew myself—sex made me feel a connection, real or imagined. Some of my friends weren't that way, and I was damn jealous of that. I barely knew him, but I liked Oskar too much already to argue about it. And it wasn't like I was seeing anyone else, so why not? We'd talked more in a week than I'd talked to some past boyfriends in a month or two. We were lucky we both had this time free from work. My doubts from earlier threatened to resurface, but I urged myself not to worry about breaking up when I hadn't even agreed to date him.

"Wow, that was fast," Oskar said when he saw me.

"Ha! I trained Bea well. Sorry you had to cut your snooping short."

Oskar stalked toward me. "I guess you'll have to make it up to me," he said in a husky voice that made my body hum.

"Yes," I said, embarrassed by how throaty I sounded.

I'd never dated a German-speaking guy before, and it turned me on in a way I couldn't understand. Ever since I'd met him, I imagined being intimate, his deep voice whispering dirty things in my ear. Sex with someone who spoke another language was different—I knew from experience. That thrill pulsed through me again. I liked variety. And occasionally I liked being submissive. The thought of that type of play in such a harsh language had my panties soaking.

He led me to the loveseat, sat, and pulled me to it. We nestled against each other. His arm draped around the back of the chair, giving us more room. His fingers tapped the fabric behind me, sending vibrations along my skin, which was already heated from his voice and my wayward thoughts. Yet both of us waited for the first move.

I was so beyond stimulated that I gave in first. But instead of kissing his lips again when I leaned in, I went for the strong jawline I'd been admiring.

"You smell amazing." I trailed kisses along his jaw toward his ear in a way that made him shudder slightly under my lips. My fingers tangled in his hair. "Very uniquely Oskar," I said in a low hum before I nibbled and sucked on his ear.

He groaned and pulled me closer, teeth scraping my neck. "Lucia, you smell like heaven yourself, like grapefruit. I find it irresistible."

He nipped along my throat, and it was my turn to squirm under his lips. I lifted my knee and scooted over so I was on his lap, straddling him. His firm hands helped me up, caressing my ass and back. Suddenly, I could feel how very hard he was. His cock strained against his jeans when I leaned in for a deep kiss. I couldn't help but rock a little against the friction between us. God, his body felt amazing everywhere it touched mine.

With a groan his mouth moved lower to trail down my neck and the swells of my breasts. My nipples wanted some attention too, and I guided one of his hands from around my back to my chest to show him what I wanted. Our eyes locked for a moment and I nodded, giving him permission to move forward as his hand slipped inside my dress and bared my left breast.

"Fuck, you're beautiful." His whisper was throaty as he dipped his head, his stubble tormenting my sensitive skin before his mouth and tongue swirled around one breast, then the other, causing me to whimper and grind against him again.

He broke away with an almost painful moan. "Lucia, my pants are killing me. Can we move to the bedroom? I swear I will stop whenever you want me too. No sex," he promised.

I stood up, feeling emboldened by my arousal. "No sex," I reiterated before I pulled my halter dress over my head and stood a moment in my black thong. A garbled sound escaped him as I turned and walked as calmly as I could into the bedroom. I heard the clink of his belt buckle hitting the wood floor as he followed me.

I sat down on the bed and scooted back so he'd have room to join me. Slowly, he crawled onto the bed beside me. His touch was gentle and teasing as he circled my breasts, nipples, and stomach. His hand slowed when he reached my scar in the center of my chest, just under my breasts. I could sense his curiosity. It was a strange thing, but I'd always been a little proud of it. I'd survived heart failure, and the odds of that were small. That scar reminded me to keep fighting, no matter the chances.

"That's from my cardiac window," I said as he traced it first with his fingers and then with his lips. My lady parts were on fire, reminding me I hadn't been intimate with someone in far too long, nor had I bought that vibrator.

"It makes you even more beautiful and unique," he said.

"You have a story written on your body, and I want to hear more about it one day."

I tapped the irregular circular scar on my right breast. This one, I didn't like. I had other tiny scars on that breast from constant ripping of tape from delicate skin. The scars were ugly, but they had saved my life. "This was the continuous IV site. I wore it for a year and a half."

He kissed it too, whispering, "What a fighter you are," before dropping delicate kisses and nibbles all over my breasts and nipples. Shivering under his touch, I regretted saying no to sex tonight. At this moment I really wanted *something* inside me.

I reached between us and rubbed his erection through his boxers. "I want to make you feel as good as you're making me feel."

He placed one of his hands around mine to stop me from touching him. "I'm serious, Lucia, only do that if you want to," he said, pulling back a bit to meet my gaze. "I'm happy to take it slow tonight. I haven't met a girl I can talk to like you in maybe forever. I'm serious about not blowing it."

I laughed at that and wiggled my hand on him under his, which made him groan. "It's a little late to take it slow. Oskar, I said no sex. We can do other, um, stuff." My cheeks warmed at my words.

He kissed me hard again and moved his hand off mine, so I could rub him and tease him like he'd been doing to me. He let out a guttural sound deep in his throat and looked at me again. "Can I touch you like you are touching me?"

I kissed him passionately, completely turned on that he kept asking my permission. "Please," I whispered as I licked his ear.

I moved his hand to my panties and let his fingers slip inside so he knew I was okay with it. As I bit and sucked on his ear, I reached inside his boxers and slid my fingers around him.

We moaned together as my hand circled up and down at the same moment his finger slid into me. A riot of pleasure rippled through me as he slipped a second finger inside and his thumb found my clit.

"Lucia, god, you're wet," he said huskily.

I whimpered into his ear and nibbled on it again. I'd always been kind of loud in bed, and Oskar didn't seem to mind. I rubbed my hand up and down him quicker, feeling him harden more as he stroked me closer and closer to my breaking point.

I could tell by how rigid he was that he was getting as close as I was. I moved my hand more rapidly, moaning more frequently and noisily as his fingers moved in and out of me, teasing my nub. I didn't know how we managed it, but suddenly we exploded together, both curled on our sides facing each other.

Oskar leaned forward and kissed me gently. I glanced down, glad to see he'd come mostly on his stomach.

"Let me clean you up," I said. "I'll be right back."

Softly, he removed his fingers and kissed me one more time before I slipped on my panties. After I cleaned him up, I grabbed a nighty and crawled back into the bed.

He rolled onto his back and pulled me partially on top of him. His fingers airily thumbed my back while he pulled my thigh across him with his other hand. He kissed my temple and said, "Thank you."

I wasn't sure if he was thanking me for our intimacy or afterward. We lay like that for quite some time until the air conditioning became chilly.

Finally, Oskar spoke again. "I'm going home Monday for ten days, but I was serious, Lucia. If you want to be exclusive, I am willing."

"Okay," I said, and I kissed his muscular chest. For someone who spent a lot of time studying, he had a phenomenal body. I guessed that might be because it seemed like all his hobbies were outdoor activities.

He tilted his head to the side so he could see me. "Okay?"

I nodded against him. "Okay." He moved to get up, and I whispered so softly I almost couldn't hear myself, "You can stay if you want to."

I snuck a glance at him again. "You're sure?" he asked hesitantly.

I lifted off him enough to crawl up to kiss his lips. "Only if you want to."

I hoped he did. I loved snuggling but knew not everyone did.

"I do."

With that, he pulled the covers up around us and wrapped his arms tighter around me. That warmth that had been expanding in my chest all night grew dangerously hot as I nestled against his heartbeat.

Thirteen

Three years earlier, Early February
LUCIA

Itching tore through my torso and chest, strong enough to pull me from my slumber. Not like no-see-um bites itchy, but a mild tingling desire to scratch permeated my body. I clicked on my bedside light and lifted up my shirt. *Shit,* was all I could think as I looked down and saw a pink rash covering most of my trunk. Lowering my shirt, I sighed and took a sip of water with my morning meds.

I shuffled out of bed with my backpack and headed into the kitchen. Twice so far, I'd forgotten my bag. Having a sharp tug on my IV and chest tape had been unpleasant enough the first time. It really made me feel like a dog on a leash, so I'd tried to avoid it since.

"Mom!" I said, as loudly as I could without shouting as I entered the kitchen. Dad worked late as a chef, so he was still sleeping.

"Lucia?" Mom twirled from the Nespresso machine and

took in my face, lips turning downward. I slugged over to her as rapidly as I could with my walker and my extreme shortness of breath.

"Mom, there's a rash on my chest." Even I could hear the worry-whine in my voice.

Her shoulder sagged as she pulled a chair out for me. "Why don't you call Dr. Steinberg, while I toast your bagel?"

"Sure, um, thanks," I mumbled as I pulled the cellphone out of my backpack.

I was eating bagels or toast every morning because some of my medicines were so strong, I'd vomit otherwise. My phone read seven thirty, but I knew Dr. Steinberg was up and at work from the times he'd rounded on me in the hospital.

He picked up after the first ring. "Hi, Lucia. How are you doing today?"

"Hi, Dr. Steinberg. I'm doing all right, but I woke up with a rash on my chest and torso this morning."

"Can you describe it for me?" And I did. "Hmm, and do you have a fever? How well do you feel overall?"

"I don't have a fever, and I feel pretty good. Normal." I laughed. "Normal for me."

"I think you have a fungal infection on your chest. Have you ever heard of diaper rash?" he said in his calm voice.

"Diaper rash?" I repeated in a quiet, astonished voice. My mom turned to stare at me, eyebrows arched.

"Um, yes. Lucia, you are taking two thousand milligrams of immune suppressants. That is four times the amount for most organ transplant patients. You are also taking a high dose of steroids. Are you still taking sixty milligrams of prednisone?"

His voice was always so collected and even. If I ever had bad news delivered, I always wanted to hear it from him. I trusted him to fix me.

"Yes."

"Lucia," he said soothingly, "this is very normal for an immune-compromised person. Do you notice anything else?

Maybe issues with your fingernails?"

My thumbnail had grown a small white spot in the center. I'd cut it out, but it hadn't worked. Reluctantly, I described it to Doctor Steinberg, who said it was also a fungus.

Great, I was covered in fungi. Just what every girl wanted to hear.

"I'm always happy to see you in the office," Dr. Steinberg continued, "but based on what you have said, this is what I recommend. First, buy Desitin, the purple one, and apply it two to three times a day. Try to limit showering to two to three times a week, because the fungus likes moisture. Now Lucia, if you get chills, a fever, or if it spreads, you need to come in and see me immediately. If it is after hours, go to the ER. Do you understand?"

"Yes. Thank you, Dr. Steinberg, and I hope you have a good day."

I was lucky to have him. I still had horrible fatigue, and the last thing I wanted was to go in if I didn't have to.

"You too," he said kindly, "and please call me in two days and let me know if it is improving. If not, I want you to come in so I can look at it."

As I hung up the phone, I turned to my mom, who'd put the bagel and cream cheese in front of me. "Thank you. Do you know what Desitin is?"

She laughed like this was a hysterical question. "Yes, of course. Don't worry, carina. I can run to Publix on the way home from your INR appointment. We need to go soon, so you should eat up."

"Thanks," I said as I took my foul-tasting prednisone before a quick bite of my bagel.

My blood levels still hadn't stabilized on the oral blood thinner I was taking to prevent blood clots, so we went every morning to test my INR and adjust my warfarin dose.

I laid out all my pill bottles in front of me as I ate. I'd counted a few days ago, and I took twenty-four pills a day, plus the heart

IV and prescription eye drops. I'd made a lot of progress, but it had been slowly sinking in that my life might never be like it once was. I knew I needed to call Ru and Paola, but every time I considered it, I found an excuse not to. Each day, each clink of the pills in their respective spots in the pill case, was like another nail in the coffin of my former life. I felt like telling my friends would be the plunge that dropped the casket into the ground.

The chair scraped as Mom sat beside me, and I attempted to think positive. She and Dad loved me so much. But I was so lonely, and she was my only friend here. I should talk to Ru and Paola—I knew it deep in my bones. And it would only get harder the longer I waited. Honestly, if I wasn't so thirsty in the morning or I didn't have an INR appointment, I wasn't sure I'd even want to get up. At the end of each day when I was finally alone in Mom's office, I sobbed over all I'd lost. At first, I was so optimistic, but now it'd been over a month. Each day I felt like I had less and less to look forward to as my dreams drifted further and further away, along with the girl I once was.

Fourteen

Present day, August 3
OSKAR

Smooth skin and warm, lush curves rubbed against me as I woke spooning Lucia. I held her close with one arm, my hand resting on the silk negligee and under her toned abdomen. Her long wavy hair spread everywhere, and her grapefruit scent surrounded me. Her body felt like heaven in my arms—lusciously rounded in all the places I liked. I was as hard as a rock with her perfect backside pressed against me, her ass cradling my cock. I wanted nothing more than to bury myself inside her, but I could wait. This girl was worth a fucking wait.

As I breathed her in, I realized I couldn't remember the last time I'd woken up with a girl in my arms. Anita, my ex of almost three years, had never liked sleepovers. It might not be manly, but I'd always loved cuddling. God, how could you not want to wake up to this?

My arms tightened around her. I was shocked by how possessive I felt about her. How much I had already fallen for her.

After last night, all I could think about was another guy touching her, kissing her full lips.

Fuck that.

Even though it had only been a week and I barely knew her, I knew I didn't want anyone else to be with her. It wasn't like I was dating someone else. She was sexy-smart and made me laugh with her dry humor. And her body wasn't just tantalizing; it was so deliciously responsive. I hardened even more as I remembered her lusty moans and the way she'd writhed with pleasure. An orgasm alone had always felt only half satisfying.

I kissed her creamy shoulder that had become visible in sharp contrast to her vibrant turquoise lingerie. My stirring roused her little dog, who ran up and looked at me, wagging its tail. I petted its head, and it licked my fingers.

Lucia turned on her back, grinning at me. "Good morning, Oskar."

She reached her arm down to the dog, where her hand quickly became covered in kisses. I half wanted to do the same. She was still pretty, maybe prettier, with sleep ruffling her natural looks.

"Good morning, Bea!" she said in a voice she only used for the dog. After a second, she rolled out of bed with a "BRB" and headed toward the bathroom.

While she was in there, I heard the sink running for several minutes and assumed she'd also washed her face. I decided to look for my clothing before remembering it was in the living room and contented myself with petting Bea. The dog was really pretty cute. It was standing on my chest, wagging its tail with its mouth open, smiling at me.

I heard the bathroom door open, and she came back with her hair much tamer. The vision of her in the soft morning light in that little nightdress made me want to tear it right off her. I felt myself grow instantly rigid again, which was a problem because now I wouldn't be able to use the bathroom.

I tried to think of some complex math as she said, "So, do

you want to get breakfast? There's this place we can walk to. It's about a mile and a half away, but the bagels are *so* good."

"Sure," I said, standing up. "Let me just use the bathroom."

I smiled, noticing her checking me out. She caught my arm and gave me a quick peck before letting me slip past.

When I came back, she was in the living room. There was a neon green and yellow bag beside her that she zipped up when she heard me. Her hand closed around what looked like a pill case.

"Wow, that was fast. Let me just get dressed."

She pulled her purse closed and dropped something in it before grabbing the bag and putting it in the laundry area. She was biting her lip and fidgeting with her nighty strap as she did, and I suddenly felt like I'd intruded on a part of her life she wasn't ready to share with me. I was curious about her medicines, but I didn't want to be pushy. I could read clearly from her body language this wasn't the time to ask.

About five minutes later, we were out the door with Yappy, who started barking at something.

"Mikey!" Lucia squealed.

Ahead of us, a typical Southern-looking guy with longish brown hair and a baseball cap loaded up a bright red pickup truck. He squatted down as Lucia and Bea ran over to him.

"Hi, hi, hi!" he said excitedly to the dog, who was clearly happy to see him. He scooped her up and gave her tons of kisses.

"Oskar, this is Michael, one of my best friends," Lucia said by way of introduction. "Mikey, Oskar." I noticed she didn't give me any descriptor like *friend* or *boyfriend*, though I didn't know what I would've wanted, anyway. "Where are you going so early?"

Michael looked up at me. "Hi," he said, before standing up with Bea and snuggling her to his chest. "I have to go to Cordele for my nephew's birthday." His nose crinkled as he said it.

Lucia's face fell. "I thought we were going out tonight?"

"I'm not spending the night!" he said incredulously. Then

he muttered, "God, no. Oh, hell no. I'll be back late afternoon, but you can text me when I'm there. In fact, please do. I'm likely to drink the whole bar if today goes like the last time." He rolled his eyes before pausing to examine me again. He handed Bea to Lucia, giving her a look I couldn't read. "What are you up to?"

"We're going to Belly."

Michael gave a nod of recognition. Suddenly I wondered how close they were. Lucia had said just last night she was all right with being exclusive. I didn't believe guys and girls couldn't be friends, but they had an intense, almost unsettling closeness.

He hugged both Bea and Lucia before he said, "We can text today, or I'll call you on the drive back about our plans."

"Drive safe and don't text and drive!" Lucia shouted.

"Yes, Ms. Farris," he responded sarcastically.

With a wave, Lucia deposited Bea on the ground. "I can't wait to get some coffee," she said, bouncing on the tips of her toes.

"Where are you and Michael going?" I asked begrudgingly.

"Oh." She waved her hand. "Just Blake's."

"Blake's?" She said this like I should know what it was. "Is that a bar?"

She looked at me in shock. "You don't know Blake's?"

"No."

"Oh, well, um, yes. It's a bar. Well, bar-slash-club. They have dancing too. Michael and I go there all the time," she said.

Michael was good-looking enough to be competition and clearly was tight with Lucia and Bea. Something in me flared at the thought of her going out dancing with him. I'd seen how people danced here, and it was much more sexual than friendly, like it was back home.

"And Michael is one of your best friends and neighbors," I stated, but even I heard the edge in my voice.

"Yes." Her voice softened, and I could have sworn a look of true contentment passed over her face. "When I moved back here, I didn't have any friends. I graduated a semester early and none of my friends from high school attended Atlanta colleges. I told you I was sick?"

I nodded.

"Well, I had to defer, so I didn't get out much. Just me at home..." She shrugged, then smiled ecstatically—full of warmth. "But then I moved in here, and I met Michael, who was just about to start law school. He was my first Atlanta friend. I don't know what I would have done without him." Her tone turned sentimental, and her eyes looked almost misty as she said it.

Great. I was competing with a saint.

"But you guys never considered dating?" I asked with some hesitation.

Lucia laughed like this was shockingly hilarious, surprising me. "No."

"Why not?" I persisted.

She giggled again. "Michael doesn't like me like that. Oskar, don't worry." When I didn't respond, she added quietly, "He'd be more into you than me. Blake's is a gay bar. Tonight, they have their drag show, and then they open up the floor. I went to college in Rome and the clubs there—well, there was more personal space and more dancing with your friends. I loved dancing, but here I like it at the gay clubs better. Feels like college again—friendly and fun."

"Got it," I said, a little embarrassed by my wariness.

She smiled slyly like she knew where my thoughts had been, but the rest of the walk was filled with her usual enthusiasm and bouncy gait. We grabbed breakfast from the place she gushed over and headed to a park across the street. She practically pranced in front of me, and I couldn't help but notice how amazing her ass looked in her shorts, my eyes drawn to it like a magnet. She had no idea what watching her walk in those tight shorts did to me.

She twisted, catching me ogling her butt, and her eyes twinkled. Or maybe she did.

When we reached the park, she took the coffee and bagel, giving me that million-dollar smile that lit up her whole face.

Something in me tightened at the sight. I felt like I was falling hard and fast for her. A little bit of ice dropped in my stomach. I'd even told her a little about my dad this week.

It wasn't just those curves—it was *her*.

Fifteen

"Hi, Ru," I said timidly, having finally gotten up the nerve to call her. Sweat beaded my temples, a combination of fear of talking to her and the effects of the medicines.

"You are the worst. Friend. *Ever*." Ru enunciated every word in the dramatic flair she sometimes had.

"I'm sorry I haven't called or taken your calls." I tapped my fingers on the deck railing and sucked in a breath for courage.

"Is graduate school that busy? Don't make me regret accepting Georgetown," she teased me, not really mad. Sometimes we went weeks without talking, though this was the longest.

"I have to tell you something. I, well, I am not in graduate school right—"

"What?" She cut me off. "Are you working? Did you decide not to go? How did I not know this, Lulu?"

I let the silence drag a moment and said softly, "I had to defer. I was hospitalized most of January."

"Lucia!" I heard the panic in her voice. "Were you in an accident?"

"No, not an accident. I, um, I got sick," I said vaguely.

"What kind of sick? It sounds like you were in the hospital for weeks."

"I have lupus and pulmonary hypertension." Already short of breath, I explained as briefly as I could what had happened.

"Why didn't you tell me?" She sounded hurt.

"I'm sorry." I felt tears sting the backs of my eyes as I said truthfully, "I thought maybe if I didn't, I'd get better. But Ru, I'm not in the hospital, but I'm not getting better."

We talked for a long time until she had to go to classes. Part of me felt relieved to have told her. Yet a bigger part, the part I feared, acknowledged I could no longer pretend this had been a nightmare, like the ones that had plagued me to the point where I had to sleep with Ambien.

As depressed as I'd been after my first shower, where my mom had to help me wash myself, I took in a calming breath and called Paola to face the painful reality once more. This wasn't a nightmare—this was my life.

Sixteen

My heart pounded in my chest, partially from nerves, partially from Atlanta traffic, but mostly from thinking about Oskar. I really had it bad. So bad. And that scared the shit out of me. At the mere thought of him, my world brightened, like I was looking at everything through rose-colored glasses. He was interesting, good looking, and smart—not to mention, I was very attracted to him. It seemed obvious, but I was picky. My lady parts tightened as I recalled our recent farewell kiss at the airport. Still, I was terrified of dating.

I'd dated quite a few guys in the three and a half years since my bout in the ICU and weeks of hovering near death. Yet Frank and Ali always hung in the back of my mind. After my breakup with Frank, I'd wondered if anyone would ever want to be with me for the long-haul—someone chronically ill.

When Mom and Michael came over with beers to celebrate, I'd realized they thought I was better off without Frank. Even knowing—yes, fuck yes—they were right, I'd cried off and on for a few weeks when sleeping alone at night. I wasn't sure I'd ever find love and my happily-ever-after.

As much as I hated to admit it, eventually I saw Mom and Mikey's point. I was healthier and happier without Frank. He hadn't been a good boyfriend, not like my first boyfriend, Raúl, or even Alessandro, until he'd cheated on me. But I'd been with Frank because I'd been afraid of being alone, afraid no one could love someone like me.

And who could?

Currently, I liked my life. Hell no, it wasn't perfect, but I was content. I wasn't sure dating would be good for me, especially if it led to someone not being able to handle my illnesses again.

These budding feelings also brought the terror of putting myself back out there. I was in a good place now, but hearing the words I'd heard from Frank again might break me. There were a lot of things to talk to Oskar about, and a lot of complications that came with dating someone chronically ill. He had his dad, so he understood a little, but it was different with a partner. I'd noticed the curiosity on his face he saw all my medicine. He'd only seen this side of me—the side of me that was happy and embracing every moment. The side that knew life was short, and the only constant in life was death, so you had to live in the now. I could only hope he would still have that fire in his eyes when I got sick and couldn't do anything fun for weeks at a time. Or when I was too fatigued and canceled our plans to sleep instead. But maybe he'd be like Ali and pretend he was all right with everything while sleeping with someone else behind my back.

I tapped the steering wheel with my fingers, huffing my worries as I drove through Atlanta traffic. There was almost always traffic here. I was only in it because I'd offered to drive Oskar to the airport. He wouldn't be back until the sixteenth, ten days away. Ten days, a normal time in between dates, but that it sounded like so long told me how I truly felt. I tried to tell my heart to chill, but it wasn't listening very well. And it wasn't just my heart—I'd enjoyed hearing German while getting frisky more than I thought I would. I was screwed. Literally, part of me hoped. And now we were dating.

The only thing that kept my worries from spiraling out of control was that he seemed as into me as I was into him. Living in another country wasn't always easy. My whole life, I'd dated guys from many places around the globe, and I understood sometimes that was tough. Even though I felt partially Italian, Alessandro and I had been brought up very differently. Rome wasn't South Tyrol, and I was also half American and born in the USA quite literally.

Oskar seemed happy I understood his language and way of life. My grandparents' culture was not so different from his; I'd spent nearly a month there every summer and it had rubbed off on me. I could see why that might draw him to me, but I was scared, too. We'd been having great fun, but work and his graduate school were about to start back up, and things could get busy quickly. Plus, his dad was sick overseas.

Take it easy, Lucia. You're just dating, not getting married.

It was four by the time I pulled into my parents' driveway after some mild cursing at the Atlanta traffic.

"Mom! I'm here," I hollered, entering the kitchen. I grabbed a Pellegrino and took my afternoon meds as she came into view.

She greeted me warmly with a kiss to my cheeks and a "Ciao, carina."

"Can I borrow your car, please? Traffic is already bad. I think I can do it all in one load in the Outback."

"Sure," she said, walking toward the basement. "I'll help you load up your classroom supplies. What do you feel like for dinner? I bought bronzino, but your dad is always willing to eat that if you want something else."

"Bronzino's good, thanks." I'd become a pescatarian the summer of my illnesses. Some studies believed hormones affect lupus. I'd felt better since I dropped the meat, so I'd stuck with it. Originally, neither of my super foodie parents liked it, but it seemed to make me feel better, so eventually they accepted it. I intensely missed amatriciana, my favorite Roman dish, but you couldn't win them all.

Working together, we loaded up the car quickly. I was right—it all *just* fit in her car. Then I felt my phone buzzing.

I had a WhatsApp message from Oskar. *My flight is boarding soon, but I wanted to say thanks again for the drive-kuss.*

I messaged back, *I hope you can get some Zzz. Drink some Augustiner for me, xo.*

"What are you grinning like that about?" My mom scrutinized me. "Is there a boy? I know that look! That is a happy sex look!"

"Mom! I am not having sex with anyone right now," I said, exasperated. My parents had me when they were both older and were still very much in love *and* lust. My mom wanted the same for me.

She winked and said, "I'll get more out of you over wine. Bring Bea when you come back from school and spend the night."

"Ma," I warned her, but I was only teasing, and she knew it.

"Of course, carina," she said. We both knew she was going to pry anyway.

I decided to indulge her, because I loved my mom and would never forget her being there for me every day I recovered and because I didn't drink and drive—ever. I'd been too blessed by my recovery to chance my life or others'.

When I got to the side door of my school, my coworker Anu was there. "Thanks!" I said as she held the door open for me.

"Of course! Did you finish your classes yet?"

"One more. How was Hyderabad?" I asked. She'd told me at the end of the school year she'd be visiting her parents in India for three weeks.

Her face turned serious as she followed me and opened the door to my classroom for me. She shook her head. "The kids don't like going to India. I don't know what to do with them. They are spoiled."

I laughed at her comments. She'd been one of my best friends at school because not only was she an international person, like I was, but her husband was a physician, and she understood about my lupus and being out sick. Their marriage made me want an arranged marriage. She was less than ten years older than me, but she'd had her son at twenty.

"You look fantastic, Lucia," she said, looking me over. "How's everything been?"

By "everything," I knew she meant my health. "I am hoping for less sick days this year."

I'd had nineteen last year, which made me feel embarrassed and guilty. It'd also had done nothing to endear me to the principal. A room change for no reason was usually the administration being petty and why I'd had to lug my stuff back and forth from my parents' place.

She nodded as her phone rang. I hugged her quickly as she whispered, "See you soon, and we can catch up more."

I went back to my car and did the rest of the trips quickly, feeling excited again now that I was back in the building again and seeing my friends. Some texts from my mom halted me from my poster hanging and reminded me I needed to hurry to my dinner date. I glanced around the room, happy once more about the school year and grateful for this job. But for a minute, my eyes slid closed and I thought about Oskar's words and my buried dream of the IMF. Suddenly, instead of posters in my hands I imagined revenue reports. And instead of helping a few students, I imagined improving the developing world's economies and traveling to faraway landscapes I'd always dreamed of visiting.

My eyes flew open, and I looked at my world map. I looked at all the countries—most of South America and Africa—that required the yellow fever vaccine. The live vaccine I couldn't take while on immunosuppressants. Even if by some chance I made it to the IMF, I'd be working at a desk, not working in the field.

I closed my eyes tightly to block the tears and stopped what I was doing, disgusted with myself. This was my life, and I was happy with it. I was healthy. I opened my eyes to the remaining bare cinderblock and swiftly grabbed my purse before hurrying back to get Bea and have dinner with my mom.

Seventeen

Holy hellfire, my throat hurt. That was what woke me up. I took a sip of water for my morning medicine as excruciating pain shot down my throat. Even my tongue stung all over. Confusion settled over me as I gained consciousness. This felt similar to strep throat, which I'd had so many times it wasn't funny, but that couldn't be right. I was taking the motherlode of antibiotics right now.

Dr. Steinberg had warned me to be careful, and honestly I thought I had been, but between Sjogren's making me susceptible to skin infections, my history with methicillin-resistant Staphylococcus aureus (MRSA for short), taking a whole hell of a lot of immunosuppressants, and nicking myself shaving my leg because I was literally tied to the top of the shower and couldn't bend down properly, I had gotten an incredibly nasty and potent infection on my shin. Courtesy of said immune suppressants, within twenty-four hours, it had spread dark pink cellulitis from my foot to my thigh. I'd been in Dr. Steinberg's clinic the last two days getting Vancomycin, a top-gun IV antibiotic. There was no way I should have strep. Vanco should have blasted that to smithereens.

I drew a steady breath. I'd see Dr. Steinberg at one thirty. Whatever it was, we would handle it. However, when I got up and opened my mouth to look at my throat. *No, no, no!*

"What the fuck?" I screamed at my reflection before looking again. Yep, still the same. My tongue was almost completely black. Not purplish, like I'd drunk too much red wine—which I hadn't—but straight-up black. I had the plague!

After what felt like the wait of my life, I sat in the exam room with my mom as Dr. Steinberg walked in.

He greeted us with a smile. "Hi, Lucia. How are you feeling today?"

"Dr. Steinberg, my throat and tongue hurt and, well, they're black." Even I heard the whiny-worried pitch to my voice.

In his unshakable voice, he said, "Can I see?"

I nodded as he put on his gloves and approached me.

"Stick out your tongue."

I did.

"Yep, it's black. It looks painful," he added sympathetically.

He stepped back, threw away his gloves, and put on a new pair. "How is your stomach? Is it itchy and red?"

"Well, um yeah. It itched super bad last night and this morning. It was a little pink, so I started using the diaper cream again," I confessed, a little embarrassed.

I hated the satire of regression my life had become. Since I'd been released from the hospital, I'd been back for doctor's appointments more times than I could count.

"Can I see?" I lifted my shirt in response, and he nodded. "Your hands, please."

I held out my hands, and he looked at my fingernails. He stopped at my thumb, which was cracked worse than normal. The white in the center had spread. Fingernail fungus, *gross*.

Finally, he said, "Lucia, you have a very bad case of thrush, a yeast infection."

My cheeks burned. "Um, I'm not itchy down there."

He laughed and quickly added, "Yeast infections aren't always gynecological. I understand why you might think that, because this type of infection isn't common with people your age, normally infants and elderly, but you are immune-compromised, and the antibiotics can take away even more of the good bacteria on your skin. I will start you on an antifungal. I need to talk to Dr. Ramsey and Dr. Manson and decide what medicines we all agree for you to take. Some of your medicines can cause liver failure, so we need to be careful about what we add. This is your last day on Vanco, too, so I'll be switching you to an oral component. Why don't we get you started on the IV and then bring you back in here to discuss treatment after we all come up with game plan?"

He inspected me thoroughly, clinically, and he frowned, eyes lingering on several bruises.

"Okay," I said in a small voice.

I kept trying to maintain a positive attitude, at least when I wasn't alone. *I'm alive. I'm alive*, I chanted to myself.

I'm alive, but shit, this life is hard.

Not for the first time, I had a horribly ungracious thought that maybe the doctors shouldn't have done so much because I absolutely hated living like this. It'd been painfully difficult to talk to Paola and Ru about their normal college lives when I'd had one only months before.

"We will also do some lab tests and get a baseline for your liver enzymes and some other things," Dr. Steinberg continued gently. "We want to be sure the thrombocytopenia doesn't come back. You are doing your INR at home, right?"

The frequency of my antibiotic use and lupus flares had given me a history of thrombocytopenia, or low platelets. I'd also been covered in bruises from that and from my blood thinners.

"Yes," I answered quickly.

My blood thinner wouldn't regulate to the correct level, and

I needed to monitor it daily. After having to pay for me go in every day to test the blood thinner, our insurance sent a home prick test I did daily. I knew how to read it and slightly adjust it.

"It was high, but I'll skip it this afternoon."

"Okay, good. I know this hurts, Lucia. We'll get you better soon, and I'll see you in an hour."

"Thank you, Dr. Steinberg," I said as I slid off the table and walked to the infusion room.

I knew he would. He'd call all my doctors and tinker with my medicines until I felt better. He couldn't cure any of my diseases, but he'd collaborate and advocate with everyone nonstop on my behalf.

I tried to act upbeat for my doctors who worked so hard and my parents who hadn't complained once about adjusting their schedules or my mounting bills, but every day that veneer got harder and harder to keep up. I'd been out of the ICU for almost a month, and it had become clearer than clear that I'd likely never work for the IMF or possibly even travel. My grandparents and their home I loved so much might be a piece of my past.

Sometimes when I woke panting and sweat-drenched from my nightmares, from the vampires that hunted and killed me, I almost wished they were real. I'd never admitted it, but the thought clung morbidly to the silent room and darkness between night terrors. At least with the sleeping pills, the sentiment didn't last long until sleep pulled me back under.

Eighteen

My heart skidded like the wheels of the bus as it pulled into the Innsbruck station. The last two hours had seemed to crawl by. *Fuck*, staying awake with the jetlag was trying. Yet knowing I was going to see my dad in the hospital after he'd been there a week while I went on dates with Lucia was enough of a guilt trip to keep me awake.

I sat up straighter, looking out the window to see both my mom *and dad* waiting for me. My breath whooshed out me as I gathered my stuff. Mom had said he was doing well, but last week had been the first time it had really struck me how far away I was from everyone. Atlanta sure wasn't Munich when my family needed me.

"Hey! Oh, I'm so glad you're not in the hospital," I exclaimed, throwing my arms around Dad first and then Mom. As I stepped back and we walked towards the car, all smiles, I couldn't help but ask, "So, everything all right?"

I could have sworn he blushed. "I was dehydrated, so it stressed my kidney. After fluid and a few days of observation, I was fine. Totally fine now. You could have stayed in Munich a few days with Gunter, like you planned."

"Gunter said it wasn't a problem," I said. "I need to see you guys too." God, it was sad how much I'd missed my parents.

"Anna's still at the house with Alex and Sophia," Mom informed me. "Hendrick had to go back to work already, but at least you get to see your niece and nephew. They've missed you."

I smiled at her rambling. She and Lucia would get along just fine. Shit, where had that thought come from?

I cleared my throat and said instead, "I've missed them. I can't believe it's been eight months since I was here last Christmas."

It seemed surreal. Mom chatted on and on about everything and Dad and I squeezed a few words in edgewise, but mainly she talked like we hadn't spoken at least once a week since I'd moved away.

Sophia and Alex ran out of the door as we pulled up. "Ugh," I grunted as I lifted them up in a huge swinging embrace. *Shit*, they certainly were bigger and heavier than the last time I did this.

The next few days flew by, and it was a relief to see Dad back at work and his diabetes appearing totally under control. Before long, my time with my parents and even hiking with my middle sister, Johanna, was done, and I found myself back at Munich Central Station.

Before I could even get off the bus into the late afternoon

heat, I heard my name. I glanced around until I caught a glimpse of Gunter, my best friend and past roommate. He hurried toward me, and his familiar face made me grin. *Fuck*, I'd missed him.

It was sweltering in the late summer sun. We wasted no time hitting the main crosswalk and hurrying up to his place. I dropped my bags, and we flopped down onto the sofa.

"I've never seen your place this clean." I was shocked. It wasn't like Gunter was messy, but his place was spotless.

Gunter just laughed. "I stay at Claudia's a lot. Her place is bigger and, well," he shook his head, "Oskar, I can't wait for you to meet her. I can't believe you haven't yet. I'm not sure what she sees in me." He was still shaking his head, but grinned as he said it.

By the look on his face, I could tell he was completely into her. I smiled because I was halfway there with Lucia, and I'd just met her. "I'm happy to meet her. Is she coming tonight?"

"Nah, man, I'm not *that* whipped. We can do breakfast in the morning. If you still want to go biking?"

"Yeah. I haven't biked at all in Atlanta. Plus, you took the day off. It seems like we should do something with it."

"Shut up. You're here. But your dad's okay now?"

I laughed. "He's totally fine. I shouldn't have changed—"

"Man, your dad was sick. Enough said, okay?"

"Okay, thanks."

He changed the subject. "What about you? Anything going on over there in America? Have you found someone who can find Innsbruck on a map?"

He burst into laughter at his own joke. God, us engineers were so awkward it was amazing either of us could find someone to date.

"I've met a girl who can find Innsbruck on a map." It'd been surprisingly hard, hence the joke.

"Really?" He turned to look at me. Something in my voice must have betrayed how much I liked Lucia.

"Actually, she speaks German."

Gunter coughed. "What? Why?"

His mouth was hanging open as I explained to him about her family. Before I could even get a sentence past her having gone to college in Rome, Gunter interrupted me, "Wow, she's cooler than you are. Do you have a picture?"

"I have one."

Originally, I'd saved her profile picture because I'd missed her. She'd sent me two more pictures at my request, although to my disappointment, nothing dirty. *Fuck*, it wasn't right how much I thought about her. We'd even video chatted once already, and we'd messaged each other every day.

"Let me see her," Gunter pressed, oblivious to my pining.

When I pulled up Lucia's picture, he whistled. "Shut up, man. You're dating her? Or is that just some random girl you know?"

I bristled slightly. My sense of humor had never been quite as self-deprecating as his. I looked at the picture, suddenly self-conscious. It was a fantastic picture; I knew because I'd looked at it every day. She was twisting to face the camera, laugh-smiling in a backless top. You could see her muscular back and fantastic ass in the shorts she was wearing. In my opinion, she was a ten, especially with her exuberance for life and her intelligence. Maybe an eleven with how responsive she'd been in the bedroom so far.

"Yes." I quietly added, "Not very long. But you know, we're a couple."

Gunter looked at her again. "I don't blame you, man. And she speaks German fluently? What does she see in you?"

I swallowed, suddenly wondering the same thing. I'd never had trouble dating before, but she was stunning. Was she too gorgeous for a boring engineer like me?

Thank god I was saved from answering by Gunter's phone ringing. Apparently, half of our friends were already in the beer garden.

"I'm ready," I said, and changed the subject to something I

knew would totally distract Gunter during the walk there. "How is everything at Mercedes?"

We'd studied at TUM together, but I'd taken the biochemical engineering track and he'd done automotive engineering.

His eyes lit up. From our previous talks, I knew he loved his job. When it came to work, asking him about it was like asking a grandma about her grandkids. After a ten-minute monologue about the latest model his team was working on—not finished at all—we got to the beer garden. With a collective groan, everyone told Gunter no job talk.

I looked around the wooden benches at my college buddies and felt like I was home. Atlanta was nice, but I couldn't wait to move back here. My friends and the Augustiner Keller beer garden were the same as always. If I'd taken the Ph.D. here, like I'd been offered, I could do this every weekend. Plus, I could visit my family whenever anyone got sick.

My thoughts were interrupted by Gunter. "You guys would not believe the hottie Oskar is boning."

"I'm not boning her. We just started dating."

Everyone laughed, and Hans shouted, "You're red. Are you embarrassed?"

Gunter teased, "Yeah, he's embarrassed about his fake girlfriend. If you saw this girl, you would not believe she'd date him."

"Oh yeah?" Peter taunted. "Call her."

"No."

Gunter and Hans laughed, and I couldn't believe they'd just had one stein.

"Fine, I'll text her and see if she's busy," I grumbled while I dug out my phone and texted, *Hey Lucia, at your favorite beer garden. Have time to do a quick video chat?*

My WhatsApp video buzzed a second later and Lucia popped up, speaking German a million miles an hour. "Hey! I only have five minutes before my next meeting, but I had a second to call you back."

"Are you really dating this dork?" Gunter shouted.

Lucia laughed and blushed. "I guess so."

My friends hooted. "She guesses so," Hans said.

"No, we're dating," she said, blushing a deeper red. She turned around and said in English, "Go on, Anu, I'll be right there." Turning back to us, she said, "Hey, I'll see you in a few days. I need to go to my meeting." She grinned the huge smile I loved. "You guys have fun and enjoy all that beer you will not get here."

"Bye. Uh, I'll call you again if I get a chance."

She shook her head. "Don't worry. I'll see you in two days. Ciaooooo. Ciao, ciao!"

She clicked off the screen, and I chuckled how she still said goodbye like an Italian even though many Austrians said "ciao" too.

Peter was the first to speak. "Gunter, you were right. That girl is much too hot for this dork."

I felt my cheeks heat even further. Ribbing went round and round. Well, at least until our beers were finished and straws were drawn to decide who would wait in line for the next round. Luckily, the conversation changed to something besides my love life. The fun times resumed, and I almost felt like college had never ended.

Still, hours later when I fell asleep that night imagining Lucia's curves, I could only hope they were joking that Lucia was way too good for me.

Nineteen

Three years earlier, Late March
LUCIA

I sat in my clinic room waiting for Dr. Manson, feeling pretty good. Finally, slowly, I'd been making progress. I drove here—alone. I was still taking it slow and couldn't walk upstairs without getting pretty bad dyspnea, but I'd stopped needing the walker. I'd even lowered my steroids, and I hadn't had to use the diaper rash cream since that adjustment. Life was weird and different, but I'd started settling into a rhythm. It was easier to be positive than it had been the first two months. I still occasionally fell asleep on a wet pillow, but not often. I'd been trying to stay optimistic as I regained small measures of independence.

Dr. Manson beamed at me as he entered the room, telling me how proud of me he was and how great I'd been doing. Both he and Dr. Steinberg were paranoid about me getting an infection near my heart pump, but I assured him I was feeling good.

Finally, he turned serious and clasped his hands behind his back. "Lucia, now that you're getting better, we need to discuss you being sexually active. I think you know several of the medications you are taking cause severe birth defects, right?" I nodded. "Before, you took the pill, but it's counter-indicated with the IV and your risk of clots. Especially because you have antiphospholipid antibodies in all your blood tests, they don't recommend estrogen birth control at all. Dr. Steinberg thinks it's a bad idea because you take antibiotics too frequently and they make it unreliable—"

"I'm not having sex," I said firmly, interrupting him. God, had all my doctors been discussing my sexual activity? Was nothing private? I motioned to my chest and hidden IV. "Who would have sex with someone wearing this?"

His face softened. "Lucia, many of my patients, even those on medicines like yours, are married."

I wanted this conversation to end, so I just said, "If I have sex, I'll use a condom."

"With these medicines, you are supposed to use at least two forms of birth control or an IUD. Most are over ninety-nine percent effective, much more than condoms. Have you ever considered one?"

I shook my head. "No." Before I lost my courage, I asked, "Will I be on these medicines forever? Will I ever be able to have a baby?"

Doctor Manson's handsome features drew tighter. He paused for a moment, looking like he was debating what to say. Finally, he said, "You are really making a remarkable recovery. So, will you be able to stop taking these medicines? Maybe, but maybe not. Most people take these medicines for life." He hesitated again. "Have you read about PAH and pregnancy?"

"A little," I admitted. "But if my heart gets better, I can get pregnant, right? It's already improving a lot, you said."

He closed his eyes and his brows drew even closer together. I knew whatever came next, he didn't want to tell twenty-one-year-old me. In the gentlest voice, he said, "Lucia, even if you stopped taking all the medicines that could harm a fetus, we would still recommend you not carry the child if you got pregnant. The American College of Cardiology and the National Health Institute recommend all pulmonary hypertension patients avoid pregnancy at all costs or terminate in the first trimester if they become pregnant. Because of this recommendation, there is very little research. But from what we have, there is a twenty-five to fifty percent chance of maternal mortality. However, medicine is improving all the time. In a decade, who knows what will have happened."

He paused and looked at me, brow wrinkled. I stared at him completely dumbfounded for a minute before saying, "You mean whether I live or die if I get pregnant is a coin toss?"

"Yes, Lucia. I'm really sorry to be the one to tell you this. But there are other ways to have a family. Adoption or surrogacy. But no, you should never carry a baby, because even if you are much better, and you do survive, the damage to your heart will be like when you were hospitalized. We can't guarantee it would recover a second time. I'm sorry."

I managed to make it through the appointment without breaking down—barely.

But when I finally reached my car and sat alone inside, I started crying. Loud, painful sobs that wracked my body. My hand found its way to my stomach. *I'll never be able to have a baby*. What else were they going to take from me? If it was much more, I'd lose any optimism I'd found—and maybe even the will to fight.

Twenty

Present day, August 16
OSKAR

Just landed. Can't wait to see you. Kuss, I sent to Lucia as I shifted my long legs in the cramped plane seats. They weren't made for people six-three, like me. I knew she wouldn't see it for at least an hour and a half, but I couldn't help it. I wanted to send it.

Being home again had made me question my need to leave. Why had I picked a program so far away? But Tech was a fantastic opportunity, and I'd been itching for a change. Still, the trip home had cemented this fact like nothing else could have: after graduation I was moving back. My family was there. My friends were there. I liked it better there. I frowned, recalling coffee yesterday with Gunter and Claudia. He'd looked at her like she hung the moon. He was happy—so much happier than I'd ever seen him. Yet some ugly part of me was jealous. I wanted what he had. At least I'd met Lucia. She understood my language and way of life.

Well, I had Lucia until I moved back. That was at least two

years away. Was there anything wrong with enjoying what was happening with Lucia now?

I shook my head and texted my mom I'd landed. *Worry when tomorrow comes*, I told myself. Then I mentally braced myself for the deplaning wait and immigration lines. Luckily, it didn't last as though as I'd thought, and after stopping in the bathroom to brush my teeth, I felt my phone vibrating.

Yay! I'm leaving here soon -xo.

I smiled the whole train ride, thinking about Lucia, yet my breath still caught when I saw her and Bea as I exited the station. She was wearing a cute summer dress conservative enough I'd guess she wore it to work, but still flattering as hell. She looked good enough to eat. Maybe she'd let me do just that. That was only kind-of sex, right? As I walked closer, I saw it was a wrap dress that had sunflowers on it that should have looked childish, yet she made it look adorable. I found myself chuckling, gravitating toward her like I was a sunflower and she the sun.

"Hi," she said with a wave.

"Hi." I took a step closer and gave her a light kiss. The dog was barking, so I bent down to pet it. "Hi to you too, Bea!"

I reached for Lucia's hand as we turned to walk toward her place. A warmth filled my chest with her hand captured in mine.

She looked up at me, smiling. "Perfect timing by the way. I just made it home and had time to grab Bea and get up here."

"Really?" I assumed she'd gotten home much earlier.

She looked sheepish for a moment. "Well, it's really busy this year. Yesterday was the first day, but they've changed my schedule." She let out a long sigh. "I'm a little nervous about it because I have three different preps, so I wanted to be sure everything was in order. I hate leaving if the classroom isn't perfect. But enough about me, tell me about the trip! Looks like you and your friends had fun. And I'm so, so happy everything is fine with your dad. God, that must have been scary! Are you tired? Hungry?"

I smiled at her fast-talking concern before I said, "Dad's

fantastic. He was just dehydrated. You saw me drinking with the guys."

"You must miss everyone so much." She squeezed my hand. "I miss my college friends from Rome too, but it almost feels like another lifetime. I still talk to my best friend, Paola, but many I've lost touch with." Her eyes held a dreamy look, and I wondered not for the first time if her health was what was keeping her in Atlanta.

"Yes," I agreed. Maybe that was what bothered me. It was good to see everyone, but we were all changing, and some of us had moved on. She was right: I wasn't that person anymore. Yet I didn't quite fit here, either.

She squeezed my fingers again, bringing me back to the present. "And you saw more family in Innsbruck?"

At least this was easier to talk about. "My sister Anna and her family drove up from Vienna to see me. Well, to see Dad, but stayed for me. They would have come to see me too. Johanna took me trekking for three days. I've missed the Alps. Then it was time to go to Munich."

"It sounds perfect," she said wistfully. "When do you go back?"

"Thanksgiving. The tickets were much cheaper than Christmas, so I decided to do the shorter, cheaper trip this year. I won't teach or take classes this summer, so I'll have more time to go home next summer. It felt long between this trip and last Christmas break." I wasn't too thrilled about a Christmas alone, but the price was too hard to walk away from.

"That's smart," she said as she opened her door.

As soon as she unhooked the dog, I dropped my bag and reached for her. My arms slid around her, my hands cupping that fantastic ass as I pulled her closer to me. I couldn't help but whisper before I kissed her, "I missed you."

"Me too," she said as our lips met.

With her body pressed against me, I was hard in an instant. She tasted like heaven, but after a moment, she pushed me away, making my belly flutter. Maybe I was reading more into this than there was. *Fuck, the guys were right.*

Her cheeks were a little. "Um, Oskar, do you still have any clean clothes left?" she mumbled.

Shit, do I stink? "Yes, um, do I smell? Do you want me to change?"

She looked up, her eyes widening. Her cheeks were fire-red now. "No, no, you don't stink. It's just…" she looked down again and played with the belt on her wrap dress, "planes are dirty. I, um…I think I mentioned I take immunosuppressants, right? Well, planes carry a lot of germs, and I was hoping you could take a shower and use this special antibacterial soap I have. I have gotten a skin infection from a plane before. It really sucked. I'd prefer not to repeat it. I'm allergic to one antibiotic and with the medicines I take, I need big-gun antibiotic therapy if I get an infection." She peered up at me with a vulnerability in her eyes, and I could tell she was embarrassed.

Now I felt like a dick for not thinking about it. Of course, planes were dirty. The first thing I'd wanted to do at my parents' place was shower. I'd just been excited to see her. I knew she didn't like talking about this medical stuff.

"Sure, I don't mind at all." I bent down and ruffled through my bag before pulling out the few clean clothes I had.

As I stood, she said, "Do you need help?"

I raised one eyebrow at her and cleared my throat. "Do you mean, like, turning on the water or washing myself off?" She just smiled coyly at me. "If you're offering?"

She sauntered into the bathroom, and I heard the water turn on. When she reemerged with her hair in a high bun, wearing nothing but lacy white underwear, I felt like I'd died and gone to heaven. My cock raised his head in agreement. I yanked off my shirt and unbuckled my pants as she stalked toward me, a playful smile on her lips.

"You're more beautiful than I remembered," I said as I reached out a hand to pull her to me. She pushed down my pants before straightening to lean in for a kiss, her silky skin pressing against me. My hands drifted over the curve of her behind, then pulled her more firmly against me, making us both groan. I moved my hands up to unclasp her bra and bent down to kiss the swells of her breasts.

"Come," she said, pulling my hand and guiding me into the bathroom.

Light steam told me the water was ready. She stripped off her panties and stepped into the shower first, before motioning for me to get closer to the showerhead. The hot water on my back did feel amazing after traveling, and I trembled slightly as she leaned forward to kiss my jaw and neck.

Her hands roved over my body as she whispered along my skin, "I don't know how you stay in shape in graduate school, but I'm glad for it." She grabbed some soap that looked like medicine, and my whole body quivered as she rubbed it over almost all of me and then herself. My cock tightened almost painfully hard as I watched her hands.

She washed her hands and smirked. "This is antibacterial soap. I don't think you want it *there*." Then she demanded, "Turn around."

I didn't think I could get any more rigid, but her bossing me around was sexy. I liked her confidence. I twisted into the water, and her hand wrapped around to hold me where I wanted it most as she traced kisses and nips along my shoulder and back. Her firm breasts pressed against me, her hand moving swifter with the water's lubricant. I had never experienced anything quite like this, and *fuck,* did it feel good. A loud groan-oath escaped me as her teeth nipped a little harder, arousing me more than I'd thought possible with a novel pleasure-pain sensation.

She inched higher and nibbled my ear as she stroked me more fervently. "Do you like that?" she asked as her hand slid faster and harder. "Have you been thinking about my hand on your cock?"

I totally lost it at her words, the strength of my orgasm

making me brace myself against the wall. She slid lower as she released me and gave me little kisses on my shoulder blades.

As soon as I could collect myself, I spun to face her and gave her a long, deep kiss. My fingers reached between us and found her folds. I turned to whisper in her ear as I caressed her entrance. "Can I kiss you here?"

"Oh yes," she replied throatily.

That was all it took: I was on my knees, at her feet, ready to feast on her. I gave her a few light nips on her inner thigh and brought my other hand around to her ass, tugging her closer. *I fucking love her body*, I thought as I glanced up at her wet skin glistening in the shower spray. Her eyes were closed, her head thrown back. Desire moved across her features.

"God, you are gorgeous," I couldn't help saying before I took her into my mouth. I knew that image was going to be seared into my brain.

She made wonderful mewing sounds as my tongue invaded her and one hand kneaded her ass, urging her closer, while the other reached up and caressed her breasts and pinched her nipples, one after the other, giving her that edged pleasure she'd given me.

"Oskar, oh god," she continued to whimper, making me feel like a god and work harder. She lasted barely longer than I had, and I had to help hold her as she moaned out her release.

I stood and cradled her. Her head and mouth found their way to the curve of my neck. Contentment, rightness seared through me as I held her in my arms. We stood there several minutes, until I noticed the water had started to cool and she shivered slightly. I stepped back slowly and shut it off as she opened the curtain and grabbed a towel. She wrapped one around herself before throwing the other one around my shoulders and stepping back into my embrace.

She was still wobbly from her orgasm, and I was happy to continue to hold her. Finally, she whispered cheekily, "Thanks for agreeing to the shower."

I laughed and kissed her forehead before stepping back and starting to dry myself with the towel. "Thank you for the warm welcome back."

Lucia left the bathroom and returned a minute later with two ice waters. That warmth in my chest burned hotter at her consideration.

As I thanked her and watched her sipping her water, I realized I was screwed. I'd never dated anyone with the level of passion she'd shown so far, and we hadn't even made love yet.

"Hungry?"

"Didn't I just eat?"

She whacked my shoulder. "Ha, ha. For real food."

I kissed her once more because I couldn't fucking help it and said, "Starving."

She said she'd start cooking and went to turn on the oven before she dressed in jean shorts and a tank top with a built-in bra. I knew because watching her put it on geared me up for round two. She had amazing breasts, and I found her scars kind of sexy. They made her unique.

Once we were both dressed, she poured us wine and chatted while she baked some asparagus and pan-seared some tilapia. I told her more details about my trip. She laughed so hard she snorted, especially when I told her about reuniting with my college buddies and named all the drinking songs we'd sung.

Then her face dropped for a moment. "I miss my Roman friends. I've only been back once in three years." But before I could say anything, she smiled, gesturing at the dinner. "I wanted to make something lighter for you because I know German foods can be kind of heavy."

The food filled up her tiny kitchen table.

"This is perfect," I said honestly. "Lucia, thanks for everything—letting me leave my car here, cooking for me...the shower."

"Any time. Hey, I wanted to ask you. Do you have classes Monday night?"

"No, why?" I asked, pausing mid-bite. It was light and fresh, like the wine.

"We do team trivia at this taco place in Oakhurst. Me, Michael, and some other friends. It starts at eight. We leave here at seven if you're interested."

I grinned at her. "Sounds great." A thrill ran through me—she wanted me to meet her friends. I shook my head at myself. She'd kind-of met mine.

By the time we finished dinner, I was yawning, and so was she, even though the sun was still out. But I wasn't ready to go home yet, so I offered to help her clean up and walk the dog. She laughed at me because I was in no hurry to go home.

"Okay, Oskar, I'm not going to kick you out this second, because I kind of like having you hanging around. I've had two glasses of wine, so I'm not working tonight, but I have to get up at five thirty. If you're interested, we can watch a movie, but then you gotta go."

I enthusiastically agreed, and we snuggled in together on her bed, hunched over her laptop since she didn't have a TV. She picked *Across the Universe*, and while I hadn't seen it, I liked the Beatles. I wouldn't have cared what we watched; I was just glad to have her warm body pressed against mine.

When it was over, the two glasses of wine I'd had were long gone. I knew she needed to get up early, so after making plans to do something Saturday afternoon, I reluctantly left her with a kiss.

Twenty-one

Three years earlier, Early May
LUCIA

"What about the Rogaine? You didn't want to pack that?" mom asked, making me laugh.

"Mom, I can't do the Rogaine by myself." I ran my hand through my hair, feeling the little stubble that had grown in throughout, hidden within the longer hairs. "But it's fine. It's growing. It really worked. I still can't believe it." It tangled easily as it grew out, but it was a relief it was growing at all, so I wouldn't complain.

"With your vitamins, it'll grow quick," my mom reassured me, but it never seemed to. I'd lost my hair twice before due to lupus but never like this. The previous two times I'd gotten a bald spot about the size of a quarter right before high school graduation and when my health kept having issues my second year in Italy. As it had grown back, it'd been an awkward cow-licked poof. But the last week in January, when I'd been released from the hospital, it was clear my hair was falling out *all* over my head from some combination of lupus flare and heavy steroid use. I didn't go bald, but it was really thin.

My mom, like always, stepped up to the plate. Twice a day, after breakfast and before bed, she'd donned gloves and used the dripper throughout my head. My auburn-golden-light brown hair had always been wavy and thick, one of my favorite things about myself. It was a unique color to me, and I'd admit I was vain about it. Whenever I looked at my brush and shower drain and clump after clump of hair was gone, it was a horrible feeling—one more thing being taken from me. But now it was finally growing. That gave me hope in a way I couldn't explain.

"Thanks for all the help, Mom." We smiled at each other in the mirror. I looked away quickly. It was still hard to look at my puffy cheeks. I compulsively double-checked the countertops and opened a few drawers. The fluid retention from the steroids made me feel like a chipmunk. Truly, it wasn't so bad. I just didn't look like I used to, with my defined cheekbones.

"Lucia," Mom said as if she knew my thoughts. "You are doing so well, carina. Finally, now you are on twenty milligrams of prednisone, not sixty. Dr. Manson says you are doing great, and you haven't even needed to call Dr. Steinberg in two weeks. Your dad and I are so proud."

I laughed again, then said seriously, "I *am* doing so much better."

"Your dad and I think it's really good you are moving out. I know, despite everything, this still feels like a sick room to you. We understand this isn't home until you can easily walk back up and down the stairs. But we want you to know if it ever feels like too much, you just move right back in—no judgment at all."

"Thanks, Mom." We walked out of the bathroom, and I glanced around. My mom had asked her yardman with a truck to help me move because I wasn't supposed to lift more than ten pounds—it would put too much strain on my heart. Basically, everything weighed more than ten pounds.

My furniture was mostly over at my new place. It was small,

so I'd needed a little table with three chairs (four wouldn't fit) and a bed. Everything else had come from around my parents' place and was old or currently unused: a tan loveseat, a coffee table, sheets, blankets, and some floor lamps. I also had an eclectic mix of dishes, glasses, pots, and pans that had outgrown Dad's restaurants. I was thrilled. I loaded my medicine bag and small duffel with clothes and toiletries I'd use right away in case I didn't want to unpack. Most days, I still had pretty bad fatigue.

Mom and I got into the Fiat 500 they'd bought me a month ago, certified pre-owned. Living in America, I needed a car, especially with everything going on with my health, but I still was astounded by their generosity. Despite all the shitty things about being sick, there was one huge positive: my parents and I were closer than ever. Unlike most twenty-one-year olds, I now thought my parents were totally awesome and didn't care who knew it. There was nothing like family when you were sick.

We pulled up at my new complex, where Dad's car was already in the lot, and Mom took my duffle down the hall to the last unit. Two months ago, I would have needed to stop during this walk to catch my breath, but not anymore. I was improving.

As we opened the door, Dad said, "Surprise!" In his arms was a tiny blond Pomeranian puppy.

"For me?" I asked in shock.

Dad squatted down and put the little doggie on the ground. I knelt too. It was so cute, buzzing around like a little bee.

"We didn't want you to be alone," Dad said gently. "What will you call her?"

"Bea, like Beatrice," I said, gently grabbing her and kissing her head. "She already makes me happy—it fits." With her pressed against my chest, I felt love and hope bloom inside me. I needed some space to recover, but my wise parents were right: this was better than being alone. "Bea, you and I are going to be best friends."

She licked me in agreement.

My parents smiled and left me snuggled on the new loveseat.

As they did, I held Bea close until she fell asleep in my arms. A few tears slipped down my face. This apartment was dumpy, but my parents had already given me so much, and I needed to get out of their house. Living in the office had been a daily reminder of everything I still couldn't do: walk up the stairs to my bedroom, go to GW, have children, and even be who I'd been only months before. I'd hated having to ask my parents to pay for this place, but they seemed to understand. I needed to keep taking steps to embrace the fact that my life was different now, and living in an office wasn't the way to do that. This was my life, whether I liked that or not, I had to keep living it.

I wiped my tears away with my free hand and petted little Bea's soft fur with the other. I took a deep breath and looked around, trying not to dwell on everything that had changed since January fifth. It was really hard, but I had to keep being brave and remembering the improvements I'd made in the last five months, not dwell on everything that was gone possibly forever.

Twenty-two

I lounged back on my loveseat, heels hurting from standing on linoleum all day in my classroom. I turned to Michael, who'd gotten distracted by a text on his phone.

"Mikey, I'm starting to really like him," I confessed. That was the reason we were waiting on Oskar. I'd invited him to trivia—I never invited guys to trivia.

"So?" Mikey said with a raised eyebrow. "From what you've told me, he's super into you, and you haven't even had sex"—he held up a hand, making a face—"or if you have, please keep it to yourself."

I leaned forward to smack him with a pillow. "We have not."

"See? That clearly means he likes you. It's almost been a month."

"We can't all be sluts." I said, then snorted, laughing into my hand at the thought of his last hookup.

"Don't." He wrinkled his nose in a grimace and rolled his

eyes upward. "He was fugly. And country. You know I hate country boys. But please, I'm going to vomit. Can we get back to you?"

I stopped laughing and chewed my lip. "He hasn't seen me sick yet, either."

Our eyes met and he sighed.

"What if he's like Frank? Or Ali?"

"Frank is an idiot," he said harshly, before pausing a moment. "You can't help being sick, Lucia. And aren't Italians notorious cheaters?"

"I know," I whined, then added defensively, "Not all Italians."

"If he can't take it, he doesn't deserve you." He shot me a grin then petted Bea nested beside us.

I leaned my head on his shoulder. "I love you, Mikey."

"Oh, Lu," he said, putting his arm around me and switching the other to pet Bea. "I love you, and Bea, too."

We were like a little family, the three of us. Mikey had been there for me when I had no one. My mom had corralled him at the dumpster one day and introduced us. As our friendship developed, he eventually confessed he'd been too shy to make friends and hadn't even been openly gay before moving to Atlanta. He was much more social now, but we'd both been there for each other when we needed it. Both too self-conscious to make friends for our own reasons.

A loud knock startled us both, and I jumped up to get it, the excitement of seeing Oskar racing through me.

"Coming!" I opened the door and stepped aside to close it before giving Oskar a quick kiss. "Hi, there."

"Hi," he said in a low voice that sent shivers down my spine.

We might not have had *actual* sex, but we'd certainly hit a few Os together. He'd spent the night again on Saturday. I was kind of getting used to having him around in a way that made my heart pinch like it did when I got nervous. This was the opposite of what I'd told myself I wanted when I met him.

Oskar turned to Michael with an easy smile. "Hi, Michael. How's it going?"

"Fine," Michael said before turning to me. "I think I left my radio on. I'll be right back."

I giggled as he left, seeing that for the blatant lie it was. But I appreciated it nonetheless. Slowly, I inched my arms up around Oskar to pull him toward my lips. As his body pressed against me as his mouth met mine. I could feel he was as eager to see me as I was him.

I broke our kiss but kept my arms around him. "Are you going to spend the night again?" I whispered. "I still have to get up at five-thirty."

He kissed me softly, arms tightening. "If I'm invited, then yes."

I inched up him so we were even closer and threaded my fingers through his hair. "You're invited," I whispered. "Oh, and I'm ready." I was telling him now because I knew enough about Oskar that to know if I told him at the end of the night after a few beers, he'd probably make me wait till I was sober, and I didn't want to wait anymore.

He leaned back to look at me seriously. "Lucia, are you sure?" I nodded vigorously, and he pulled me flush against him again, but before I could kiss him again, he spoke. "I can wait. I don't want to unless you're okay with it." His hand rubbed soft caresses on my back.

"You're not seeing anyone else?" I half-teased.

"No, of course not." He looked offended I'd even asked.

"Then I'm sure. But Oskar?" I pulled back, and meeting his gaze again. "You'd better make it worth my time," I said with a straight face before dissolving into giggles.

With that, he hiked me up and fused us together—mouths and bodies. I lifted my legs and wrapped them around his waist, meeting his ardor with mine.

My lips inched lower, and I peppered kisses along his chin and neck as he gripped my butt, grinding us together. "Oh, I can promise you that," he said. A loud knock on the door made him lower me. We both glanced down at his obvious erection, and I giggled again and petted him once as he said, "I'll just go to the bathroom first."

When he'd closed the door, I let Michael in and checked that everything was in my purse. My alarm for tomorrow was set, and I had my keys. When Oskar came out, I went too, and then we left.

Monday trivia was something we tried to do every week, and between the groups, we manage to do well in most categories. I didn't know anything about pop culture or sports, but I could locate every country on the map and was good at history and math. I needed a team. Oskar fit right in with my regular crew. He was the science component we'd been lacking.

Throughout the game, we kept giving each other steamy glances and stealthy lingering caresses under the table, our minds clearly on the promise of later. Even though the night was fun, we were both eager to say goodnight to Michael.

As we entered my place, Bea greeted us with her happy run from the bedroom, which always made her furry paws slide a little bit on the wood.

"I need to walk her," I said to Oskar. "You can stay."

I felt suddenly nervous, even though I was horny as hell and knew I wanted this.

"I'll come," he responded immediately.

We ambled around the little pond and I scolded Bea for waking some ducks. As we walked, I asked cautiously, "Um, have you ever been tested?"

"Tested?" Oskar asked, unsure. I watched the light go off in his head. "Yes, I went to the doctor when I was back home. Everything was normal. And you?"

"I'm normal too. I got tested after my ex broke up with me." I laughed. "Well, normal down there, anyway."

I couldn't resist the joke. The idea of my health being normal was ludicrous.

Bea accomplished what we went outside for, with me luckily only getting three mosquito bites as she did. Once we were back inside, I fidgeted with the speaker a minute, trying to calm my nerves.

Oskar came up behind me and started kissing my shoulders. "You still want what you said earlier, Lucia? You seem tense. It's okay if you changed your mind. I can still spend the night."

He pulled me back so I could feel every inch of him against me. His body made mine heat up like a popsicle in a Georgia summer—completely melting against him, fire raging through my core.

I twisted in his arms and said firmly, "Oh, I want you to make good on your promises."

I watched surprise and passion flash across his face before my mouth crashed against his. Our tongues tangled, and he found my butt again with his hands, like he loved to do, and pulled me up so I was tight against him. My legs wrapped around his waist and he took us into the bedroom, our lips never leaving each other's.

I was greedy for him as we walked, wiggling against his hard-on and pulling off his shirt. He was forced to break his kiss to pull his shirt over his head before taking off my tank top as well. Then he knelt on the bed, laying me down gently, his firm body pressed against mine. Flames of desire coursed through my body as he started to kiss my neck and breasts. I tugged at his pants as his fingers worked on the buttons of my shorts.

In a minute, we were both in our underwear. He pressed back into me for a moment before rolling onto his back, pulling me on top so I straddled him. He broke the kiss to undo my bra. As he did, he told me, "You're in charge, *Süsse*."

His words dampened my panties more, as did his kisses to my breasts. His hand slipped into my panties and into my folds, making me gasp. I moaned as I rocked against his hand and fondled him with mine.

"God, you're soaking wet for me, and I love it."

"I want you inside me. Now," I ordered him as I pulled away from his fingers and rolled off onto my back. I slithered down my panties, and as I did, he got up and grabbed a condom from his jeans' pocket on the floor. He slid it on and kissed me once before coming back to the bed. Thankfully, he only teased my folds a moment before slipping inside. Pure bliss filled me, and I knew he felt the same from the ragged moan that escaped him.

When he began moving, I rocked with him, digging my heels into his lower back and making strangled, mewing moans and *god yes*es.

His German "oh yeah" sent me over the edge, and I screamed a release loud enough I thought Michael might have heard down the hall.

Oskar paused a moment, kissing the underside of my jaw and letting me savor my hazy post-orgasm bliss. Then he rolled so I was on top, and the new friction had me moaning again.

"Oskar, your German does something magical to me. Keep talking."

His eyes flashed—he liked me being bossy—and he obliged by talking dirty to me.

Fuck, I loved it.

Finally, he told me how beautiful my face was when I came, and I shattered again, spasming around him, sending us both over the edge at the same time. I collapsed on top of him and he held me close, pulling my face into his neck and softly caressing my back. After several moments, when the air conditioning started to feel cool, I slid off. He got up to throw away his condom, pressing a kiss to my forehead.

When he came back, I'd slipped on my panties, but otherwise I was still in a post-gasm daze. He pulled on his boxers, slipped into bed, and drew me on top of his chest, snuggling me closer and settling the covers around us before I fell into true oblivion— happy, warm, and held next to his beating heart.

Twenty-three

Three years earlier, May 26
LUCIA

"Lucia, why didn't you visit for your birthday?" Paola whined at me. "Last year we had so much fun in Istanbul!"

Istanbul—that's what I'd done for my twenty-first birthday. Look at how far I'd fallen. A used loveseat in a rickety apartment. This was my new cool place to be.

I took a steadying breath before responding, feeling like a broken record. Paola had been having a hard time understanding I had a chronic illness and that I was still sick.

"I can't fly that far. My doctors won't allow me overseas yet. Actually, I can't fly at all yet."

"When are you going to get better?" Paola asked. "We miss you."

"I don't know," I choked out, even though my eyes stung and my throat was constricted with emotion. I'd made one friend here, a neighbor. Months here and one friend. She couldn't know how much I missed her and the *l'amicizie di Roma*. I was saved from embarrassing myself by a loud knock on my door.

"Paola, I have to go. Thanks for the birthday wishes."

"Ciao, Luci. Auguri!" she said as I ended our video chat.

I hurried to the door and opened it, knowing who I was expecting. Ru stood there in a micro-dress I'd never be able to rock with my curves.

"Birthday bitch!" she shouted as she barreled into me.

"Happy graduation!" I said enthusiastically, hugging her tightly. I'd known Ru since kindergarten, but this was the first I'd seen her in months, even though we'd talked weekly, if not more, since I'd admitted to being sick.

She broke away, holding out a gift bag and a bottle of Prosecco. "Shall we?" she said, motioning to the bottle.

I nodded and took the bottle as she bent down to pet Bea.

"Hiya, Fluffy!" she said, before yelling to me in the kitchen, "We're going to celebrate tonight—birthday and graduation!"

I smiled at her words, trying to feel happy and not think about what a step down this was from my birthday last year as I opened the bottle and brought us two glasses.

"To us," I said, as we cheers-ed and took a sip.

"You look great. I like that dress." She studied me more critically. "I mean, if I didn't know you, I'd say you look normal. I still can't believe everything that's going on with you."

I smiled my thanks but didn't feel like it. My face was still so puffy from the steroids—normal, but not me. I was wearing a high-necked backless dress, so at least my port site and IV were concealed. I'd learned how to walk with my purse and I did appear "normal." I just could never forget my bag. And it was amazing most people never noticed, never saw something out of place.

When I didn't respond, Ru continued. "This place is cute and you're starting graduate school, right? In two weeks?"

I took another sip of my drink before responding. "Yes, finally."

I'd been getting better and better, and although I was a far cry from my former self, I needed something to do besides sit around and think about all the changes in my life. I was doing better, but my life was nothing like my college years—*la dolce vita Romana*. Still, I wasn't as depressed as I'd been living at home. Now at least I had a budding friendship with my neighbor, who was new and friendless in Atlanta. And a puppy had been a welcome consumption of my time. Bea completely lived up to the name, "she who make happy."

"When are you moving?" I inquired.

She'd gone to NYU for International Business, and she'd been accepted into an MBA program at Georgetown, her top choice, for the fall. She was super-duper Ivy League smart.

"I already moved, actually," she admitted. "But I wanted to fly down for your birthday and see my parents before my summer internship starts June first. Maybe you can visit me?"

"Maybe," I said noncommittally. I wasn't comfortable traveling yet, which was so unlike me. I used to take advantage of the fifty-euro tickets all over Europe. Now I was stuck, and sometimes it felt suffocating.

"Come on, open your present," Ru pushed.

I smiled and opened the gift bag. As I did, I had to lock my jaw not to show my face fall. It was a blouse—a low-cut blouse. The kind I always used to wear. The kind of clothing I'd never wear anymore, because it showed my IV site. Even if I got it out, I'd likely have a scar.

Hoping I was showing a great fake smile, I said, "Wow, it's so cute, Ru. Thanks."

She didn't seem to notice that I freaking hated the shirt and everything it represented.

"Yay! I knew you'd like it—it's so you." She downed her drink and poured me another as we caught up. She was only half-wrong. It *had* been so me, but not anymore. Finally, an empty bottle later, she asked, "Ready?"

"Sure." I got up, feeling a little tipsy. I'd barely had a sip of alcohol in months because I was taking so many medicines.

We walked fast enough to a bar a few blocks away that it made me breathless. As soon as we got inside, Ru ordered us each a shot of tequila. I wanted to say no, but it felt nice being a normal birthday girl for a few minutes, so I said nothing. I drank mine with a slight grimace. I could already feel the buzz working itself warmly through me. Sure, I wasn't supposed to drink too much, but one had ever told me I *couldn't* drink. It was my birthday after all.

After a little bit, Ru started talking and flirting with the two guys beside us. Suddenly there were four tequila shots in front of us. I debated the shot a minute, then didn't want to make a scene, so I just took it, but I warned Ru, "no more," as I did. My catheter was rare enough that if I went to an ER, most likely no one would even know what it was. I couldn't get sloppy drunk.

One of the guys, Max, sidled closer to me. Our thighs rubbed as he started asking me all about myself and laying on the pickup lines, one after the other. He was cute, with piercing blue eyes and fire-red hair. For a few minutes, I attempted to forget everything going on in my life. I found myself laughing and flirting back, having an amazing time for once. His interest in me felt addictive, and I didn't realize how starved for it I'd been—just normal interactions with people.

Over the next two hours, we drank two more drinks, but I switched to sparkling water for the second. It was wonderful to have someone's undivided attention on me and not full of sympathy. Yet suddenly, everything was spinning as I stood to go pee.

Shit. I was drunk.

Attempting not to wobble on the walk back to my barstool, I told Ru, "Hey, sorry, do you mind if we bail?"

Ru looked at me with disappointment, then nodded, likely seeing I was smashed. "Only if you and Max exchange numbers," she teased.

"No," I said, a little harshly. What was I going to do with Max's number? Go on a date and show him my heart pump?

Yeah, no thanks. Tonight was a one-time deal. I softened my tone. "Come on, Ru."

Just then, Max stood. "Hey, where are you sneaking off to, birthday girl?"

"Lucia's drunk, so we are bailing," Ru informed him.

He had the courtesy to look chagrined at that. "That's my fault, so you can't leave until I get your number to make it up to you next time. Us gingers have to stick together."

His lips quirked in a charming way, but I said firmly, "Sorry, Max. It was nice to meet you, but I think this was a one-time thing."

I tried to be polite, but it clearly wasn't enough, because a look of irritation flashed across his face. "Come on. I bought you two drinks. No number?"

I ran my hand along my hidden IV inside my purse and said through clenched teeth, "I offered to buy one of the rounds of drinks. I'm sorry. Ru, come on."

"Unbelievable," I heard him muttering as we walked away.

I felt like the walk to my place was twice as far, and my head was spinning a little.

"Lucia, he was cute, and you guys seemed to hit it off," Ru said when we were almost back to my place. "What's your deal?"

"My deal, Ru," I gritted out with exasperation lacing my voice, "is I have a fucking IV in my heart."

"I'm sure some guys would be fine with it. It's not that bad."

I pushed open the door and we stepped inside. I slammed it shut, shaking with rage. "Yes, *it's that bad*!" I was yelling now, but I didn't care. "My life fucking sucks. I can barely even walk around. I take twenty-four fucking pills a day. I can't go back to Italy. I can barely live on my own. My dream of going to the IMF is gone. I'm completely mooching off my parents. *My future is gone*. Did you know I can't even have kids? *Never*." I felt my breath coming in pants as I glared at her. "And what do you think sex would be like with this between us?"

I pulled out my pump and shook it at her. Sympathy and

sadness flashed across her face. Seeing that, I broke down in tears.

"I fucking hate this thing!" I pulled on the IV tubing. Of course, it didn't do anything because my skin had grown around it for five months, but Ru got a frightened look on her face.

"Stop, Lucia!" Ru grabbed me and held me in a firm hug.

I sobbed into her shoulder and whispered, "It's that fucking bad. I'd rather have died than have to live with all my dreams taken away."

"Shh, let's get you to bed. It'll be better in the morning," Ru cooed. She led me to the bed and tucked me in. I eventually fell asleep crying, with Ru rubbing my back and snuggling Bea, who was attempting to cheer me up by licking my eyes.

I woke up with a terrible headache and my tongue stuck to the roof of my mouth. Nausea rumbled in my stomach. Extreme embarrassment washed over me as I turned to look at sleeping Ru, getting semi-tangled in my IV tubing and needing to tug my backpack closer. Nausea threatened to overwhelm me as her eyes opened.

"Ru, I'm really sorry about last night—"

"No, I'm sorry. I know you're taking a lot of medicines. I shouldn't have pushed you to drink. And who you give your number to is your own business." I nodded, and she took my hand in hers. "Are you okay though, Lulu? If you're depressed, it's okay to get help. You scared me when you grabbed your IV like that..." Her voice trailed off.

I squeezed her hand and a few tears leaked out. "I'm all right. It's just, my whole life has changed. My dream of working for the IMF is gone. My health is gone. I don't know about dating, but I'm not ready yet. It's been hard. And I'm lonely. Everyone's been great and helpful, but I feel like no one knows what it's like for me. I've tried to have a good attitude because my parents and doctors have done so much, but it's hard to live like this. I don't want this to be my forever. I want to support myself again. I want to travel again. I want my life back."

She brushed my hair with her other hand. "It's all right to be sad and angry," she said softly. "You've been through a lot."

"I know, but I have to keep fighting to be happy for what I have gotten back, otherwise I'll never be able to handle it. The alcohol brought it out. I can't drink as much with these medicines."

She nodded. After a while, she left me in bed nursing a terrible hangover, but told me to call her anytime, day or night, and she'd always be there. I felt horrific from the drinking and my outburst. I didn't feel that angry all the time. I was still determined to get better, and I had, little by little, every week. I'd taken steps back, but I was improving. I hadn't spent this birthday in a club on the Bosphorus, like I had for my twenty-first birthday in Istanbul, but I was alive. I knew my own words were true—I must focus on what I could do, not what I couldn't. Otherwise it was just too much to handle, and I wouldn't be able to keep swallowing my pills and mixing my IV.

I was lonely though. I moaned at the pain in my stomach and petted Bea, wondering if loneliness was all my future held.

Twenty-four

Present day, August 25
OSKAR

I glanced down from the loveseat to where Lucia was sitting cross-legged on the floor with her fluffy dog in her lap. With one hand, she was absentmindedly petting her dog. In the other, she held a pink pen that flew over the pages of an assignment. A class roster sat beside her, mostly filled with numbers. I couldn't help but smile as I looked down at her, realizing this was what was missing with some of the other girls I'd dated. I liked that she taught and was in graduate school. She was busy and utterly focused on that work, as was I.

We had wanted to see each other but were both so busy. She'd had grading to do, so we'd settled for this study date. Maybe it wasn't the most fun thing we could be doing, but if I had to work this Saturday afternoon, it was nicer to do it with her. I knew her bedtime was around nine thirty, or at least that was the last time she usually ever texted me back, and she used weekends as catch-up. That was fine with me; my program was demanding.

I grinned, thinking about how we'd started this morning. We'd attempted to work at my place—I couldn't believe she still hadn't seen it, and I had a bigger table to work at—but my roommates had kept coming in and making noises or talking with her. I could tell Lucia was distracted. When Ryan had come in with his friend Sam, Ryan had blatantly checked her out. Luckily, Lucia had been looking at her paper, but I'd frowned at him.

Ryan had gotten her attention when he said, "Oskar, is this your girlfriend? She's so pretty." Lucia had blushed and been friendly, but I could tell his flirting was making her uncomfortable. He hadn't let up, though. "Lucia, are you going to Shoot the Hooch with us next weekend? It'll be awesome! And you can bring some friends." I'd barely controlled my eye rolls. This was exactly why he was single.

She'd looked to me, because I hadn't mentioned it yet, not knowing if I'd wanted to go or not, but it sounded intriguing. I'd shrugged. "I haven't done it yet."

"Next Saturday and we'll bring all the beers," Sam had continued. "It'll be great! We can barbeque after at our place. My girlfriend, Shelly, is coming too." He muttered, "She'd like more girls."

"Are you guys doing the two-hour or the four-hour tubing?" she'd asked.

When they'd said two, she'd agreed and then whispered she wasn't getting much done here. She'd looked stressed and since I had tons to do too, so I'd asked if we could go to her place instead, which she'd looked relieved to hear. I told her I'd pack a bag and meet her there. When she'd gone, Sujit had congratulated me on how attractive she was. I shook my head at him, agreeing, but that wasn't my favorite thing about her. We'd talked every evening since I'd gotten back, and I was falling harder and harder for her. He'd smirked like he understood. He was engaged to a girl from back home in Delhi.

Now, as I looked at her with the quirky side ponytail she'd just pulled to the side to work, I found myself distracted by her.

Sujit was right: she was beautiful, and we'd been working for hours. From my vantage point, I could see she was on the last paper for that class. So maybe I could convince her to break. I saved my work, and, as if she could read my mind, she pivoted and grinned at me.

She stood up, gently moving her dog, and stretched her back. Her fantastic ass was right in my face, and if I wasn't horny before, I certainly was now.

"My back is a little sore. Would you mind giving me a back rub?" she asked innocently. She had terrible posture while grading, so I wasn't surprised.

"Sure, Süsse," I said closing my computer. I liked talking to Lucia in German, not only because it was my native tongue and I enjoyed her accent, but also because she'd told me it really turned her on. She'd also admitted she liked using lube. I found it extremely attractive she knew what she liked in bed and wasn't shy to tell me. Her loud moans turned me on, and I wanted to do what she enjoyed. The sounds of her ecstasy made me come harder than I ever had before.

I followed her into her bedroom, which even with her windows closed was bright with afternoon sunlight. She turned and smiled at me one more time before stripping off her long-sleeved shirt and lying face-down on the bed. I wasn't really sure I'd be good at this, but when I started working on her neck and back, I realized she really was tight.

She groaned a little under me and said, "Oskar, that feels so good."

At that noise I couldn't help but lean down and kiss her back. "You usually say that when I'm doing something else, Süsse."

She turned her face so she could see me. "What do you have in mind?" she said huskily.

I kissed her gently. "Close your eyes and I'll tell you."

I'd noticed she *really* liked hearing me tell her what I wanted to or planned to do. So, while continuing rubbing her back, I unclasped her bra. "First I'm going to rub your back some more."

I did, but I also leaned forward and nibbled her back and then said right in her ear, "Then I'm going to rub your beautiful breasts."

As I said it, I reached under her and caressed her tits. I loved them. They weren't huge, but full and perky. Her nipples were so sensitive, and she always made the most wonderful sounds when I touched them. She rewarded me with a muffled whimper.

"Then," I rubbed my bearded stubble along her back, "I'm going to stick my hand in these shorts and touch your pussy. Is it wet for me, Lucia?"

"Yes," she moaned, and when I unbuttoned her shorts and slipped my hand inside, she was certainly slick for me. I wasn't wrong—she loved dirty talk.

I moved my finger in and out of her wet pussy as I rubbed myself against her round behind. "Lucia, what do you want?" I asked as I nibbled her shoulders again.

"I want you," she said into the pillow.

I pulled down her shorts and exposed her lacy panties. I stood and took off my pants and boxers, keeping a hand on her back to keep her from getting up as she wiggled. When I lay back down, I softly bit her lower back, making her cry out, before I rubbed my dick along her ass cheeks and up her back. "What part of me, Lucia?" I demanded.

She whimpered but didn't say anything. I reached under her and gently pinched her nipple. At that, she moaned out, "I want your cock."

I rubbed against her again, teasing her. "Like this?" She mewed, and I continued playing with her with my words and body—rubbing her clit, pinching her nipples, and pressing against her. "Where do you want it, Lucia?"

She moaned into the bed and I wondered if I'd pushed her too far. Then she said, "Oskar, I want your cock in me. *Now.*"

Her words pleased me on some primitive level, and I flipped her over, more turned on than I ever remembered being in my life. I rubbed myself on her through her panties as I reached for her bedside table and the lube I knew she liked. I put on a condom and pulled off her panties, then rubbed some lube on my fingers and teased her with them. With my other hand, I caressed her breasts as she whimpered and moaned.

I leaned down and kissed her neck. Bit her softly a few times. "Beg me."

She obliged me by squirming against my fingers. "Please, Oskar. Give it to me. I want you deep inside me."

I pulled back and put one hand around the back of her head as I slipped the other out of her and threw her legs over my shoulders. "You want it hard, Lucia?"

"Oh, please," she managed right before I thrust deeply into her. "Oh, god," she screamed out as she lost it around my dick, nearly taking me with her.

I barely held back as she clenched around me, but I wanted to give her more of that pleasure. I knew she liked dirty talk, and I'd just seen how much. When she came after a minute like that, I really felt like a god. I moved slowly and gently in and out of her as I felt the after quakes of her orgasm.

Her eyes flashed open, dazed, and I asked, "Did you like that, Süsse?"

She nodded, and I thrust a little deeper, drawing another moan from her.

"Do you want another one?"

"Yes," she whispered huskily, and started moving with me. I pounded her hard and fast, moving to caress her breasts. While kissing me intensely, she pulled me in closer and deeper with a passion of her own. I knew I couldn't last much longer with the exquisite sounds she was making under me. When she moaned out her release for a second time, I gladly followed her.

I quickly got rid of the condom and pulled my boxers on before drawing a still very naked Lucia on top of me to snuggle. She wrapped one leg around my waist and gently kissed my chest. She looked up at me with those hazel eyes I adored. They were drowsy from our lovemaking.

"Your eyes are so warm, Oskar," she said with a smile as she played with my hair. "I've always had a thing for brown eyes. I think they're sweet."

I kissed her hand and threaded our fingers together. "Lucia, you are irresistible."

"Really?" she said with a hint of a tease, and she kissed my chest some more.

Despite the intense orgasm I'd just had, I felt myself responding to her touch.

"Irresistible?" She slipped her hand from mine. She and her mouth shimmied lower, and I went from waking up to half-mast. She slipped her hand inside my boxers, and I was surprised I felt like I could go again, or that she could after two orgasms.

When she slid my boxers off and started kissing and sucking me there, I couldn't control my moaning or fisting her hair. "Irresistible? I meant insatiable."

Lucia stopped as I was getting close and leaned forward to whisper in my ear. "I'd rather you come in me, because I'm wet for you again too." She put a condom on me as she straddled me and rode me like a pro. "Touch me," she ordered. This time she was the one commanding and I was eager to obey—to please her. I palmed her breasts as she rocked against me hard, in the way I knew from last time hit her g-spot. She lifted almost all the way off and pushed down deep.

Fuck! She was going to make me explode before I could make her come. God, she looked amazing on top of me and felt even better. My talking always seemed to take her over, so I bit out, "It's okay to come, Süsse. I know how much you like my dick."

As I'd hoped, she lost it at my words. After a few more tugs on her hips, I followed. She collapsed on top of me and we lay like that, sweaty and wrapped in each other's embrace. If I wasn't sure before, I was now: I was completely addicted to Lucia Farris.

Now Lucia was napping on top of me. I couldn't resist watching her face, softened with sleep, as she did. I was tired from the fantastic orgasms she'd given me, but I was enjoying watching her and feeling her warm body snuggled against me too much to join her. Something unfurled in my chest at the sensations.

For a while, I got lost in my thoughts. Between our conversations on walks and dinners, the trivia game she'd brought me to, and our phone chats, I knew she was smart—certainly the most intelligent girl I'd dated—as well as the most sensual. Sex with her was wild—the best I'd ever had. My arm tightened a little around her. For someone outwardly conservative, she was so free in bed, which delighted me. I loved how well our bodies responded to each other and that she knew what she liked, because no one wanted to have sex with someone who wasn't enjoying it as much as you were. I hadn't wanted anything serious when I'd asked her out, but she had been hooking me deeper and deeper.

Almost of their own accord, my fingers stroked some of her silky hair back so I had a better view of her face nestled on my chest.

Her phone started vibrating nearby and woke her up. She rolled over to grab it. "Hi," she said sleepily.

Her volume must have been turned up because I heard a teasing male voice on the other end. "Are you napping?"

Jealousy roared through me as she giggled back, still naked in bed with me. "Maybe."

"I thought we were grabbing dinner. I'm getting hungry. I wanted to see when you wanted to go."

She groaned into the phone, and I was about ready to kill the guy on the other end. I'd never felt jealousy like this. I wasn't sure I'd ever been jealous before, but she made me greedy.

Then I heard, "Is Oskar still there?"

"Maybe." She giggled again, turning on her back to peer up at me.

"Oh, lord." The Southern voice shocked me into realizing her very gay best friend was on the other end. His voice picked up in volume. "Oskar, do you want to join us for burgers?"

She lifted her head and looked at me, raising an eyebrow in question. I replied in a loud voice, "Sure. Thanks, Michael." My heart was slowing down, but I was shocked by how much the idea of her flirting with another guy bothered me.

"But I want to walk, Mikey," Lucia said. "We've been studying and grading all day and I need some fresh air and to stretch my legs."

Michael continued speaking in a discernable but grumpy voice. "Fine, but I'm hungry. Can we go in fifteen minutes?"

"Nooooo. I need to shower and walk Bea. Can we do thirty?"

"Fine, just knock when you're ready." The phone clicked off.

Lucia looked up at me, and I reached down and kissed her. "Nice nap, Süsse?"

She kissed me back then jumped up. "Yes, but now I need to hurry. No play time, but you want to join me in the shower?"

I happily agreed, and true to her word we tried to get through it quickly. I was ready while she was still in a towel, so I offered to take out her dog. She rewarded me with a fantastic smile, so it was totally worth it to walk little Fluffy, who liked to yap at huge dogs. When I came back, she was ready with her hair in a French braid and wearing her usual shorts that tormented me. I grabbed my wallet from her bedroom, where I noticed she'd changed the sheets and made the bed. She was a little fastidious with her sheets, but I guessed if she was worried about skin infections, it made sense.

Hand in hand, we knocked on Michael's door, then took the two-mile walk Lucia liked to her favorite burger place. It was just past the bagel shop she favored. While walking, Michael asked about her Labor Day plans, so she told him about "Shooting the Hooch." He told us he was going to Florida with his friends. He didn't sound too excited, but he could be deliriously so. I'd gotten to know him well enough that I knew Lucia had enough enthusiasm for the both of them.

At the burger bar, Lucia told us to grab a table and offered to wait in line and buy our food. I'd tried to protest, but she waved me away, saying I'd gotten too many meals and technically right now she made more than me. With a tease that she was my sugar mama, making me whisper words of retaliation in her ear, she pushed us away.

Michael and I found a table outside after a few circles. "I'm really shocked Lucia's going tubing with you," he surprised me by saying. His voice held a mix of scorn and disappointment.

"Why?" I asked, confused. He hadn't seemed shocked I was napping at her place and didn't comment on our hair being wet, so what? So far, he'd always been friendly to me.

"Um." He cleared his throat. "Oskar, the river is pretty freaking sunny." He said this like I was an idiot.

My own anger rose in response as I snapped back, "Well, I hope so. It'll be cold if it's raining."

He gave me a look, like I literally might be the dumbest person alive. "I'm just surprised, like I said. You seem to really like Lucia, and it doesn't seem like something you'd want her to do. You know, be in all that sun. *She has lupus*." He said the last bit like I was a total moron and I tried to remember what she'd told me about lupus, and what I'd read.

Shit, she wasn't supposed to be in too much sun. She'd asked about the length of the trip before agreeing. She always had that sunscreen smell, long sleeves, and a cap when we went on walks. Damn, I was such an idiot.

My face must have shown my shock because Michael said, "Just take care of her, okay? She's really tough, but she's fragile, too. Sunscreen is not enough to prevent a flare. She can't get too much sun. Period. When she gets sick, it's really bad."

Lucia waved excitedly to us with a number and dropped some empty plastic cups on our table, saving me from farther awkwardness.

"I'm so excited for my French fries," she said, plopping down beside me and bouncing slightly with anticipation. She was easily the bubbliest person I'd ever met.

"Lucia, are you going to be okay tubing next weekend?" I asked her, sticking with English because Michael was here.

She glanced at us both and I could have sworn silent words were fired between her and Michael. After a pause, she said, "I have a UVB shirt, and I'll wear a hat, and I'll be, like, totally white with sunscreen. It should be good. It's only going to be two hours."

"We don't have to." My hand found her thigh under the table and squeezed. I really didn't want her to get sick because of something stupid like this.

She tried to smile, but I could see some pain in her eyes. I knew she had four autoimmune diseases and had been very sick once, but she had been tight lipped about it. She'd only given me the minimum about her conditions and history—like it was so far in the past it didn't matter.

"But Oskar, I *want* to go," she said, her eyes never leaving mine.

I reluctantly nodded, I didn't want to fight, but worry gnawed inside me at what Michael had said. I broke her gaze, realizing it was frightening how much I cared for her. Tubing was nothing compared to her health.

She brushed her thigh against me, and her fingers threaded with mine under the table. I met her gold-flecked eyes again and nodded a second time, releasing my grip on her leg and starting to eat. I'd mention it again later. Maybe her answer would be different when we were alone.

Twenty-five

Two and a half years earlier, Late February
LUCIA

I eyed the vascular surgeon as he prepared the biggest needle I'd ever seen. Anxiety coursed through me. Not for the first time, I wished my Hickman catheter was being removed by general anesthesia, not local.

"Little prick," the doctor warned.

I tried to take a calming breath. Months and months had culminated in this day. After I'd been on the IV heart medication for over a year, Dr. Mason had declared my PAH stable and in enough remission to stop the IV medicine.

My eye widened slightly as they sliced my breast tissue that'd grown around the catheter. With a little wiggle and a strange but unpainful sensation, the tubing pulled from my superior vena cava to my subclavian vein before the area was quickly stitched and covered with gauze. And like that, the IV medication was done.

I drew in a deep breath of relief and then looked at the

surgeon and smiled. I could have lived on the continuous IV forever—I'd met people who did. But it had always felt like a leash, a tether holding me down. It had been the one obstacle I'd struggled to live with, and now when I looked down at my chest—it was gone! It had saved my life, but I didn't want to need to wear it forever. Even if it was just symbolic, I felt more like myself then I had in over a year.

Since my birthday almost a year ago, I'd barely had any alcohol and hadn't had another breakdown, but I hadn't dated anyone, either. I hadn't wanted to with the line and sinker attached to me. There were times when I'd been desperately lonely and without my parents, Michael, Ru, and Bea, I wasn't sure I could have done it. True to my words to Ru, I'd adjusted to my new state of life and had been working toward a MAT in addition to the economics master's since January. I was planning to be a teacher. This wasn't the path I would have chosen, but it was the path I was on. I was trying to look forward with joy.

I closed my eyes and tried to contain my tears of elation. I could travel to Europe again for the first time in almost a year and a half. Life wouldn't be what I had once hoped, but I was going to keep living it all the same.

Twenty-six

Present day, September 1
LUCIA

Oskar had asked me twice since last Saturday night if I was sure I wanted to go tubing with him and his roommates. I'd given him a firm yes. Mikey had been a pest about it too. This was something I couldn't have done three years ago, and I wanted to do it. Honestly, Michael was probably right to be concerned, and no, I probably shouldn't go. But it was just two hours, and I'd wear sunscreen. I should be okay.

I thought.

I hoped.

I hadn't gotten too much sun in more than three years, so I wasn't really sure. But two hours should be fine. At least, that was what I told myself.

A loud knock had me running and Bea barking. I was in my bikini and shorts, having just applied my first layer of sunscreen, but I ran anyway. When I saw my oldest friend, I squealed like a piglet.

"Ru Ru!" I shouted as I grabbed Bea and threw open the door. She was inside in a second, hugging me tightly.

"Hi, Lulu."

Ru and I were similar. Her parents had wanted her educational track in more than just English. She'd taken a Mandarin and Spanish track, while I had taken a German and Italian one. Somehow, we'd stayed close through it all, even after having spent years away from each other for college, graduate school, and work. Now she worked for Coke but was only rarely here and mainly based in Shanghai, where she lived with her boyfriend. She traveled to South America frequently, too, and occasionally Europe. We didn't see each other much, but we kept up via WhatsApp. And after the last few years, we were closer than ever. I was saving every penny up to visit her next summer. I was supposed to finish my second master's by then. I'd been all over Europe, but I'd never been to Asia, except Istanbul. I really wanted to and felt safe knowing she'd be there in case anything happened to me.

"I missed you so much! How's Edward?"

She laughed and flipped her long hair. Since high school, she'd gotten more and more confident, and living in a country where men outnumbered women by more than thirty million had done some serious things to her ego. I still loved her. Just because she liked to flirt and shop, she wasn't any less smart. The girl was a brilliant loyal friend who'd been there for me through thick and thin on countless phone calls.

She pulled out her phone and showed me her WeChat. Edward had left her at least ten messages and hearts in English and Mandarin today alone. She'd sent one back.

I snorted and pulled her toward my bedroom. "Come on, let me finish getting ready."

She eyed me as I pulled on my collared button-down UVB shirt.

"Are you wearing that?" she asked with a wrinkle of her nose. Sometimes it was still hard for her to understand how much my lupus scared me. Your body shouldn't attack itself.

"I can't get too much sun," I said in a slightly exasperated tone. More than eighty percent of people with lupus had issues with the sun.

"I know," she said, sounding apologetic. She tried to grab Bea, who was jumping around on the bed, wagging her tail in a frenzy. "Are you bringing that sunscreen?" She motioned to the bottle sitting in my bike basket.

"Yes." I slipped it into my bag. "Thanks for reminding me." I glanced around to see if I'd missed something.

"Good." She gave me a once-over and conceded, "It's not too bad." Then she clapped her hands and said excitedly, "Tell me about Oskar before he gets here, and then we can catch up on the other stuff later!"

I opened my mouth to start talking, but a loud knock had us smiling and looking to the door. I whispered, "*Wǒ xǐhuān tā.*"

I like him. I knew a few phrases in Mandarin after more than fifteen years of friendship.

"Girl, that smile says it all." She bumped my shoulder and grabbed Bea. "Oh, you little fluff, I caught you now." She kissed her head as I opened the door.

"Come in," I said in English, cluing him in that I had guests. "This is Prudence, my oldest friend. Ru, this is Oskar."

"Her boyfriend," he added with a big smile as he held out his hand.

I gave him a quick kiss on the cheek. "My boyfriend," I agreed. "Let me get my stuff."

I grabbed my bag and a six-pack of beer. I heard Oskar and Ru politely making small talk. She said he could use her Chinese name and nickname, Ru.

She leaned in and whispered, "*Ta shi hen hao.*" *He's very good.*

We got to the North Atlanta rental site around noon. Sujit, Ryan, Sam, Sam's girlfriend, Shelly, were already there and politely introduced themselves. We gathered our stuff as Oskar shucked his shirt. I ogled his flat stomach and light dusting of hair on his sculpted chest as I applied a final layer of sunscreen.

He caught me checking him out and leaned in to whisper, "Like what you see?"

"Mm-hmm," I whispered back with a kiss.

God, we were getting cheesy, and I didn't even care.

In her tiny bikini, Ru was getting ogled herself by Ryan and seemed to eat up the attention. She was just wearing that and a big hat with massive shades. I knew from all our talks she really liked her boyfriend and would never cheat on him. But since she'd moved to China, she'd become an almost professional flirt. The male-to-female ratio over there could do that to a person. Her boyfriend put up with it, and his parents apparently loved her.

We crowded onto the bus, and some rowdy guys in the back who looked like they were in a fraternity started singing as we drove upriver. They must have been at least already a few beers in. Ryan, who was also from Atlanta, asked Ru and me the last time we'd tubed down the Chattahoochee. We looked at each other and laughed—it had been the summer of senior year. It had been a while ago, but I thought I remembered we'd both gotten super burned; today I had my shirt, and we'd put on tons of sunscreen. Ryan seemed disappointed Ru had a boyfriend and started flirting a little less and talking to Sujit more until we finally got there.

"Jesus, I need some beer for this!" Shelly moaned as we got in the tubes, trying not to let our bodies touch the frigid water. "Babe, can you toss us some Blue Moons?"

Sam tossed them to us as we twisted to grab them without touching the water. As soon we'd drank one beer and with a second in hand, we got more comfortable. Shooting the Hooch, as Atlantians called it, was mainly drinking and sunbathing, which was why Michael had originally disapproved of me going. There were almost no rapids, and it was more a social event, like tailgating—a Southern ritual.

Sam and Ryan were at least a beer ahead of us and started

singing Georgia classics, like "Chattahoochee," to which we couldn't resist joining in. I filled in for Oskar and Sujit when the Southernisms got too thick. It was nice to talk to Sujit a little, who I knew was Oskar's closest friend stateside. He had a nice, laidback personality, so it was easy to see why the two got along. Oskar was right: Ryan was nice, but a little abrasive.

Talk turned to jobs, travel, and family. Shelly and Ru had both studied business and got along smashingly well. Several beers in, we were all laughing. I'd gotten lazy as the alcohol ran through me and stopped trying to keep my feet out of the water; my toes were most definitely numb. I'd kept switching my beer from hand to hand, but my fingers were freezing, too, a combination of the beer and needing to stick my hand in the water so our tube avoided rocks.

Oskar noticed them and said, "Good god, what's wrong with your fingers?"

My Raynaud's was acting up, no surprise. Eight of my fingers were bright white. I wiggled them at Oskar, slightly tipsy or maybe drunk—it was hard to tell when you were just lying in a tube, not walking. Then I looked at my toes, which had gone numb an hour ago, lifting them out of the water and wiggling them at him too.

"Raynaud's," I said nonchalantly.

I couldn't resist reaching over and touching his belly. It was warm, and I giggled when he flinched and hissed out, "They're frozen!" He took them in his hands and rubbed them. It burned and tingled as they started to regain feeling.

"I've told you about this," I said. I wasn't sure whether it was frustration over having four freaking autoimmune diseases or over the fact he didn't remember that turned my voice sharp. Despite the alcohol in me, I wondered if my lupus was flaring. It shouldn't have been this bad. My PAH medicine usually helped control it. Well, the water was cold enough, I supposed.

Shelly and Ru were distracted, and Oskar must have heard something in my voice because he switched to German. "I haven't seen it before," he said softly, still rubbing my fingers. "Are you okay?"

"I've only known you in the summer," I bit out. Then I softened my tone at the flicker of something that flashed in his eyes. "It's fine." I glanced at my watch and grimaced. "It's been more than two hours—*closer to four*—and this water's freezing. The sun isn't helping."

Oskar looked around. We were floating past a few buildings, but our surroundings were mainly residential and the Chattahoochee National Recreation Area. The parking lot was nowhere in sight. "Are you all right?"

I laughed. "What are you going to do if I say no?" God, these beers were making me bold.

"Lucia," he said in a warning tone. "I don't want you to get sick."

His tone sobered me, and despite the beers and the heat, I felt an icy fear grip me.

"I don't either. I'm having fun, but I thought it would just be two hours." I sighed. "I have to tough it out until we get back to the parking lot. Either I'll be okay, or I won't. Unless you have a helicopter, we have to wait it out. Honestly, I won't know until tonight. If I get too much sun, I might get a rash or a fever." I shrugged, trying to be nonchalant, but I was getting a little nervous. "If not, I might get a flare. My rheumatologist is good; he'll take care of me." I never would have agreed to four-plus hours in the sun, if I'd known.

I squeezed his hands and looked into those beautiful molten brown eyes, my heart skipping a beat. *Please don't let it be a flare.* That could mean joint swelling or even organ problems. I hated taking steroids. I didn't want chipmunk cheeks or for my hair to fall out. Was that vain? Maybe.

Suddenly, I felt close to tears. The ice in my belly chilled further. I really didn't want Oskar to see me sick. I knew I should have never agreed to date him. I liked him way too much already. It was going to hurt if he couldn't handle this—oh god, it was really going to hurt.

He kissed my fingers, which were now bright red from his rubbing, indicating oxygen was reflowing to them. "Let me see your toes," he demanded, and I twisted my tube so he could grab them.

He rubbed them like he had my fingers. The de-numbing sensations started again—tingling almost to the point of pain, but more annoying than anything else. It was really sweet of him. I'd always thought feet were kind of gross, but appreciated what he was doing. It made me feel a little mushy, and the beers only accelerated that spreading warmth deep in the cavity of my heart. The icy fear of him leaving me was now battling the warmth of him taking care of me, making me icy-hot.

"I wanted to try it," I admitted softly. "It's hard, always watching everyone else do something you can't do. When we get to the endpoint, I'm going to swim. I don't care how cold it is. I told you about the PAH and the heart IV. For more than a year, I couldn't swim or bathe—just shower with tape tightly covering the site. I thought I might never swim again." I motioned around us to the beautiful sunny day and our friends laughing and drinking. "I thought I'd never do anything like this again. I might not do tubing again, knowing it's far more than two hours, but I don't want to live my life afraid of being alive."

He tickled me, making me squirm. "You are the most alive person I've ever met."

His gaze was intense, making feel me all kinds of heat—desire and something else, something that terrified me.

Please don't break my heart.

A few minutes later, we saw the disembarking point downstream. About thirty minutes later, given the river's slow crawl, we were there. After turning in our tubes, we all dared each other to jump in. I finally stripped off my shirt, and Sujit asked about my scar.

I teased him, telling him the truth. "I got stabbed in the heart with a knife."

He looked poised to ask more, but Oskar took that moment to toss me in and dove in after me.

He came up, sputtering, "I think my dick just froze off. Is this enough swimming?"

I couldn't help the burst of snort-laughter that escaped me. There were children nearby, so I was glad he'd said it in German. Teeth chattering, I nodded, and we waded out. We toweled off and drove five minutes away to Sam and Shelly's apartment complex on the river. Everyone had known to eat a big breakfast, but now it was past five and we were all starving.

The girls ran inside place to change as the boys headed down to gear up the grill. We fired up some hamburgers—and veggie burgers for me—in a shady spot by the river Oskar had asked them to switch to. By the time Oskar drove us back to my place, despite how careful I'd tried to be, there was red all over my body in places the shirt didn't cover. I shuddered—I'd gotten sun fever, and I'd be in for a shivery night.

We bid Ru goodnight and both of us showered. I was going to see her and her parents tomorrow for dim sum. My hat and sunscreen had kept my face mostly shaded, but the V of my chest and legs were burned. Despite having worn the shirt most of the day, I had the usual rash on my left bicep and used some steroid cream on it before washing my hands. I was shaking with cold, and I pulled on leggings and a long-sleeve. Something hurt on the back of my left thigh, and I wondered how I'd bruised it.

"Are you okay?" Oskar asked, his voice full of concern.

My fingers were white again. I shook my head and just got in bed and curled up under the covers. It was eight thirty, but I was really tired. My whole body was wracked with tremors. Usually, when I'd gotten sun fevers in the past, I'd be fine the next day.

Oskar got in bed beside me and pulled me against his warm chest, which helped a little. It did more than heat my body—it made me feel safe and cherished.

"Are you okay?" he asked again. "I can take you to the

hospital."

"No, no. I'm fine. It's a sun flare. Michael was right. I'll see how I feel in the morning. You don't need to stay over; I'm sure it's too early for you to go to sleep."

"I'll stay," he whispered to my temple as I fell asleep.

I woke up in the morning unusually tired, but the fever was gone. The back of my thigh was pinching me painfully, and I'd have to go to the bathroom at some point soon and check it out. My knees hurt, and a quick touch told me they were swollen.

I woke Oskar with a kiss. "Hey, thanks for everything yesterday. You were so sweet," I told him as his sleepy eyes opened.

"Of course," he said softly as I played with his hair. "Do you feel better?"

"I'm still a little tired."

"That's it?" His eyes held concern as they took me in.

"My joints have some fluid on them," I admitted. "I think I need to cancel trivia. Between all the fun and feeling like this, I don't want to start the school week behind."

He looked disappointed but nodded. Canceling plans because I was sick made an icy guilt settle in my stomach.

"Can we get some coffee before you kick me out?" he asked. I nodded, and he continued, "I need to go to my lab, too. Remember, I don't have service there, so if you need me, send me a WhatsApp."

"Okay," I said and slid out of bed to start the coffee.

As I did, my thigh pinched again. I stopped in the bathroom, grimacing when I glanced in the mirror. It looked like the start of a staph infection, but with the spreading redness and pain, it already seemed pretty bad. I quickly pulled my leggings back up to send Oskar off, praying, *Please don't get sick*, even though it never seemed to help.

Twenty-seven

Present day, September 8
OSKAR

"How's the grading going?" I asked Lucia, noticing her frown.

"Ugh," she groaned. "I hate being out of school."

She leaned back, eyes closed, and her silky hair fell on my legs. She was down on the floor hunched over the coffee table, how she preferred to work. No thanks—I was on the loveseat. I didn't understand the purpose of her desk, which I'd only seen holding papers. She didn't even own a chair for it.

I rubbed her shoulder and leaned down to kiss her temple. Opening her eyes, she turned so her back cracked before she rested her elbows on my legs. Her gorgeous eyes pivoted to meet mine.

"It's okay," she muttered. "But that sub was not me, though. All these assignments are a mess. I don't know if the kiddos didn't understand or were goofing off"

I stroked her cheek with my thumb as she continued to hold me with her amber-flecked eyes. "I'm sorry you got sick. I'm sorry we went tubing."

I felt guilty I hadn't talked her out of it and worried what could have happened to her. Something inside my chest constricted a little as I looked at her still slightly wan face. I dropped my hand.

She shook her head. "You told me not to go. Michael told me not to go. I shouldn't have gone." Her expression fell, and she whispered so quietly, "It was fun."

Her words pinched that same part of my chest.

"Come here, Süsse," I said, gently patting my leg while saving my work and closing my computer.

She stood, and I pulled her onto my lap, crushing her to me. I hadn't told her, but she'd scared the shit out of me last week. This was the first time I'd seen her since the morning after we went tubing. I'd been irritated she was blowing me off until she finally admitted she'd been sick. She felt so good nestled against me, I just held her there a moment, rubbing her arm.

"Look at all the things you can do," I said. "Tubing wasn't *that* fun."

She didn't respond, but her arms tightened around mine and I rested my chin on her head. God, I'd been so worried about her. When we'd woken Sunday morning, her fever was gone, but her knees were about twice the size of normal and the rash was still on her bicep. She didn't take off her leggings, but I found out later she had an abrasion that'd turned into a nasty infection.

She watched it on Sunday, but on Monday evening it got worse, or so she told me, and she spiked a fever. She'd gone to see her doctor the following day and apparently had had a fever of 103 and a softball-size infection on the back of her thigh from dirty river water and the rubbing tube. She'd missed work every day this week except Friday and looked honestly like a fragile shell of herself. It frightened me as much as my growing feelings for her.

She'd said it sometimes happened with the sun—that it messed up her immune system, and she was on immunosuppressants. I hadn't seen her leg, although she said it looked normal now.

She'd have to take antibiotics for fourteen days total.

Having her in my arms loosened something that had been tight in my chest all week. "I missed you," I couldn't help saying.

Those were words I could form for how I felt. I wasn't sure when my feelings for her had gotten so serious, or whether that was a good thing. I wasn't staying in America forever. We were probably both setting each other up for something painful, yet I wanted to pull her closer, not back away.

She kissed my neck. "I know. Me too." Her voice was muffled by my skin. "Oskar, if you really want to be my boyfriend, this will happen a lot. I get sick *a lot*," she added with emphasis.

My arms tightened involuntarily at her words. "I *am* your boyfriend, and I don't mind helping out."

As I said it, I knew it was true. I wished she didn't have to deal with all this crap, but it didn't scare me away. She was an amazing girl despite it all.

Just then, there was a knock on the door, and I moved her off me to answer it. We'd ordered pizza, something we hadn't done before. Normally she spoiled me with her cooking, and she took after her chef father. But she'd admitted the antibiotics and fighting the infection made her tired, and she looked it. She'd also confided somewhat reluctantly if she didn't eat carbs with the antibiotics, she threw up, so pizza seemed a good choice.

We ate dinner, and I let her get caught up some more on her work. Then we went to bed just to rest for the second time in a week. With the comfort of holding her in my arms, I fell asleep before I'd even planned on it.

I woke suddenly to her sounds of distress. She was moaning, "No, no, no," and whimpering. Her breath was coming in pants, and she had a light sweat on her brow as she thrashed around. Bea, I noticed, had wisely climbed over to my side of the bed.

"Lucia, wake up," I said, slightly shaking her.

She awoke with a gasp, her eyes wild with terror. "It's just me, Oskar," I said gently, rubbing her arm. "You were having a dream. It's okay."

Her eyes calmed a little bit, but her breath sounded as bad as it had that day we'd met hiking. "Ca—can I turn on the light?" she stuttered.

"Of course," I said, still stroking her arm.

She sat up and turned on the lamp, then wrapped her arms around herself and reached for my hand.

"What did you dream about?"

She frowned and said, "Vampires."

"Vampires?" I asked, mildly shocked. Sure, vampire shows and movies were scary. Yet it was kind of a strange nightmare to have and still be so upset about.

"I have a recurring dream about vampires. It's never exactly the same, but in the end it is. I'm hiding and alone. Then they find me and kill me by ripping open my throat." She shuddered as she said it. She squeezed my hand. "At least this time, you woke me up before they killed me." She tried to smile, but she still looked panic-stricken.

"Um, Lucia," I said hesitantly, "you don't believe in vampires, do you?"

"No, Oskar." But then she said, "The vampire's inside me." She closed her eyes and a few tears leaked out, startling me. I squeezed her hand, not certain what she meant or what to say, but luckily she continued. "I started getting this dream when I was released from the hospital, and I thought about it really carefully during that first year. I realized the vampire is lupus, it's PAH, it's all this crap living inside me and attacking me when I least expect it. *It always finds me.* I can't escape it because *the vampire is inside me,* waiting, hidden, to prey on me." She took a deep breath and wiped her eyes. "The medicine I take for lupus can cause night terrors. I've gotten better about this dream. You get used to medicine after taking it for years. In fact, it hasn't happened since the night of the hike where we met, but the antibiotics I'm taking can also cause vivid dreams."

I sat up and pulled her to me. She clutched me hard and sobbed into my shoulder. "I can never escape."

"Shhhh, Süsse. You're going to fight it like you always do."

Her words saddened me in a way I couldn't even formulate thoughts about. In all the time I'd known her, she was usually so exuberant. To see her this way felt wrong.

We stayed like that several minutes until she finally whispered, "Why do you like someone broken like me? You're so perfect, Oskar—nice, smart, fucking hot as hell, good in bed. Why put up with me?"

I heard the vulnerability in her voice, and I didn't like it. She was a beautiful, intelligent, and successful girl—not to mention, considerate and funny. I was the lucky one.

I kissed the top of her head. "You're all those things too, Lucia." I had only known her a little over a month, but what I'd gotten to know, I couldn't resist.

She pulled back and kissed me. Her face was wet from her tears, but it was a hard, deep, soul-burning in a way that I couldn't help but feel aroused by. Suddenly, I noticed her chest pressed against me and her fingers pulling me closer, drawing me in deeper. My hands roamed her body.

But this was wrong. She'd been sick.

I pulled back. "You're still recovering, Süsse."

"I'm fine," she said, leaning in to kiss my neck the way I liked. "I put on a Band-Aid before bed. You won't touch the infection on my leg."

"Lucia." I gasped as her hand slid down to rub me. "It's you I'm worried about."

"Please," she whispered.

Her eyes met mine, and there was no way I could resist that look and that plea.

I reached for her with more than just lust. Seeing her sick had awoken something protective in me I hadn't known existed. I tore off her shirt. I wanted to kiss every part of her body so she knew what she meant to me. I started with her eyes, still wet from her tears, and worked my way south to her cheeks, her lips, her neck. By the time I reached her breasts, her grip on my dick told me I wouldn't make it much farther unless I wanted to risk coming in her hand. An oath escaped me when she pushed back my foreskin, her other hand was pulling down my boxers.

I pulled off her leggings and panties and rubbed myself against her. She looked at me with such a look of adoration, I couldn't help but plunge in. She was wet and warm around me. I moaned—it'd never felt this good before.

Shit, it had *never* felt this good before. I didn't put on a condom!

I moved to pull out, but her hands and legs tightened around me, stopping me.

"Lucia, condom," I somehow managed to pant out.

She still didn't release me. "It's okay. I have an IUD, and we've both been tested. *It's okay*," she said again as she pulled me in deeper.

There was no arguing with that, and nothing had ever felt this good. I'd never had sex without a condom. Ever. I leaned down, and our mouths and tongues tangled as I thrust into her, feeling her anew. Her sweet ecstasy grew, and I knew with how good this felt it'd soon be over. I reached between us and rubbed my thumb on her clit. When she came with my name on her lips, I flew over the edge as she clenched around my dick. My vision momentarily hazed over in the afterglow of the most intense orgasm I'd ever had. I pulled my hand from between us and tried to carry some of my weight, but I mostly collapsed on top of her with my face pressed to her neck.

"Lucia," I whispered reverently to her as her hands caressed my hair and back.

When we finally got up, Lucia insisted I shower with her antibiotic soap, "Just in case."

She redid the sheets and threw the others in the hamper as I washed. Then she rinsed herself off and rejoined me in bed. I eagerly spooned her lush body that fit perfectly against mine.

My eyes felt heavy as she whispered, "Thank you."

When I woke up with Lucia in my arms and the sun on her brilliant auburn hair, I'd never seen anything more beautiful. Lucia made me feel something I knew I'd never felt before. Holding her felt right in a way nothing ever had.

For how long, though?

"Morning," she murmured sleepily, oblivious to my inner turmoil.

I couldn't resist tightening my arms around her and nuzzling her neck. I wasn't going anywhere yet. While I was here, I'd do everything right. "Lucia," I asked carefully. "Will you tell me about your medicines today?"

She stiffened. Every time I'd spent the night, she'd taken her daily pills when I was in the bathroom. But I didn't want her to feel like she had to hide from me. I'd been scared last weekend. If I ever had to take her to the hospital, I should at least know what medicines she took.

With reluctance, I relented. "It's fine. You'll tell me when you're ready." I kissed her temple and moved to get up, disappointed she didn't trust me.

She halted me by threading our fingers. "I'll show you."

She kissed me softly and got up. Soon I heard the coffee maker kick on in the kitchen. When I finished in the bathroom, I found her on the loveseat with the dog, waiting for me. She looked timid.

"I just want to know all about you," I said.

She took out a bunch of pill bottles and the four-a-day pill case she carried in her purse. This was the first time I'd gotten a good look at it.

She picked up one of the bottles. "This is Pilocarpine. I take it for Sjogren's to produce saliva. Sjogren's affects my glands. My body attacks my glands—tear glands, saliva glands..." Her cheeks pinkened, and she looked down. "It makes my skin dry, which is why I'm more likely to get infections. It's why I prefer to use lube. Otherwise, after a few minutes, sex starts to hurt and I'll bleed."

"I'm glad you told me."

I knew she liked lube and was always wet when we started, but that made more sense. I understood this was hard for her to talk about, but I wanted her to know I'd like her anyway.

"I take prescription eye drops, too," she continued. "Otherwise my eyes get dry and scratchy. It sucks."

I'd seen her use the eye drops. She took out four pills and plopped one in each section of the case, then put that bottle back in the bag.

She smiled at me and said, "I always joke it's good I have Sjogren's because it's my alarm clock. The pills really only last four and a half to five hours. If I'm thirsty, I realize I missed a dose of medicine."

I put my hand on her thigh as she took out another small pill bottle and shook out three pills.

"The type of pulmonary hypertension, PAH, I have is rare. I have group one, and less than two in a million people have it. I take three Viagra a day for it," she said with a wink, "but, well, they call it the generic name, sildenafil, when it's used for PAH. It helps keep my veins open."

"Really?" I asked.

"Don't take with grapefruit," she said, laughing, and handed me the bottle to read. "I'm really lucky it's the only PAH medicine I take. I used to take four. Amazingly, controlling my lupus has changed my PAH to an annoyance from a life-threatening disease. My doctors were surprised. Also, it helps with the Raynaud's, the issues with cold intolerance in my hands and feet. It's more of an annoyance than a danger—at least, mine is. Some people have it worse."

She finished with a shrug, trying to downplay her conditions. She took out a large bottle, and I put the sildenafil back in her bag.

"This is mycophenolate mofetil. We all call it CellCept, even though it's generic now. It's an immunosuppressant. I take twice the dose of an organ transplant patient. I used to take four times more, but now I'm a lot healthier. It's only approved for lupus if you've had organ failure, and not at all in Europe. It has some bad side effects. I had some GI issues," she picked up an aluminum pill container, "so now I take probiotics."

"And it's better?"

She smiled. "When I'm not on antibiotics, yes. The only step up from immunosuppressants is chemotherapy or IGG, and some IV infusion therapies. Luckily, I've never had to do that." She picked up the sixth medication. She was so calm about it all, but I guessed she'd had three and a half years to get used to it. "This is hydroxychloroquine or Plaquenil; it's a staple drug for lupus. It's actually an antimalarial. I'm still confused how it helps, but it does." As she put two in her pill case, she said casually, "It can cause blindness, so I go to the eye doctor twice a year to monitor my eyes."

I squeezed her thigh.

"This is iron. I have iron deficiency anemia. It's fine if I take iron, no big deal, but otherwise I want to sleep, like, fourteen hours a day. Sjogren's, iron deficiency anemia, and Raynaud's are found often in lupus patients. And finally, vitamin B. It gives me energy and helps keep my hair healthy."

"So, you take eight prescriptions plus two vitamins? Fourteen pills a day?"

She fidgeted with the bag's zipper and finished quietly, "Probably forever."

I threaded our fingers together. "Thanks for sharing with me, Lucia. I told you my dad has diabetes. It's different, but he has to do his pump and shots a few times a day too. He has to worry about his eyes, skin infections, and his kidneys, too. *I get it*. It was brave of you to tell me about it."

Finally, she looked up with those green-gold-speckled eyes I adored, and I saw a torrent of emotions there. I couldn't help but kiss her.

I said softly as I leaned back, "I like you, vampires and all."

Twenty-eight

September 29
LUCIA

"The view up here is super!" Oskar exclaimed, making me smile.

I tugged his hand as I pivoted to soak up the view of Atlanta and the tri-skyline of downtown, Midtown, and Buckhead. Because of our busy schedules, quite a bit of our hang-out time lately had been spent doing schoolwork. Dating had been possible, if not optimal. At least we were in the same boat.

But with this gorgeous late September day, and the fact Oskar had never done Stone Mountain, we were here. I'd never liked that it was a Confederate monument. But it was the largest single piece of granite in the world, so I'd always chosen to overlook its carved defacement, which only encompassed about five minutes of the pretty three-hour hike. It was a mile hike up and down, then five miles around. The best part was that it was less than half an hour from my place.

It'd been almost a month since my nightmare, and in that time Oskar had been amazing. Most of the time I was normal

Lucia, but some days I was more tired than others. I'd tried to keep it from Oskar as much as I could. Even though I hadn't been diagnosed until college, I knew I'd had this disease since I was a child. Besides the occasional flare-up, I could usually manage what I considered an average life—outside of my pills and more sporadic doctor's visits, not much different from anyone else. There was just one thing I hadn't talked to him about: I couldn't have kids. *Ever*.

That conversation wasn't something I wanted to have right away. If Oskar was like most guys, even hints about kids too early on would scare him away. We'd been dating two months, and the way we spent time together, well, there was something more than casual dating going on. At least for me. While there'd been no *I love you*s, it was obvious something more serious had been happening between us.

At the same time, I felt it was only fair to tell him before it was too late. He might not be okay being with someone who couldn't have kids and give him a family someday. And if he wasn't, I needed to let him go. I promised myself I would talk to him about it soon. The way I already felt, if this went on too long, I'd be crushed. I already felt like I might be pretty bruised. Heck, what a liar. I *would* be crushed.

"Ready to do the loop?" I asked, nerves jumping. I needed to talk to him.

"Sure," Oskar said, turning with me.

The trek down was nicer for me because I didn't have to fight my defective pulmonary artery. At the very bottom, the Cherokee Trail started. It had always surprised me how few people took it, compared to how many climbed up to the top. It was normally nice, quiet, and scenic. Plus, it was shaded.

Oskar surprised me about two miles in, right before we hit the lake, by saying, "Your parents live in town, right?"

"Yes. So far, I've protected you, but we're close, and they're interested in you."

"Protected me?" Oskar asked in a strange voice.

"Well, I mean, you know the inevitable family dinner."

I winced even as the words escaped me. Was it too early to even say that? He stopped, and I almost ran into him.

"I wouldn't mind meeting them," he said seriously.

I couldn't take the look in his eyes, and I wanted to talk to him about the impossibility of kids before he met them. I knew my parents would like him; everyone liked him.

He stepped closer and gently tilted my jaw up, cupping my cheek. "If my parents lived here, I'd want you to meet them."

I glanced around the trail and saw we were alone. I sucked in a deep breath. "Oskar," I said. "There is something I want to tell you before you meet them." I risked glancing up at him, and those warm eyes held me captive. The coward that I was, I couldn't help but stretch up and touch my lips to his one more time.

What if he didn't want me after this?

Despite my attempts at being strong, I felt tears slid down my face. Oskar felt them too and jerked back. His hand came to my cheek again, his eyes searing into mine.

"Lucia, what is it?"

I held his warm chocolate gaze and said in a quiet voice, "I don't know if we will still be together in a month or a year, or if you want me for the long haul. It's too early for that, and I *don't* want you to think about it yet…but there is one thing you should know as we continue to date, in case it gets to the point where you'd consider a future with me." My voice cracked and more tears slipped out. "Because I have pulmonary hypertension, I should never get pregnant. Many women with PAH, their hearts can't recalibrate postpartum. About a third to half of those mothers die, depending on the study. Knowing that, *I* will never get pregnant."

My heart skipped a beat, and my stomach grew queasy as emotions raced across his face.

I sucked in a quick breath, hoping I wouldn't vomit, before continuing. "That's what I want you to think about before you ask to meet my parents. That's what I want you to think about before you want me to meet yours."

I wiped my tears away, unable to speak or face him anymore and resumed walking. After a moment, I heard Oskar's footsteps behind me. He didn't speak, so I didn't, either. A few minutes later, we got to the lake, where there were several families with strollers. I kept walking past the crowded section near the parking lot, not wanting to see families right at this moment. I reached a deserted spot, found a big rock, and thumped down.

I gazed out over the lake and struggled to calm my mind, stomach, and heart. Inside me, something was breaking. I wondered if this was where Oskar would leave me. Frank hadn't wanted kids and didn't care. Oskar would be a good dad; I knew that deep down.

Heat seared my thigh as Oskar sat down beside me. He still hadn't said anything but took my hand in his. I felt his gaze on me, but I kept mine on the lake—calm, blue, tranquil. Everything I didn't feel. If I looked at him, I would lose all the composure I'd mustered.

"Lucia." The way he said my name sent shivers down my spine. When I didn't look at him, he said softly, "It really sucks, what you just told me. I always thought one day, I'd meet someone I'd want to start a family with and get married and do that. I haven't felt that yet."

His words cut me like a knife, and I trembled.

"I like you a lot," he continued quickly. "I'm still interested in dating you and seeing if, one day, I feel that way about you."

I turned to look at him, open-mouthed. What was he saying?

His eyes held mine, and he said slightly wistfully, "You'd be a wonderful mother."

At that, I did shatter. I closed my eyes as the tears poured out. My free hand involuntarily went to my stomach. I loved my mom and had always pictured being a mom someday myself— decorating the Christmas tree, reading bedtime stories, playing tag. So many images flashed through my mind. Gone. They had all been taken from me.

"Christ, Lucia. Look at me." His hands came to my face. "There is more than one way to have kids. There is adoption. There is surrogacy. There is foster care. You love your students. I can't imagine you not having a family, if you wanted one."

"Yes," I said, dropping his gaze. "But that's not acceptable to everyone."

His hands fell from my face, and his voice hardened a little, "Lucia, I'm not ready to get married or have kids. Or talk about getting married or having kids."

"I'm not either, *Oskar.* I still barely know you! But I thought you should know. If you stay with me, I don't want you to find this out when you're thinking about those things."

I couldn't help but close my eyes again. Hot tears ran down my face, despite my best efforts.

With a deep breath, I forced myself to open my eyes and look at him. "I just thought you had the right to know before you got too attached. I don't want to waste your time. I like you too, Oskar. I like you a lot. But if this isn't something you can handle, then I need to know. You can sleep on it. You can think about it. But if this is a deal-breaker, please tell me. If it's okay, I won't bring it up again. We might break up next week, or we may date for years before we ever want more. But if it's a deal-breaker, please let me know before I consider that commitment."

We held each other's gaze a long moment, and terror gripped me as I waited for his response. Finally, he leaned in, kissed me chastely, and pulled away before our eyes met again.

"I would never leave someone for something they can't control," he said.

"You don't have to tell me now. Think about it," I insisted.

He stood up and held his hand out for me. I took it. "You said what you needed to say. You're right; it's good to get it out in the open now. Thank you for telling me." His words were so stiff. "I said what I needed to say, but can we drop it?"

I nodded.

He looked relieved, a small smile curving his lips and his shoulders softening. I felt some tension leave my body before he said, "I still want to meet your parents, but no more medieval baby talk, okay? Let's just keep letting things go on like they are, slow and steady."

I couldn't help but laugh as relief poured through me. "No more *medieval* baby talk, baby," I teased, giving him a quick kiss. I wrapped my arms around him and he held me close. Warmth filled me up from the inside out.

We fell back into our normal rhythm for the remainder of the walk. I couldn't believe he was okay with still dating me, even knowing I'd never be able to carry a baby. An incredible burden had been lifted, as awkward and horrible as the conversation had been. The fear of this talk had been festering inside me, and I felt freer for airing it out.

When we finally got back to my place after dinner, I nearly pushed him into the shower. He'd never seemed more attractive to me than he did at this moment. I peppered kisses all over him. He tried to touch me, but I halted his hands.

"Let me," I begged.

He held my eyes, then nodded.

Right now, I just wanted him to know how much he meant to me. I knelt down and took him in my mouth as the water steamed around us. I used everything I had to pleasure him, my mouth, my tongue, my hands. He groaned over me and cupped my jaw and pulled my hair, thrusting and moaning as I sucked him hard. My core tightened and dampened, knowing *I* had created that fervor. His fingers in my hair and his cock in my mouth stiffened at the same time as I swallowed his release with the "*Lucia,*" he gasped.

He pulled me up to him and held me in his arms as the water teased my aroused flesh. With slow sensual circles traced on my back, he started telling me all the ways he planned to make me moan and scream his name. God, he'd barely even touched me, yet I was slick with anticipation as he hardened again. I *really* liked his German dirty talk.

Much later, as I lay curled in his warm arms, his hand on my stomach, our fingers intertwined, I felt something close to bliss. He'd made good on almost every dirty promise. I was sated and sleepy. My ex hadn't wanted kids, so my inability to have them had been a relief for him. But *I* wanted children someday. Oskar still wanted to date me, even knowing my options were unconventional. He'd said nothing had changed, but for me, everything had. I wiggled back against his chest, snuggling closer, and he murmured sleepily in my ear.

For the first time since I'd met him, I fell asleep in his arms, optimistic that one day, he might still be in my future, and that might not be a scary thing.

Twenty-nine

October 8
OSKAR

A nervous tension ran through me as I shuffled up to Lucia's door. I was going to meet her parents tonight. I'd asked for it—kind of—but I still wondered, what if they didn't like me? Or was I being a moron? I wasn't staying here forever. But it seemed wrong not to meet the family she was so close with when they lived five minutes away and she spoke of them incessantly.

I let out a breath before knocking on the door. Despite what Lucia thought about herself because of her medical issues, she was a catch. My friends' words echoed in my mind: *What's she doing with you?* Not only was she trilingual, but she'd earned a master's degree by twenty-three and would get a second by twenty-five. And she'd done them with incredible grades.

I knew her mom was an academic and a professor, but her dad was a self-made man with a culinary degree. From what Lucia said, he worked almost all the time—six days a week.

It is going to be fine, I assured myself as I knocked on the door.

Fluffy's barking and some muffled shushing made me smile. After a moment, Lucia opened the door, looking a dream in a fitted cream sweater and skinny jeans. I salivated, imagining her backside in those pants. Her eyes shone as she took in my sunflowers.

"Are those for me or my parents?" she asked hesitantly.

"You," I said as I pulled her into my embrace.

I loved the way she fit against me, her breath fanning my neck. She always smelled amazing, a scent like grapefruit but uniquely her.

I whispered in her ear, "I realized we've been seeing each other a while, so I thought..."

She pulled away, smiling. "So I haven't scared you away yet?" she teased.

She walked away to put her flowers in a vase. I followed her so I could watch her incredible ass. It wasn't an expensive gift, but I'd wanted to do a little something for her, since she did so much for me. She'd changed my whole outlook on Atlanta. I guessed that was why I'd suggested meeting her parents. Considering I wasn't staying in America, I sort of regretted it.

She caught me looking and raised an eyebrow.

I coughed and said, "I asked to meet your parents, didn't I?"

"Yes, and we should probably go." She paused and then asked, "Do you mind if we take Bea? She likes going over there and playing with their dog."

"Sure," I said, and we headed out the door with Bea in tow.

It was very close, and just a few minutes later, we pulled up to a cream-painted brick house with dark brown shutters. Shit, her family must be rich.

"Here we go," Lucia said as she got out of the car with Bea.

I grabbed the bottle of wine I'd bought and put my hand on the curve of her back as we walked up the front porch steps. Her mom opened the door as soon as we knocked and waved us inside. She gave Lucia a quick hug, kissed Bea, and then turned to look at me with gray eyes. She had straight light brown hair.

"Hello, I'm Maria," she said with a slight accent.

"Oskar." I held out my hand. "Nice to meet you."

She smiled warmly at me in a way that made me feel comfortable, but her eyes on me were intelligent and observant.

Lucia bent down, petting both dogs, who wagged their tails and ran circles around each other.

I heard Lucia's dad before I saw him. "Lucia," was spoken in such a way that I knew he loved his daughter possibly more than anything in the world.

Lucia jumped up and hugged him before turning to me expectantly. He was a solid man and despite almost a full head of gray hair, he stood sure of himself and sturdy. Lucia looked so much like him, from his remaining ginger coloring to his height, unlike her petite mother.

He stuck out his hand and said in a deep voice, "Oskar, nice to meet you. You can call me David."

His eyes went to the wine I brought, and I felt a touch apprehensive, as I knew chefs could be picky.

"*Nebbiolo.*" He said the word slowly and then gave me a big smile. "Well, I know one of two things, either you have good taste in wine, or you are good at listening to Lucia." He looked at her, his eyes softening with affection, and his smile widened. "This is her favorite." He chuckled. "Well, favorite besides Brunello, but we can't drink that every day, now can we?"

In that moment, I was certain of one thing: if I hurt Lucia, her dad would never forgive me. She was his world.

"What are we eating, Dad?" Lucia asked as we walked into the kitchen. The little Pomeranians zipped in front of us, yapping excitedly to each other.

"We are having a harvest salad with Rocchetta cheese, risotto with mushrooms and truffles, the three of us *brasato al Barolo*—that's beef—and Lucia's favorite, tiramisu." He grinned at her. "So yes, we can drink your wine."

"Goody!" Lucia said, clapping. She walked behind the

kitchen island to get glasses. "Everyone's drinking? This needs to aerate."

Murmurs of assent went around as Lucia opened the bottle and poured the bottle into a fancy decanter, like nothing in my own home. Her mom motioned for me to sit, and her dad washed his hands before turning to check on some of the food he was preparing. I offered to help, but he firmly said no.

When Lucia brought her dad a glass a few minutes later, he told her, "Thank you, baby," before shooing her away.

Then we sat down at the dinner table, and now that he wasn't cooking, David's full attention fell on me. "So, Oskar, you're from Innsbruck?"

"Yes, but I studied in Munich."

"And biochemical engineering, correct?" Maria asked.

I nodded. "Yes, with a concentration in biomedical engineering."

"Fascinating," she said. "Why that?"

"My mom worked at a company that made hearing aids, and my dad has type one diabetes. I was always interested in medical equipment and drugs. With this degree, hopefully I can help a lot of people. Not like being a doctor, but quality control in my own way." I smiled at Lucia. "Like Lucia's obsession with the UN."

Both of her parents' gazes swerved toward her, and she blushed.

Her mom said in a low but firm voice, "Lucia, I thought you didn't want to do that anymore?"

Her cheeks turned redder. I didn't know what I'd said wrong.

"Lucia's a really good teacher," her dad said. "What job is more important than that?"

I cleared my throat uncomfortably. "I meant her paper. Lucia's thesis."

"It's okay, Dad. I gave up on working for the IMF," Lucia said before she took a rather large gulp of wine. She turned to her mom and thoroughly changed the subject, "Mom, I think I mentioned Oskar and I normally use German. It's been nice to speak it so much again." She smiled at me, her cheeks losing a little color. "Although Oskar says I have an accent from Oma and Opa."

Her mom switched to German, her first language, to tease me, "And what about you? Do you speak like a Southerner?" Her accent was much stronger than Lucia's.

I responded politely, but with a grin, "I speak the best German, like all Austrians—Austrian German."

She and Lucia laughed before Lucia switched back to English. "We speak mainly Italian at home, but if it's just my dad and me, we tend to fall into English. German, not so much."

"That's fine, Lucia," her dad said with a smile. "So, Oskar, why choose to study in America?"

"Well, Georgia Tech is one of the best biochemical engineering programs in the world. I preferred an English program since some international firms require higher English competency. When they offered me a spot with a stipend, I couldn't refuse. Plus, I wanted to travel a little, too. I'd always lived within two hours from home and wanted an adventure."

"And Atlanta, you like it so far?" he asked politely as he served me some of the beef.

I looked at the delicate curves of Lucia's face, at her full lips, before I turned back to her dad.

"Yes, I like Atlanta. Honestly, though, I've liked it more since I met Lucia." She looked up at me and smiled. "My first year was busy with the courses, and I didn't have any German friends. It feels more comfortable speaking German again. Plus, she knows the city well. We're both studying almost all the time, but we make time to do some fun things. It's nice to be with someone who understands my schedule's busy. And she's busy herself, so I don't feel as bad working long hours in the lab."

David smiled at Maria. "That, I certainly understand."

I cut into my meat at a pause in the conversation and took a bite. I could immediately understand how the man could own two restaurants. Not that I'd doubted it with Lucia's cooking skills.

"This is incredible," I told him.

He smiled and let me eat a moment, while Lucia and her mom chatted with her dad occasionally joining in. "When you graduate, where do you see yourself?" her dad asked me.

"Well, ideally, I'd like to work in innovation, more than maintenance, and hopefully with equipment, medical equipment. Although I wouldn't mind working with drugs, it isn't my first choice. And there is also the government sector." I paused a moment. "And food, but I like food like this and don't want to mess with it too much. That wouldn't be my ideal job."

"I mean, where?" His eyes pierced mine—I was trapped. "Will you go back home?"

I should have known he was waiting for the kill. I saw Lucia and her mom turn to look at me too.

"I don't know," I managed to choke out. "Likely not home. Innsbruck doesn't really have that type of job. Maybe, but the chance of getting a job there is small—minuscule. Maybe somewhere in Austria, perhaps the south, Graz, or certainly Vienna. There are more jobs in Germany, especially Frankfurt or Hamburg, many in Munich, which feels like home and isn't too far."

He wasn't done. "So you'll be returning to Europe?" I heard the concern in his voice.

His wife shook her head slightly, and it suddenly dawned on me that he'd pulled his wife away from her family. He could be afraid life may serve him the same fate back.

I risked a quick glance at Lucia, before saying truthfully, "I'm not sure. I have almost two years before I needed to decide. There are also so many jobs in America, more than Germany or Austria." It wasn't a lie. For every one job in Germany there were maybe ten in America. Compared with Austria, maybe twenty. But before I'd met Lucia, I knew one hundred percent I wanted to move back.

I looked at her beautiful profile out of the corner of my eye before focusing on my food. Now I felt more conflicted. I liked her like I never had another person, but Atlanta wasn't home. A light sweat broke out on my brow and I wondered again why I'd wanted to meet her parents. Maybe this had been a mistake. I was still ninety-five percent sure I'd move back, but I had time to decide.

"Dad, tell me more about Regina?" Lucia asked, changing the topic to her dad's newest chef.

He became animated as he discussed her and some of her new ideas. I was grateful, even as I knew this was something that would come up again. I'd answered honestly—I didn't know. Lucia was the most amazing girl I'd ever dated. I didn't mind America, at least not since I'd started to date Lucia. But I missed my family, my home. With all her health issues, I didn't get the impression she'd want to move back overseas. We'd never discussed it. Yet as I watched her laugh at something her dad said, my insides felt funny.

Lucia's mom brought me back to the table by saying, "I hear you and Lucia have been to some of the Carter Center talks?"

"Yes. We didn't go to the last one, but we hope to go to the next one—it's a medical panel. Lucia always knows what's going on around here. It's brilliant."

"It's amazing what medicine can do," she said with a smile. "Have you been to the CDC Museum? I think you'd like it."

Atlanta was world-famous as the home of the Centers for Disease Control and Prevention.

"No, we haven't been."

"It's open till seven on Thursdays if you both are interested. Lucia hasn't been, either. Like the Carter Center, it's free."

I agreed we should, and she asked me more questions about some of the other talks we'd been to. I noted Lucia got her hunger for learning from her mom. Well, maybe both her parents. Her dad seemed plenty passionate about food.

Dinner finished without any more major hiccups. When Lucia and her dad went to his computer to check out his new menu, I offered to help her mom clean up.

It was just her mom and me, so I asked the question that'd been burning inside me, falling back into German. "Can I please inquire, why do you not want Lucia to try to work for the IMF?"

I knew Lucia's answer, but I thought there was more to it.

Her mom sighed and turned to me. "The health insurance you can buy just isn't very good, and it's very expensive. The health laws here are changing." She turned back to the pan and scrubbed hard. "Not every Ph.D. program offers health coverage. When they do, it isn't always great. Some of her medicines are thousands of dollars with poor insurance. Many economics programs are full time, so she'd have to leave her job. So she'd lose her insurance. Also, the IMF is usually contractual work, not employee, so no insurance. But mostly the job travels all over, so who knows what coverage she'd have when she gets ill." More scrubbing. "She wouldn't be able to work there the way she'd like. Her immunosuppressants don't allow her to take live vaccines. She can't get the yellow fever vaccine, so she can't travel to much of the developing world. She'd be stuck with a desk job."

She looked so crestfallen, and I felt that way too.

"Lucia is so vibrant, so healthy," I said.

Her mom stopped washing the dish a moment to stare at me. "She's been so sick before, Oskar. Her father and I can't bear to think of her sick like that again if she stops her medicines." She punctuated every word: "*She could die.*"

A sliver of guilt and sadness crept through me. I knew Lucia enjoyed her job, but I also felt she'd rather work in comparative politics than teach them. From the stories she'd told me, I knew she loved traveling. So many places she couldn't go—it must break her heart.

Lucia came in, interrupting us with a blinding smile. "Is it time for tiramisu?"

Her mom put the last plate in the dishwasher and said with a twinkle in her eye, "Yes, carina."

Of course, it was as good as everything else we'd had. By

this point, I expected no less. Her parents were friendly as we left, her dad giving me a warm handshake and her mom double kisses on my cheeks.

On the short drive home, I said quietly to Lucia, "I'm sorry for talking about the IMF. I didn't know about the yellow fever vaccine."

She put her hand on top of mine on the shifter. "It's okay." Her voice was small but firm. "Look at all I can do, and at all I have. I can't be resentful."

We were silent the rest of the drive. I was grateful but not surprised she didn't ask about where I'd want to live when school finished. She never had before. We both were enjoying a good thing while we had it. Let tomorrow worry about itself. Yet when I watched her enter her place, I felt like I was starving for her. She handled everything with such grace, and she really was beautiful, inside and out. I wanted to go home one day, but I wanted her, too.

I stepped closer to her, slid my hands to her hips, and pulled her toward me. She tugged me down to meet her lips with an urgency that matched my own. Her hands tangled in my hair and drew me closer. Neither one of us spoke about it, but both of us seemed to feel the weight of the questions about the future, and we needed this moment.

I led her to the bedroom, slowly slipping off her sweater and tank top. I sat her on the bed and knelt down to take off her boots and jeans. I trailed kisses along her inner thighs, stomach, and breasts before coming back to her mouth. When I was within reach, her hands worked nimbly on my own sweater and belt buckle. I didn't want to think about the future or if we might want different things. Right now, I just wanted her fully and completely.

I pulled back to cup the back of her head. Our eyes found each other as I slid into her tight body, making her gasp. It was intimate, holding eye contact; it was like she could see into me. I moved slowly at first until I couldn't take it anymore. I rolled onto my back, pulling her with me.

"I want to see your beautiful body," I told her, pushing her hips down hard.

She moaned and sat up straighter, taking one of my hands to her breast as she rocked. I loved to watch passion play across her face in this position. She was greedy for her orgasm on top and knew just what to do to reach it. She pushed and rocked against me until she quaked around me. Watching and feeling her release brought me to mine with a few more rough pulls of my hands on her hips.

As she slumped over me and I kissed her shoulder, I realized that while I didn't know if I wanted to stay in America, I didn't want to lose her. My arms tightened around her at the thought, almost as if I could halt time.

Thirty

October 9
LUCIA

Beep, beep, beep. The loud chiming of the alarm at five thirty had Oskar and me both groaning and snuggling deeper into the covers. I took a moment to bask in waking up in his arms before the day rushed ahead. He clutched my stomach as he mumbled in my ear. His stubble tickled me as warmth, more than just from his broad chest, spread through me.

Oskar, my boyfriend.

He stayed over several nights a week. We both preferred to be here, rather than hanging out at his place. Lately, sex between us had been even more tender and passionate.

I smiled, thinking about how sweet Oskar had been last night, how intensely he'd held my gaze while we made love. I swallowed deeply and slid out of bed to turn on the coffee maker. I did my morning crunches with more vigor than normal, thinking about what had sparked Oskar's spectacular lovemaking last night.

He planned to return to Europe after graduation.

Of course, none of my medical problems bother him, I thought bitterly. He was just enjoying this while it lasted. He'd never planned to be stuck with me long term. He'd never planned to be there when I couldn't have kids.

I crept into the bedroom and stealthily grabbed Bea and a sweatshirt, suddenly needing to be outside. Bea did her business fast, like I trained her do when I was too sick to walk her far, but was excited to keep going when I took her on a much longer walk than usual. The fast-paced walk matched the speed of my heart as I thought about what it would do to me if Oskar went back home.

Did this relationship even mean anything to him, or was he just having some fun while he was here? I hated the way my belly fluttered at the thought.

I'd finally calmed down by the time I got back and grabbed a cup of coffee. It must have been must be six fifteen by now because I heard Oskar's alarm going off from the bedroom. I tried to focus on my inner serenity from the walk. I poured him a cup of coffee, took it to the bedroom, and turned on the light.

"Morning, Süsse," Oskar said as he sat up in the bed. He leaned against the headboard and reached for the cup.

I gave him a quick kiss and hurried back to the shower to rinse off. I was about to turn it off when I heard, "Wait, I need to shower too."

He stepped in behind me and grinned at my shower cap. He never stopped teasing me about it.

I gave him a quick ogle before I said, "I need to get ready. The shower's yours."

His face fell, but he nodded, understanding I couldn't be late to work. "Thanks for taking me to meet your parents," he said from the shower a few minutes later.

I was at the bathroom mirror, starting on my makeup. "I think they liked you."

"What's not to like?" he joked as he turned off the water.

I admired the broad planes of his chest and rigid torso as he pulled the shower curtain open and wrapped the towel around himself. I kind of agreed with him.

"Ha, ha, you are such a tease," I responded, and started brushing my hair out of its messy bun.

He stepped behind me, and I felt the heat of him on my back all the way to my core as our eyes met in the mirror.

"Oh, right, that's you." He kissed my bare shoulder with his stubbly beard, sending a tremor rippling through me. I felt warmth and saw my skin flush as he whispered huskily, "I like everything about you. Everything, Lucia."

I shook my head at him and stepped into the bedroom to get dressed. "Do you want breakfast? I have yogurt or a banana."

He followed me into the bedroom and dressed too. "Can I eat both? I am buying the groceries this weekend. I feel bad I'm always over here eating everything."

"Okay," I agreed, since it was true, not that I minded. I liked cooking. But food was expensive, especially since I tried to buy more organic-type foods, which seemed to help my lupus. We ate a quick breakfast before we both ran out the door.

"See you Thursday evening?" Oskar confirmed with a kiss at my car.

"Thursday," I said as I headed to school.

We'd fallen into some patterns. Mondays we did trivia, when we could, and Oskar spent the night. Tuesdays and Wednesdays, we went our own ways. I did yoga Tuesdays, and Wednesdays I had a night class. Fridays and Saturdays, we almost always spent together, either getting caught up on schoolwork or trying to fit in something fun. Some Sunday evenings I tried to work at Aperitivo so I could save up for my trip this summer. It was really nice how things were now, but it would really suck if he moved away.

I fiddled with the radio, trying not to dwell on how disappointing it had been to hear that. I'd known in the back of my head it was a big possibility, and I'd avoided asking. But hearing it aloud confirmed all my fears.

School was close, so it wasn't long until I was there and in my classroom. I quickly clocked in on the computer and double-checked everything I needed was on the whiteboards, just as I heard, "Ms. Farris?"

I stood, saying loudly, "Come in!" to the two students who'd clearly arrived for tutoring. The students knew I got here early, and my door was always open.

"Good Morning, Ms. Farris," Cody and Jenny chimed.

"Morning, guys. What's up?"

"Can you help explain the difference between the Schengen Area and the European Union to us?" Cody asked nervously.

We had a test on Wednesday. I smiled at Cody and Jenny and motioned them in.

"Sure, guys, come on in. Do you have the graphic organizer?"

They got it out, and we spent the next twenty minutes reviewing the similarities and differences. Then the bell rang, and I stood outside the classroom with my other colleagues to monitor the halls. I waved to Anu, who smiled back.

The day passed quickly after that, which was one of my favorite aspects of. I was so busy, running to and fro, I didn't have time to worry about anything else—like the fact my boyfriend planned to leave me.

When all the students left, the second part of the job began— the grading, planning, copying, and logging grades. While at my desk, I looked down at my phone and saw I had a few messages.

One from Mikey confirming a late dinner after yoga, to which I responded, *yes*. Before I got up to finish re-arranging the room for the test tomorrow.

The others were from Oskar and I didn't want to respond right now. I wondered fleetingly if I should just save myself the heartbreak and end it. God, if I was this gaga over him now, it would be so much worse in a year and a half. I'd started getting used to waking up beside him. My eyes felt dangerously close to tears at the thought of him leaving.

"Ms. Farris?" interrupted my pondering and desk pushing.

I glanced up in time to see Ms. Blakely, the principal, entering my room. Suddenly, I felt slightly nauseous, and my back started sweating. She'd gotten colder and colder as my sick days had tallied up last year. I was one of the only remaining teachers she'd made move classrooms between summer and this year. What did she want?

"Hi, just back here! Moving the desks a little for the test tomorrow."

"Oh good, Ms. Farris, you're still here," she said as she briskly walked over to me. "I wanted to ask you about your sick day scheduled for Monday. We don't like teachers taking doctor's appointments on Mondays or Fridays. Can you please reschedule it?"

I felt myself heat and perspire further at her words.

Reschedule it?

"Um, Ms. Blakely, my rheumatology appointments can only be scheduled on Mondays at the hospital I go to, but I can schedule my next appointment at the other hospital he practices at, so I can take a Wednesday off next time. I won't be able to reschedule it for a few months because the appointments get backed up. I'm also seeing two other doctors, my pulmonologist and my optometrist, afterward. I have read the handbook, but I didn't know this was a school policy." I was rambling. Beads of sweat rolled down my back. *Gross*, I hated nervous sweats.

She frowned. "Not a policy, but a preference." A loud sigh. "I guess if it is too late to change it, just make sure it's not a problem moving forward."

I nodded, and she left. My Raynaud's had flared up because I was nervous, so I rubbed my fingers. My students had done really well last year on the AP exams and the parents had been happy, but *everyone*—staff, parents, students—had talked about my number of sick days.

I took my afternoon meds early, my mouth suddenly dry. I distractedly massaged the sudden pinching in my chest. I needed this job. Without it, I wouldn't have any insurance. I was glad I had yoga this evening because now I had two things stressing me out. I might have to buy some wine to go with that dinner I'd planned for Mikey.

Thirty-one

October 11
OSKAR

I gritted my teeth and flicked my pencil to the edge of the lab table, where it rocked along the edge precariously. I leaned back in my chair and ran through all the alterations to the formula I'd tried today, but the project Sujit and I were working on for our interdisciplinary course was a disaster. Sujit was a macrostructure engineer, and we were trying to find the optimal chemical strength with plastic tubing durability.

It wasn't going well.

"Oskar, can I use our calculator?" Sujit asked, interrupting my teeth-grinding from his seat near our bags. "My phone died. I forgot they change the Wi-Fi password and it was roaming."

"Shit, I forgot too." I hurried over and pulled out my phone, which read 7:37 p.m., and keyed in the new internet code. "Shit," I whispered again under my breath, not believing the time.

There were so many missed messages from Lucia on WhatsApp, since there was no service down here. My heart sped up. I'd gotten so wrapped up in our project, I'd forgotten it was Thursday—I was supposed to meet Lucia for dinner. I opened the app.

12:36 p.m.: What do you want for dinner tonight?

4:54 p.m.: Did you decide about dinner?

5:15 p.m.: I'm just going to get stuff for pasta, so we can work through lunch this weekend and eat leftovers. I have a midterm paper due next Wednesday.

7:15 p.m.: Oskar, I'm starving. Are you still coming?

7:16 p.m.: Hey, I just noticed none of these are delivered. I just sent you a text…hope everything is all right.

A second muttered oath escaped me.

Sujit glanced up. "Are we done for tonight, or do you want to keep going?"

My stomach rumbled loudly in the silence of the lab. I shook my head. "We've been at this for hours. I think we should sleep on it or at least eat first. I need to call Lucia. Can you give me a minute?"

He nodded, and I stepped into the basement hallway with my phone.

Lucia picked up after two rings. "Süsse, I'm still at the lab."

A beat of silence, and then: "Oskar, I get it." Her voice was clipped in a tone I wasn't sure she'd ever used with me.

I tugged at my collar. "I should have let you know sooner."

"Yes," she said, still terse.

"They changed the Wi-Fi code, so I just got your messages." She was silent an uncomfortably long moment as I rubbed my stubble. Belatedly, I added, "I'm sorry."

"Ah, there it is."

I winced at her words. That should have been the first thing out of my mouth. "I didn't realize it was so late. This project isn't going well," I confessed to her. Fatigue and hunger washed over me, along with the intensification of the headache I'd been battling.

Her voice softened. "Oskar, I'm not mad you're at the lab. I'm sitting at home working too. I'm *frustrated* you didn't tell me you weren't coming for dinner. That you didn't tell me *anything*."

"Well, I haven't eaten yet, either. I didn't realize how late it was. It's no excuse, but there are no windows here. The time just slips away."

Concern entered her voice, making me feel guiltier. "I have leftovers. Did you still plan on coming?"

I don't deserve her.

I glanced at the lab door, and my stomach rumbled again. My brain was too fried for any more work on this project tonight. I couldn't do anything until I ate, and I still needed to do some readings before class tomorrow.

"Can I talk with Sujit and call you back in a few minutes? I've been in here since one and feel like a lab rat."

She laughed, but said, "I'll be here," and clicked off the phone.

I opened the door and realized my hands were sweaty. She'd deserved the apology; I was appalled by how rude I'd been. I wiped my hands on my pants as I said to Sujit, "Can you be here tomorrow at seven thirty in the morning? I think I'm done with this for today."

"Agreed," he responded, and we both packed up our notes,

books, and laptops.

Mist hung heavy and eerily in the brightly lit car park. Walking briskly, I called Lucia back and told her I was on the way. I couldn't tell from her voice if she wished I'd just stay home, but I didn't want to end the evening on this note. Guilt was sitting sour in my belly. One of the things I'd liked so much about her when we'd met was that she was teaching and in graduate school. I believed she'd understand when I needed to work and couldn't play as much as I'd like to. And she had. God, she was understanding and worked her ass off, too. But she was absolutely right: working too much was different than blowing someone off.

I tapped the steering wheel as a light rain started. Booming thunder and heavier rain followed, remarkably lightening my headache with the change in barometric pressure. As traffic across town crawled in the deluge, I tapped faster on the wheel—I didn't really have time to see her tonight. If I'd just responded to her earlier, I wouldn't have to be heading over there to make up at all. I had to do those readings sometime tonight, too.

Cars filled every spot on the street near her complex. I finally found a spot nearly two blocks away. I cursed, realizing I didn't have an umbrella. Man, was it pouring in true Georgia style now, lightning briefly illuminating the dark cloudy sky. I tucked my backpack and duffel bag under me the best I could, but I was dripping by the time Lucia opened the door for me. She looked adorable in a baggy teal sweatshirt, rainbow sleep shorts, and her big fluffy slippers.

Her eyes widened as she took me in. I dropped my stuff and kicked the door shut before the dog escaped.

I pulled her toward me. "I'm sorry. I'd never blow you off intentionally."

She squeaked a little in protest. "You're all wet."

I kissed her neck and whispered back just below her ear, "I bet I can make you all wet. If I do, will you forgive me?"

She quivered slightly at my words but tried to step back. I didn't let her escape, but instead picked her up, carried her to the bedroom, and laid her on the bed.

"I'm sorry," I whispered, kissing along her lips and jaw.

"I thought you were hungry, and now I'm getting wet."

I pulled back to see her face and cup her cheek, bringing her gaze to mine. "Oh, I'm hungry all right, and I'm enjoying making you wet."

Her eyes flashed and her skin flushed under me. My smile broadened. I trailed light kisses on her neck as my free hand rubbed her pussy through her thin shorts. She panted in my ear as I drew back and found her eyes. "I'm here to kneel at your feet and beg forgiveness. To kiss you and make it better."

Her breath caught and her skin flushed even more, but I wanted to be sure this was the best way to show my remorse.

"Would you like that?" I asked as I caressed her soft cheek. I tapped my other hand against her entrance, still demanding her gaze. "Should I kiss you and make it better?"

Her lips turned upward. "It had better be a damn good kiss. And take off your shirt—it's getting me wet in a way I'm not enjoying at all."

I chuckled as I complied with her demands. Kneeling, I pulled down her elastic shorts and kissed my way from her inner thighs to her center. When she was squirming under me, I grinned before I plunged my tongue and fingers into her. I worked her over with my mouth and rubbed my finger on her clit until she was quaking, a hand fisted in my hair. She was making those sounds low in her throat that I loved.

When she finally came, screaming, "Oh, god," I glanced up at her face. Her hair was in disarray, and her eyes were closed with her lingering release. Even wearing a sweatshirt, she was spectacular. I kissed her inner thigh once more and pulled up her shorts.

Her eyes opened and met mine. "Fine, you are forgiven," she said quietly. "But next time, it'll be easier for you to just text me back."

"Easier, but not more delicious," I teased as we both stood.

She still looked delectably disheveled.

She shook her head. "Let's get you some dinner. I don't know whether to be satisfied or irritated. You've probably ruined me for more work tonight." She yawned as if to verify her words.

I threaded our fingers together and whispered with a kiss to her temple, "Oh, you're satisfied, S*ü*sse."

She pushed me playfully. I mock-stumbled as I entered the kitchen but realized she was right. If I'd just responded to her earlier messages, she would have understood and I could still be in the lab. Quickly exchanging my wet clothes for some I'd brought, I looked at her love-mussed hair and felt a tenderness and a warning not to let her distract me from the reason I was in Atlanta.

Thirty-two

November 17
LUCIA

Mom and I sat spread out at their kitchen table, nursing our coffees while peering over our large grading piles of writing assignments. I yawned, letting my thoughts wander momentarily to Oskar. He'd left yesterday, Friday, for Thanksgiving back home while I was at school. Well, not really Thanksgiving, since he didn't celebrate, but visiting family before the Christmas holiday prices soared. It made perfect sense: he had a week off and it was one of the cheapest times to fly internationally. Yet I missed him already, which was bad. I was too used to having him around—in my life, in my bed, practically living with me. The fierceness of my longing for him pierced me, completely distracting me.

Last night I'd had a fun night in with Michael. Recently, we'd been doing shorter things like a quick dinner or walking Bea, but yesterday had been cooking and then binge-watching movies all night like we hadn't done in a long time. Yet when I'd gotten into my cold bed, it was lonely without Oskar's warm frame at my back spooning me or pulling me over his chest. He'd stolen my heart. By the time I'd heard he might leave, it'd already been too late.

I frowned and turned back to my large stack of grading. I needed to focus because Thursday morning we'd drive up to Ashville to see Meme and Papa, my dad's parents, and my aunts, uncles, and so many cousins. It was a full two days between driving, eating, and visiting, so both Mom and I had wanted a head start on grading. I bemoaned the fact that I'd given an essay test to all three sections of comparative politics—at five-plus pages each, I had more than three hundred pages of grading spread before me. Mom and I sipped our coffees in silence, except for the sound of pens across the papers.

After an hour, I'd graded seven out of seventy-five. I glowered at the pile and got up to get more coffee—everything was better with coffee.

"Would you like more coffee, Mom?"

"Sure," she said with a sigh, pushing her pile back too. "I swear I'm never teaching Neorealism again, no matter how much I love those films," she grumbled. "I think half the students just wanted an easy class to watch movies in."

I risked a glance at her latest paper and grimaced. It was bleeding with comments.

"Distract me," she said. "Tell me more about Oskar. He seems to really like you. There's something in the way he looks at you."

He'd done coffee again with all of us last Sunday, in between my dad's brunch and dinner shift.

I shrugged and put my mug down to stretch my back. If Oskar were here, he'd help me by rubbing it for me. The thought made me smile.

Mom was still looking at me, so I said, "He's nothing like Frank or Ali." I sat back down. "We're both happy, I'm sure he is, and he's here another year and a half." I shrugged, trying to display a calm I didn't feel.

"Okay," Mom said, but her eyes told me I hadn't fooled her. "But Lucia, I think you should at least think about what happens when he graduates. It's clear you really like him. If you have different ideas about the future, isn't it better to know now than in a year and a half?"

"Yes," I whispered.

The problem was that I did know Oskar wanted to move back if given a choice. There was nothing wrong with dating casually in a relationship that wasn't going anywhere, but my heart was involved, and I believed his was too. I frowned into my coffee. Or maybe it was just mine.

"Would you move with him if he asked you?" Mom didn't let up, and like a good mother, she seemed to read my thoughts.

"Mom," I said, exasperated. "No, I wouldn't. We've been dating just short of four months. Ask me if we are still dating in a year."

She leveled me with a serious gaze. "I've never regretted moving here with your dad. He's the love of my life. America is not Europe; both have their share of good and bad. I don't have to tell you about moving to another country, you know. We didn't have any family in Rome when you moved, and I didn't worry. But I worry with your health now. You are doing so well with your doctors and medicines. If you move, it'll be different." She shrugged. "Maybe better and cheaper, maybe not. But likely different."

Reluctantly, I agreed. "That's my concern too. It'd be wonderful if it's cheaper, but what if they don't allow me to take CellCept over there or they change my PAH and Sjogren's medicine?"

CellCept was only prescribed in the US for patients with organ failure, like I'd had. But I knew it wasn't allowed in Europe. Another immunosuppressant was, and the girls I knew who had taken it hated it. Maybe the doctors over there would prefer the more traditional steroid use, which I loathed. Change could cause lupus flares, and I was so stable now.

"I'm nervous that if I switched everything up, I might flare again," I admitted.

I always thought of my autoimmune diseases like a whirlpool. Once one of them pulled you in, you didn't know what would happen, or how long it'd hold you in its grasp until you could escape. It could be one health issue after another for months. But if you stayed outside that whirlpool, you could tread water for weeks, months, even years without issues. Sure, you always knew you were in the water and couldn't stop taking the medicines, but you could live your life without major hiccups. Moving abroad and changing several medicines simultaneously could easily suck me right back into that whirlpool I'd fought for more than two years to escape.

I had my lupie friends who'd had kidney failure, normally the first organ to be susceptible to a flare; who had constant chronic pain and joint inflammation, which I normally only got if I ran or was in the sun; or already had progressive osteopenia in their twenties from long-term steroid use and had to constantly monitor their bodies for broken bones. That wasn't where I was with my disease.

My lupus had been so bad leading up to my organ failure and PAH diagnosis, but now I was able to live a fairly normal life. My pill-popping and overzealous sunscreen use was just a fact of my life. If I moved back to Europe, my treatment might change and destabilize me too. According to the Lupus Foundation of America, eighty-nine percent of lupus patients found it hard, or couldn't work full time. I was working and pursuing a graduate degree. I didn't want a health setback.

After a moment, Mom nodded and touched my hand. "That's my concern, too. Maybe it'll be so much better and cheaper for you, but if it's not, you won't be covered here anymore. And I won't be there to take care of you."

I stood to get more coffee to give me something to do, even though I was close to jittery with the amount I'd already had. Her words echoed my own fears—that I'd need my mom to take care of me forever.

"Mom, we have a lot of time. Let me just take it day by day, okay?"

She smiled at that. "You are good at day by day. Oskar seems like a great guy, and you seem to genuinely care about each other. But you're right. In six months or a year, you both may have had enough."

Her words weren't quite convincing.

Oskar had been great so far. When I was tired because of work or school, he never made fun of me if I crawled into bed at eight thirty at night. Sometimes he joined me, or others I'd simply wake, and he'd be there. He was very understanding of my health issues. It was obvious: I had it bad for him.

My phone started ringing, surprising us both. Funny, it was Ru. I clicked to answer, thinking she couldn't possibly be in China, because it was ten thirty in the morning here, so it'd be at least elven thirty p.m. there.

"Ru?" I said when her face popped up on WhatsApp.

"Hey!"

"Um, I'm with my mom," I said quickly, because of the time of day she was calling and the fact Ru had no filter. I loved Ru, but with our schedules and time changes, we messaged more than we spoke on the phone.

She laughed. "Hi, Mrs. Farris!"

"Hi, Prudence."

"What's with the call this time of day?"

"Oh, I'm in the Frankfort airport." She panned the camera around. "My flight to Shanghai is in an hour. Sooooo, I have been talking with Edward again, and we really want you to come and visit this summer! We were thinking June is best for us. I can take a week off too, so we can travel around some. What do you think? I won't take no for an answer! Oh, and you can bring that fine Austrian, too, if he has time."

She talked so fast, I couldn't get a word in.

"She's going," Mom said.

"I've been saving up for it," I said before either of them talked over me more.

"Yesssss! It will be so much fun! I haven't been to Southern China. I'm sending you some links. Did you get them? Don't you want to go here with us?"

I clicked the links, momentarily halting the video function. The scenery was fairytale-like with beautiful small wooden boats and jagged limestone mountains. I popped the video back up.

"This is Southern China?"

Ru nodded with a smile. "The best part is I haven't been there either. It's all close together, and Edward can rent a car."

"I'll check out these links. If I can afford it, it'd be amazing."

"Oh, my flight's boarding! Shoot, I forgot how early Germans do things. I love you, babe. We will talk details soon—I have vacation time for Lunar New Year. Edward and I will both be in town—double date! Bye, Mrs. Farris. Please don't let her talk her way out of going."

My mom laughed and said, "Bye, Prudence. Safe travels."

When we hung up, I couldn't help but smile as I turned back to my papers. I had always wanted to see China, and what better way than with Ru and Edward? If she was there, I'd feel safer, because if I got sick, she could talk to the doctors for me.

Thirty-three

November 22
OSKAR

"Is it too late for coffee?" I joked to my mom when I joined her outside the ski rental return, where she was waiting for me. "I'm getting old." I lifted her skis to carry them back to the car for her.

"It's never too late for coffee," my mom responded. "Come, I know just the place."

My mom guided me through the snow-covered streets of St. Anton to a small pastry shop. I loved skiing and the smell of winter. Or maybe I just loved Austria.

She'd taken two days off to drive us here and ski with Johanna and me. We'd stayed at my sister's hotel for free because it was early in the ski season and it wasn't fully booked. It'd been nice spending all day with my mom and sister, plus having two dinners with Johanna's husband, Peter, joining us. It wasn't a long drive back to my parents' home in Innsbruck, but an hour and a half in the fading light and curvy alpine roads would make the coffee welcome.

I logged in to the Wi-Fi while Mom used the toilet. My phone started dinging with messages from Lucia. One said, *Happy Thanksgiving! Things I'm thankful for: Austrian bed warmer. Brr it's been cold without you. xo.*

I couldn't help my grin. I sent her some pictures of the slopes and typed back, *I'm grateful to be that bed warmer. Kuss.*

We'd constantly been messaging and even video chatting, but I was shocked at the intensity with which I missed her. I kept wishing she were here for me to show her something or introduce her to someone. She was so enthusiastic about normal life that I thought traveling with her would be amazing. I'd love to take her skiing here and fly down the slopes together. And her text reminded me how much I missed being in her bed—not that the thought was ever too far away.

Mom came up just moments after our coffees arrived. She looked at me meaningfully. "I know that smile. Tell me more about Lucia."

I started telling her some of the things I'd already mentioned, about how intelligent and considerate Lucia was, and then I said, "I have a serious question. You married Dad, even knowing he had juvenile diabetes. I've mentioned Lucia has a few autoimmune diseases, and she told me she'll never be able to have children. It scares me a little."

"Do you love her?"

Her question startled me. I looked down into my coffee and took a sip. She'd never asked that about Anita, my ex, even after two-plus years. Memories of Lucia flashed through my mind—the sound of her tinkling laughter, the warm feeling of her hand in mine, the sated look in her eyes when she snuggled after sex, her intoxicating grapefruit scent that always clung to my skin, and that fire in her voice when she spoke about something she was passionate about. An intense feeling fluttered in my belly.

"I think so."

When I said that, she turned more serious. "It'll be hard, Oskar. If you stay together, you'll see her sick, and sometimes you might see her sick more often than healthy. It's very hard to see someone you love hurting often and falling seriously ill. It'll be a financial hardship, whether you move back to Europe or stay in America. Being sick is expensive—the drugs, the procedures, the time off work. Sometimes your dad worked part time. But do I ever regret it?"

She looked at me hard in the eyes while I held my breath.

With absolute conviction, she said, "Never. Because of who your father is, he loves me more. He knows at times I've struggled to maintain my job and take care of him and our family. And that I could have picked someone without health issues, but I chose him. No one could love me, or our family, more than he does. He knows how precious life is and how beautiful love and family are. Anyone could die at any time, but being with someone chronically ill, well, a lot of the time, they live life remembering that. The rest of us forget how easily it can all be taken away. I don't know Lucia. But should this affect your decision to be with her?" She shook her head. "No."

I nodded as she finished off her coffee. My mom was so right. Lucia had that sparkle of life she'd described. I kept seeing her face, imagining her saying, "We made it," on every hike we'd done. Or picturing her joy every time she saw Fluffy. And I'd never forget the passion she brought to making love to me. My skin was permanently imprinted with the sensation of her holding me so tenderly, our limbs intertwined as if I were the most important thing to her in the world. I realized at that moment that I loved Lucia. I didn't just think it.

"I love her," I whispered.

Now I could only hope she loved me back.

Mom smiled at me in a way that made me think she'd known this before I did. "And it's so good she speaks German. My English is not what it used to be. And you said she's a dual Italian citizen, so if you both wanted, she could move here easily. She wouldn't even need a visa. Soon she'll have two master's degrees, so it would be easy for her to find a job."

Then I spoke my biggest fear out loud. "I don't know if she'd move back to Europe, because of her health. We haven't talked about it. She might be afraid because if she gets different treatments here and gets sick, she won't have insurance to go back to her old doctors."

Mom regarded me with zero judgment. "Do you love her enough to stay in America for her?"

I looked around the quaint Austrian pastry shop that smelled like bread and coffee. Outside, snow was piled high on the alpine slopes I loved to ski and hike. This was what growing up had been like. Austria had been a wonderful place, surrounded by some of the most pristine mountains in the world. And Austria had world-class public services, including healthcare and education.

"I don't know," I said, and it scared me I wasn't sure. I loved her, but was love enough?

I wouldn't mind living in America for a few more years. America had many positives too. And so much diversity in food and culture I liked. Drug and medical equipment innovation there were arguably the best in the world, and that excited me. But what if we stayed together and I got tired of it, but she wouldn't move here? There were more jobs for me in America, but I wasn't sure I wanted to be stuck there *forever*. I wasn't sure I wanted to give up my family and my country.

My mom seemed to understand and touched my hand gently. "Keep dating for a little while and see how you feel. You have only been together four months."

I nodded and finished the coffee, which wasn't sitting quite as right anymore. "I have time. We should go, so Dad isn't waiting."

She nodded, but before she got up, she said, "I'm glad for you, Oskar. I don't remember the last time I saw you this happy. I know you're an engineer and want your plans all laid out, but sometimes life is for living in the now. The future will right itself."

Thirty-four

November 22 –Thanksgiving Day
LUCIA

I gritted my teeth as I endured my cousin, Coralee. She'd cornered me in a hallway, which was the only reason I was still talking to her. There was alcohol here somewhere. For what felt like an hour, she'd been telling me as she bounced her latest baby on her hip that I needed to settle down, or else it'd be too late to have kids of my own.

I was twenty-four, not forty-four. Jeez.

She was thirty, had three kids already, and felt like everyone else should too. As she pestered me, she stepped closer. Lila, my niece in her arms, plopped a warm, moist chubby baby hand on my chest as she did. God, I hated it when people nagged me about kids. I couldn't have kids, so it knifed my chest every time. And second, even if I could have them, it was none of her business.

I tried to tune her out as I made a face and wigged my fingers into Lila's fist.

"And when are you going to be done with school?" Coralee

didn't understand I was no longer working on my undergraduate degree. That I was working on my *second* master's degree.

"In May. Sorry, I need to answer this," I said, glancing down at my phone. It wasn't a phone call, but I'd had too much of Coralee by sentence two, so I didn't feel too guilty about faking it. Too many parts of me worried she was right. Also, as sweet as Lila was, holding her hand was bittersweet.

While I edged away as I heard Coralee say to someone, "Bless her heart."

I tried not to clench my jaw as I peeked at my phone in the hallway. I saw the gorgeous pictures from Oskar's two days of skiing. My belly dropped at his smiling face with his mom and sister.

He belongs there.

My eyes had dangerous moisture as I sent back, *I can't wait to go skiing!*

Both Tyrol and South Tyrol were exceptionally beautiful places with the tall Alps and the wooden lodges. It was a little too quaint for me to think I could live there, like my grandparents or Oskar's sister, full time, but I could visit. Anytime I'd enjoy a visit. I was excited to go skiing in a few weeks and see my grandparents and cousins. To see my less nagging family.

My parents and I always left on Christmas Eve to visit my mom's parents in South Tyrol. Not only was it great to see them, but the skiing was amazing. I'd grown close with my mom's parents after spending a month with them almost every summer of my life.

And unlike Dad's family, they never asked when I'd get married.

I looked at the Thanksgiving table, and suddenly I wasn't excited to sit down. Soon the comments would start that I was still a pescatarian. The nag, nag, nag of Dad's family wore on me.

I thought back to the conversation I'd had with Mom on Saturday. Would it be so bad to go back to Europe? I'd loved living in Rome and visiting my family in South Tyrol. In either

Germany or Austria, healthcare should be good. I asked Oskar to send me pictures if he saw any Christmas markets open yet. Europe could be a wonderful, magical place to live. But I worried too much to truly consider moving there.

When Oskar didn't respond within a few minutes and the message showed as undelivered, I figured he must already be driving back to Innsbruck. Maybe I'd catch him later. It was weird without him, given how much I'd gotten used to having him around. Unable to delay anymore, I slid my phone back into my purse and dragged my feet to refill my water glass.

As I'd expected, Thanksgiving dinner was fairly dreadful. My dad's family could be condescending to my mom, who, like me, was tri-lingual. She taught at a prominent American university, and yet sometimes they acted like she had trouble following in English. The problem was their accents were terrible. It was often painful to watch, but Mom bore it all with a smile.

They also had little comprehension of my health situation, which always frustrated the three of us. Coralee's husband asked me if I was better yet, like he always did. I said I was doing well. I didn't explain that autoimmune diseases lasted a lifetime, for what would have been the hundredth time. He invited me to go to the Outer Banks with them next Fourth of July. I smiled and politely declined. I didn't remind them, yet again, that I was allergic to the sun.

At least it wasn't an election year.

However painful Thanksgiving dinner had been Thursday afternoon, breakfast the following morning with my Meme and Papa was nice. Dad's parents were sweet but more traditional than we were. They asked me if I'd been to church lately. I was relieved when Coralee's son spilled maple syrup and orange juice, forcing us to react quickly and end that conversation. The answer would have been no.

My mom huffed, "My God, I need a drink," when we finally filtered into dad's car for the three-plus hour drive back to Atlanta in the afternoon.

Dad thanked us for doing our familial duty. Even though we all loved his family, we knew we were the odd ones out, living in the big city and different from the rest. Dad understood this applied to him too. He had never considered moving back to Ashville. Atlanta was plenty close to his family for him. And even though Meme and Papa were much closer geographically than Mom's family, we saw them both with equal frequency. But I felt much closer to Oma and Opa, who I spoke to more often.

I texted Michael and we made plans to get drunk and forget our family blues asap when I got back. I was busy studying and grading so often, I rarely drank, except an occasional beer or wine at dinner or trivia night. The last time I'd been borderline drunk was tubing on Labor Day. But after two days with Dad's family, I agreed with Mom: a drink sounded in order. Poor Michael had it worse than me. He was still not out with his conservative Christian Southern family. At least I didn't have to hide my sexuality.

My family was annoying, but the annoyance came from a loving place, at least. I told Michael not to text and drive and was about to put away my phone when Oskar messaged me a picture of him and some of his friends, steins in hand, from one of Munich's legendary beer houses. *Prost, Süsse*, he'd written.

I recognized Gunter, his best friend. My heart seized at his grin. He looked so happy surrounded by all his pals from college.

He looked so happy *there*.

I sent back: *Wish I was there. xo*. But I didn't get another message until we were almost back in Atlanta. My heart sank deeper as I kept checking my phone.

Me too. I'll take you here someday. Sweet dreams and see

you Sunday. Kuss.

His message made me feel a little better, but I still had an unsettled feeling he belonged there.

And I didn't.

When we turned onto my parent's street, we were all relieved to get out of the car. It was a beautiful drive through the mountains to Ashville and back, but Dad's family always made even the scenery seem a little miserable.

I grabbed Bea, who'd stayed with my parents' dog sitter, and texted Michael we were on the way home. The street out front was completely empty with many in the complex heading home for the holiday or shopping on Black Friday. I banged on Mikey's door when I passed it and left mine cracked. A minute later, Michael trudged in. One glance at his face said it all. He looked like I felt.

I hugged him. "Mikey, is it too early to start drinking?"

"No," he said immediately. "It's five thirty."

He picked up Bea and squeezed her to him. By the slump of his shoulders and the way he cradled Bea, I could tell this visit had been bad for him too. I grabbed us two beers and thunked down on the other seat as he smothered Bea in kisses.

"Dish," I said.

He took a big sip of his beer before saying, "My sister-in-law is pregnant, *again*."

I almost spewed my beer. God, I loved his snarky quips.

He petted Bea and rolled his eyes. "Everyone asks if I'm seeing someone."

"Guessing you didn't mention Patrick?"

He just gave me a look and snuggled Bea once more. "They're terrible, but they're family, which is better than no family. I'd have no family if I came out to them." I patted his hand. "Everyone asked when I'm going to settle down and start making babies myself."

"Me too." I leaned forward to clink our glasses. "To the two of us." I looked at Bea. "The three of us."

We continued drinking and venting for another beer before we ran out. It was seven by then, so we wandered down the street to a bar. The smart thing to do would be to eat something since breakfast had been a long time ago, but that wasn't what we were in the mood for. Instead, the drinking continued. Michael had in the last three years steadily grown a larger friend circle than me, maybe because I was always studying. His phone kept dinging and vibrating the bar.

Finally, I asked, "What, Michael?"

He put down his phone and said, "Interested in going to East Atlanta?"

I couldn't remember the last time Michael and I had gone out dancing. Maybe the end of summer? I probably shouldn't. The last time I'd drank this much, I had a terrible hangover. Truly horrific—vomiting until six p.m. Copious amounts of alcohol and immunosuppressants didn't play nice together.

So naturally what came out of my mouth was, "Heck yeah!"

I motioned, hopefully politely, for the bill, and paid for our drinks.

Michael pulled up his rideshare app, and a few minutes later we were on our way. We met up with his usual crew, sans Patrick, who was home for the holiday. They gushed about this new cutie Michael had been dating. Michael clarified that Patrick was *not* his boyfriend, but the look on his face said they weren't far off.

We had at least one more drink before heading to the best gay dance venue in East Atlanta, or at least we thought so. I'd always loved dancing at gay clubs because no one ever rubbed their boner on me—it was like dancing in Europe. A girl should be able to enjoy dancing without getting dry-humped-molested on the dance floor. Better yet, since I had a boyfriend, it was guilt-free fun. If anyone bought me a drink, I reciprocated—that was the expectation and nothing else. The only issue was there was a lot more drinking with the reciprocity; it was hard to refuse when someone handed you a drink. As a result, I had two drinks past—I thought—where I would have normally stopped.

We danced with his friends until the wee hours of the morning before hailing a ride home, sweaty and exhausted.

Stumbling out of our ride, Michael offered to walk Bea with me. *Oops*, we should have stopped the drinks at twelve and just kept dancing. I'd had enough to drink that even though I was happy, the slightest thing could tip me over that emotional point. Which was another reason I rarely drank so much—it certainly could make me depressed.

"God, you're special sometimes," Mikey joked as I tripped on a rock.

I turned to Michael and said, totally serious, "I don't want to be special."

He looked at me, hearing the tone of my voice, and sighed. Suddenly, I felt hot tears on my cheeks. I just wished I was normal. Just a girl like everyone else.

"I'm freaking broken!" I whined out. I started sobbing more violently.

"You aren't broken," he said, pulling me into a firm hug. "Lucia. You. Are. Drunk."

 Despite my tears, I giggled at his dry humor before I cried into shoulder. "I won't be enough, Mikey. He's going to leave me. Did you know that?"

"What is your drunk ass talking about? That boy is obsessed with you. I know. I'm a boy." He shook his head at me as he led me inside.

"I'm not enough. He is going to leave me!"

"He is not going to leave you. You are awesome. Oskar likes you because you're smart and pretty, and the nicest thing that's ever happened to me."

"Aw, I love you, Mikey."

I hugged him again. He was my best friend. What would I do without him?

He squeezed me back. "I love you too, drunkie."

I pushed away, walking toward the apartment. "But he is seriously going to leave me. Give me my phone. I'm going to leave him first. I can't do this anymore."

I reached for my purse, but Michael took it and pushed Bea and me into the house. "Hoe, no! You're not calling him. You really like him. Friends don't let friends drunk dial. What the hell are you talking about?"

I plopped down heavily on the loveseat, my heart pinching, and the tears slipped out again.

"After graduation. I'm too scared to move back to Europe, but he wants to live in Austria or Germany," I sobbed out. "When he graduates, he will leave me because I have all this crap and I'm afraid to move back overseas. And Mikey? I think I love him. I know I do. It's going to kill me. I need to just end it now. If I stay with him another year and a half, it *will* kill me."

I glanced up, and his eyes held concern. He pulled me close so I could continue crying on his shoulder.

"Sweetie, we can talk about it in the morning, but do *not* call him now. Sometimes these things right themselves, okay? Everything seems worse when you're drunk." He looked at me critically. "Not that you'll feel better in the morning."

"I hate drinking," I mumbled. "Next time, only dancing. I'm going to hate myself in the morning."

I could tell by the amount of spinning I felt that I really would. The combination of stress from being with Dad's family and wondering about my future with Oskar, with anyone, had made me want to just let go for a little bit, to let the fun continue, even when I knew I should have stopped. Seeing Oskar looking so right with his friends and family had sent me over the edge. But drinking to escape my problems had not helped me escape them. I knew I'd feel like shit for this.

"You are, but I promise you'll hate yourself more if you call Oskar and dump him," Mikey said, letting me pull back. "Let's get you some water."

So he did and I drank it, trying to halt my crying. I already regretted trying to drink away my frustrations with the things I couldn't change in my life. "I just want to be normal," I moaned.

"Do I need to take your phone?"

"No. I won't call, but this isn't over. I still think it's better to end it now."

"Go to sleep, Lucia," Michael said, and led me to the bedroom.

I rolled into bed without even shedding my clothing. I buried my face into the pillow, emotions choking me. This fear had been building since it slipped out in October that he wanted to move back. I should have never dated him in the first place. My whole body convulsed as I sobbed. I must have eventually fallen asleep because I woke up and had to run to the toilet and vomit. Repeatedly. Bright morning light glared at me, making my temples and eyes hurt.

I texted Michael, *I feel like shit. Sorry I had a meltdown. Ugh, I'm never drinking again.*

I frantically searched my phone to make sure I hadn't called or texted Oskar last night—well, his morning—and a breath of relief flew out. I hadn't. Then depression hit me as hard as relief. I thought I was relieved, but I wondered again if I should just end it now. Throughout the day, I alternated between staring moodily at the corner of my bedroom wall and at the back of the toilet. I hated myself for drinking, for torturing myself with this relationship that was going nowhere but heartbreak.

Michael didn't text me back until hours later. *Don't worry, you were okay until the end. You're just worried about Oskar, but not everyone is like Frank. Love you, my little drunkie.*

Thanks (: I still feel like shit. Please don't take me drinking again—just dancing next time.

My head was pounding, and although I was sober, I still felt the nagging anxiety why someone as wonderful as Oskar was dating someone like me. Would my life be better in the long run if, like a Band-Aid, I just ended this now with a quick, painful tug?

I groaned around the house all day. I never wanted another hangover in my life.

Thirty-five

November 25
OSKAR

It was a gorgeous late fall day outside the airplane window when we landed in Atlanta. It was so mild, the foliage was still beautiful, spread below the windows. As I took in the three skylines of downtown, Midtown, and Buckhead, it reminded me of the day Lucia and I hiked Stone Mountain. She had been so vulnerable when she told me about not being able to have children. She'd gone through so much, and I would do anything to take it away from her. I never wanted to see her cry again like she had that day.

She was such a special person. I couldn't believe how well she put up with my long hours in the labs and how she still made our study dates so fun. Or how well she took care of me. She genuinely seemed to love to cook for me and spoiled me by bringing me coffee in bed.

From what I could tell, she worked hard at her job and was well-liked. She was passionate when she talked about her lesson plans and students or showed me their projects. The trivia and cultural events she'd taken me to never failed to remind me the girl was brilliant, in addition to being gorgeous. Snuggling with her was amazing, too. I didn't know how I got so lucky. I smiled—*I love her*.

Still, I worried about our future. When I powered on my phone, I saw a message from her. *Surprise! I'm going to pick you up, so you don't need to take the train. Let me know when to leave the cellphone lot. xo*

I replied, "*Süsse, thank you. I can't wait to see you. Kuss*, I replied, knowing just how damn lucky I was.

Time seemed to drag as I made my way off the plane and through the stations of the international terminal. It seemed like an eternity before it was time to tell Lucia to pull around. She jumped out of her little Fiat when she saw me, and I drew her in for a crushing hug. Her scent enveloped me and I greedily breathed her in.

"I missed you." I nuzzled her neck, before I pulled back, not wanting to give her the plane germs.

She smiled at me as we hurried back to her car, but I got this tingling feeling I couldn't explain—something was off with her. We chatted about our breaks on the drive to her place, and I figured I must have just imagined it. *I'm tired*, I told myself. But I just had this nagging sense something wasn't right.

When we entered her place, I bent down to play with little Fluffy before shedding my jacket and turning on the hot water in the shower. I stripped off my shirt and grabbed Lucia's hand, pulling her into the bathroom with me.

"Are you going to join me?"

She surprised me by letting go of my hand and saying, "No, I don't have time. I need to work tonight at the restaurant."

"Tonight?" I could hear how hard my voice sounded. "But I just got back."

She gave me an apologetic look. "I'm sorry, Oskar, but some servers are out of town for the holiday. Plus, I need the money to visit Ru. I'll see you tomorrow at trivia."

I reached into the shower and turned it off. I picked my discarded shirt up off the floor and put it back on. "I can just shower at my place, then. I don't want you to be late." It came out harsher than I intended, but she looked relieved.

"Thanks," she said as she headed into the bedroom and slipped into her work tank top.

"You should wash your neck."

"Sorry?"

"Your neck." I motioned to it. "I nuzzled you when you picked me up."

She nodded, turned on the bathroom sink, and scrubbed her neck with a washcloth.

As she did, I said, "Okay, well, can I come over after you're done working?"

I felt like I was begging for scraps now, but I'd missed her so much. I'd just realized how much I loved her, and wanted to hold her perfect body all night long. I certainly wouldn't mind doing more than holding, either.

She turned off the sink, wide-eyed, drying herself with a towel. "But I'll be late. It could even be after midnight." She glanced down and muttered, "I'm sure I'll be too tired for sex."

I swear I saw red for a minute at the assumption I just wanted to see her for sex. Something weird was happening; normally she was as eager as I was, if not more so.

"I just wanted to hold you, Lucia. *I missed you.*" I placed an emphasis on the last bit.

She blushed and grabbed her purse. She kissed me lightly and said, "I'd like that if you aren't too tired. I missed you too."

We walked out together, and I headed home, trying to reassure myself I was just worn out and reading into things that weren't there. Yet I couldn't shake the feeling that Lucia seemed off, and I didn't like that. Maybe she was just feeling guilty.

Just before ten, I was barely holding my eyes open when I received a text from her that she was on her last table. Since I was showered and ready, I just headed over to Aperitivo. I could give her a ride home since I knew she normally took the train. I hated her taking the train with her server cash on her.

I got a message right as I pulled in. *Finishing up (:*

I froze as I entered the restaurant. Lucia was sitting at the bar, laughing with one of her coworkers who had a drink in his hand and was raising that drink toward her. As I watched, she stood up and gave him a giant hug before turning to walk toward the door and me. She halted and raised her hand to her heart, eyes wide as she saw me.

"Oskar?" she said as I stepped forward.

Some of my irritation must have shown on my face because she skidded to a stop and chewed her lip. The guy at the bar jumped up and put his arm around Lucia's shoulder. I realized I'd taken a step forward and clenched my teeth in a jealous rage like nothing I'd ever felt before.

He smiled at her, oblivious to my mounting urge to punch him, and said with a broad grin aimed at me, "Is this your boyfriend?" He held out his hand, but his face fell a little as he looked at me. He took a step away from Lucia.

"Oskar, and you are?" I hated how rough my voice sounded.

"Enrique. I've worked with Lucia for years. You're a lucky guy," he said, mirth still on his face, but the longer he looked at me, the more his grin slipped.

He glanced at her with a raised eyebrow.

"Oskar, Enrique found out he just got into medical school, so I bought him a drink. Enrique, we should probably go. Oskar flew in from Munich this afternoon and looks tired."

"Yep, tired." His gaze ran over me again and he smirked. "Thanks for the drink, and see you next week!" he said enthusiastically to Lucia.

We walked out, and Lucia said as we reached the car, "I didn't realize you'd be getting me."

"Obviously, Lucia."

"What does that mean?" she said, slipping in the car.

"Well, you and Enrique just seemed pretty cozy." I gripped the stick shift, my knuckles white.

"He got into medical school!" Her voice held some of the fury I'd been feeling. "I wanted to congratulate him. We've known each other a long time, and he's been serving and working as an EMT. This is a really big deal for him."

I didn't respond because I was so annoyed by how jealous I was. I didn't like the guy I was right now. I trusted Lucia. It was just seeing her like that and how she didn't seem too eager to see me. It had hit a nerve.

Lucia laid her hand on mine on the stick and softened her voice. "I'm sorry. I was about to leave, and he told me. It seemed like the right thing to do—to buy him a drink."

A breath escaped me, and I responded in kind with a softer, lower voice. "I saw red, Lucia. I'm sorry. I don't know what came over me. I've never felt jealous like that before. I felt like you weren't excited to see me earlier and then I saw that…you're just really special to me."

I should have told her I loved her, but I got scared. What if she didn't say it back? God, I'd just acted like a huge dick.

The rest of the short ride was silent and tense. I could have sworn something else was going on with her. At least Lucia left her hand on top of mine, and I was grateful for that. I squeezed her fingers as I drove.

We'd just made it to her street, but neither of us had gotten out yet. Cold mist hung in the air from the evening storms.

Lucia turned to look at me, her eyes full of emotion. "Oskar, what are we doing?" she whispered, her voice cracking. I didn't understand her question, but before I could ask, she added, "I don't think I can do this anymore." Her shoulders dropped as the words came out.

Tears were running down her face in earnest now, and I said dumbly, "Do what?"

"Date you." Her words were barely audible.

I felt my mouth drop as ice hit my stomach. I thought I

might be sick—that I might actually vomit. "Lucia, I trust you. I'm sorry I was jealous. I had no reason. That's not the type of person I am—controlling and envious of every other guy. You know that. I'd never micromanage you. You can buy a hundred guys a drink. I'm just tired from traveling. I'm sorry. Please don't leave me over that." I heard the desperation in my voice, but I didn't care. *I was fucking in love with her.*

She shook her head. "It's not that. Oskar, we are setting ourselves up for more pain. You are going to move back to Europe. I'm not."

"It's in a year and a half."

"Yes." Tear continued down her face, smearing her makeup. "And if it hurts this bad now, it'll be worse then."

In an emotion-choked voice, I reminded her, "You're an Italian citizen. You're fluent in German. You could live in Austria or Germany without any visas. You could come with me."

I threaded our fingers and looked at her, but her gaze was stricken, and her crying intensified. Seeing her like this was knifing into my gut. I just wanted to pull her to me and make it stop.

"No, Oskar. I don't want to move back." She looked right at me. I could have sworn she saw into my soul. "Would you promise to stay here?"

Words and breath lodged in my throat. I opened and closed my mouth several times, trying to respond, but I couldn't lie to her.

She leaned forward, and her lips landed on mine in an angel kiss that tasted salty like her tears. She leaned back and opened the door. Just before she stepped out, she whispered, "Goodbye, Oskar."

As the door shut, I felt something warm on my cheek. I reached up to touch it as my mouth formed her name. My cheek was wet. I was crying. Because the love of my life had just walked away from me and I had no words to stop her—except for lies. I stared at the door and closed my eyes. It felt like my heart had just been ripped out. I wanted to chase after her, but part of me knew she was right.

I didn't know what to do.

After a few minutes, I started the drive back to my place, more confused and heartbroken than I'd ever felt in my life.

Thirty-six

November 26
LUCIA

My eyes stung with dryness. They scratched, tearing up as I opened them to hush the alarm's wailing. My face was swollen, and for a moment I was disoriented. Then last night came crashing back over me.

I left Oskar.

New hot tears streamed down my cheeks as acid churned in my gut.

"What have I done?" I whispered to the room. Bea heard me and sensed my distress. She came up and licked my wet face. I petted her softly. "Oh, Bea."

I curled onto my side for a few minutes before I forced myself to get up and turn on the coffee maker. I threw my hair into a bun and stood under the shower at a near-scalding temperature. Water and tears mixed interchangeably down my face. I repeated to myself, *I did the right thing.* But if that was true, why did it hurt so bad?

I walked Bea quickly and tried to steady myself while I did. Walking had always had a calming effect on me, but it could only do so much for my blue heart. I could only drink a few sips of coffee and couldn't bring myself to eat anything. Nausea rumbled in my stomach, even as I continued to convince myself I'd done the right thing. I should have never dated him. I'd resigned myself to being alone and I was happy. But this—this hurt.

I dressed like a zombie. On the drive to work, I kept crying. What had I done?

I pulled into the parking lot and checked my makeup in the mirror. I wiped away the smudges, but nothing hid the haunted look in my eyes or obvious puffiness of my face. Some tears slipped out, so I waited until I could control my emotions.

The day was busy, as always. There was no time for moping. But when I sat down in my empty classroom for lunch and glanced down at the zero new texts on my phone, I pushed my lunch away again, unable to stomach food. I had to go to the bathroom before the bell rang and fix my tear-smeared eyes again.

Some of my students asked if something was wrong, but I lied to them like a pro, using my best teacher voice to say, "Allergies." Anu couldn't be fooled, though, and as all the kiddos left, she walked across the hallway to my classroom.

"Lucia?" she said hesitantly.

I let my face fall into my hands and cried, hunching my shoulders as I stepped back into my room. Anu rubbed my back as I explained everything.

She looked at me with her cinnamon eyes and said, "You should get back together."

"I can't. My health…"

"If you like him this much, you'll find a way to make it work. I'll be right back."

She returned with a spicy hot tea. We sat down as I talked and sipped it. It burned my insides yet made me feel a little warmer.

"Thank you."

"Think about what I said," she told me when she left twenty

minutes later.

When I got home, I took Bea on a long walk and tried to convince myself yet again I had done the right thing. My health was fragile, and I couldn't risk any more harm. There were seven billion people on the planet, six million in Atlanta. I'd find someone else. I would be fine.

I'd never been as relieved for graduate work as I was that night. I poured myself into it. A loud knock on the door made me jump. My heart galloped in my chest. I was half-dreading and half-hoping it was Oskar.

I peeked and saw Michael. I let him in. He looked me over, taking in my ratty PJs and puffy eyes.

Shit—trivia.

"Big paper?" he asked, looking me up and down. "You could have texted me."

At his words, I broke down again and sobbed out in a rough voice, "I left him."

Michael cocked his head, and then his eyes flashed with understanding. "Noooo. Please tell me you didn't?"

I didn't respond. I just picked up Bea and cuddled her on the loveseat. Michael sat down and wrapped his arm around my shoulder, and I cried into his chest.

"Luci, nooooo. Why did you do that?" he asked as he stroked my back.

I reached for a tissue before responding. "I couldn't keep doing it, knowing we had no future. I told him I wouldn't move to Europe. He said he wouldn't stay here. He looked devastated, but he hasn't called. He hasn't texted. He didn't chase after me.

He knows I did the right thing."

I leaned back and petted Bea some more, staring at the ceiling as hot tears leaked down my face.

"I'm sorry," Michael said, squeezing my shoulder.

"Please go to trivia," I said softly. "I love you, Mikey, but I want to be alone. I don't want to talk about it. I'm not ready for our friends to know." I turned and tried to smile. "Go see Patrick. He seems nice. It seems like I'll need to live through your relationship for a while."

"Are you sure?" he asked hesitantly.

I nodded. "Super sure. You know the only thing worse than a breakup? People asking about that breakup."

He pulled me close to him and I snuggled in for a minute. "I love you. I'm here if you need anything, okay?"

"Thanks. I'll be fine. It'll hurt for a while, but I did the right thing."

After he left, I needed to immediately get back to my work so I wouldn't focus on Oskar. I'd finally gotten into the zone and was fixing my final paper's annotated bibliography when my pulse quickened at the sound of my phone ringing. I glanced at the screen, and the queasiness I'd felt all day amplified as I read, *Oskar Riedl.*

I turned it facedown but couldn't get back my focus. Finally, ten minutes later, I gave in to the temptation and looked at the screen. I had a voice message.

With a shaky breath and hand, I hit play. "Hi, Lucia. Please, call me. I, um, Lucia…" His voice broke midsentence in a way that sent tears spiraling down my face. "Don't leave me," he finished.

I turned the phone over again and hunched over in almost literal pain. My stomach hurt so badly I thought I may be physically sick.

It took about an hour, but I was able to get focused on the sources again. As nine o'clock rolled around, I was exhausted from the emotional battle today had been and the fact I hadn't had an appetite all day. I replayed his message once more before I fell asleep on a tear-drenched pillow.

When my alarm went off, my eyes felt worse than yesterday. I glanced at the screen and saw a message from Oskar. It was a simple, *Goodnight, Süsse*, yet it kindled a fire of hope deep inside me.

Tears leaked out again during my morning rituals. I was physically ill after taking my morning medicine, which made me force myself to eat crackers—*something*—for the first time since Sunday.

At 6:17, I got a text message. *Lucia, please call me.*

I cried when I saw it, but luckily the day passed with busy numbness.

When yoga got out that evening at nine, I had another voicemail from Oskar. It was short again. "Please call me. I miss you. God, I miss you so much." It was painful to ignore him. Even though I was exhausted and got into bed late after my shower, sleep was hard to come by.

I had the same two messages as I readied myself for my Wednesday. Getting through the day seemed to be even harder than the previous two. As I left my evening class that night, my phone started ringing, Oskar's name flashing.

When I got home, I played the message. "Lucia, please. I don't want to harass you, but please, can we talk? Please." His voice cracked. "Just meet up with me and hear what I have to say. If you don't want to get together after that, fine. Just don't leave without me getting to see you one more time. Without talking one more time."

I clicked off the phone and curled into bed, snuggled around Bea.

When my alarm went off Thursday morning, I stared listlessly at the ceiling. I dressed nicely, hoping it would make me feel better.

It didn't.

Even if my clothes were nice, my eyes still looked haunted. At lunch, when I replayed all of Oskar's messages and tears streamed hot trails down my cheeks, I decided to go see him after work. He was right: he deserved closure. I would sit down and explain to him about my medicines and why I didn't want to move back abroad. Explain why it had to be over.

My palms were sweaty, and I kept biting my lip on the drive across town to Georgia Tech. I paid for parking and dragged my feet to his lab, practicing all the things I would say. I was glad I hadn't eaten lunch because my stomach was turning so much, I was afraid I'd vomit. I pulled on the lab door, but I'd forgotten it was locked.

I breathed heavy a minute, just staring at the door. Then I pulled out my phone. I closed my eyes and realized I wouldn't be able to see Oskar. It would just be too hard.

I opened my eyes and was about to walk away when I heard an accented "Lucia."

Hackles up, I looked into the deep brown eyes of Sujit.

"Lucia," he repeated. "I'll let you in. You know how bad the reception in the lab is."

I nodded lamely and followed him inside the double doors.

"Do you remember where our lab is?" he asked politely.

"Yes, thank you," I said quietly, surprised my mouth worked at all.

"Good." He smiled faintly. "I'm glad you're here. Whatever it is, I hope you work it out. Oskar's been so down he won't even watch cricket with me." His eyes twinkled once as he finished with, "Good luck," before he turned and walked away.

With a deep breath, I turned to walk down the stairs and

went deeper into the labs. When I got to his office, I counted to thirty before I knocked on the door.

Oskar opened it and just stared at me, opening and closing his mouth, before he finally said, "Lucia." With that, the spell seemed to be broken, and he repeated, "Lucia, please come in."

He stepped to the side, and I entered his lab, careful not to touch any chemicals or tables. He led me to his desk and motioned for me to sit in his chair. He pulled out a plastic one and slid it close. We stared at each other for a minute. It seemed neither of us knew what to say. Then he pulled out his phone.

"I'm nervous," he said. "You know I'm not as good with words as you. Can I play this for you?"

I nodded, my own belly in knots. Seeing him did funny things to my insides.

His phone started playing Jack Johnson's "Better Together" as he took my hand and threaded our fingers.

I started crying. When I looked into his molten chocolate gaze, I saw moisture in his eyes.

He spoke over the song. "Lucia, I don't know everything, but I know this: I want to be with you."

I held his gaze just a heartbeat, then I leaned in and gave him a soft kiss. His hand cupped the back of my head, and he deepened our kiss but kept it tender. After a minute, he pulled back and flashed me his dimple. His free hand wiped my tears away.

"I don't know what will happen tomorrow, or at graduation, but I know I want to be with you figuring it out," he said softly. "Not being with you, it hurt. It hurt so bad."

A tear leaked out of his eye. I brushed my thumb against it before I said, "I missed you so much, but I'm scared."

He squeezed my hand. "I'm scared too." He stood and pulled me up with him. He folded me into his embrace and inhaled deeply. "I'd rather be scared with you than lonely by myself," he whispered in my ear.

I rubbed my face against the side of his neck, enjoying the

tickle of his stubble. I squeezed him back. "Me too."

He kissed my forehead. "Let's get out of here," he said, and let him lead me up and out of the lab.

I was still scared about the future, but I had to agree with him on one thing: *we were better together*.

Thirty-seven

December 21—Winter Break
OSKAR

Thank fucking god this semester was over, I thought as I pulled up to Lucia's place. I was worn out. I'd managed, barely, to see Lucia almost every day since our breakup. We'd both been intensely busy with the end of the semester, but not seeing each other hadn't really been an option. We'd both seemed a little desperate—like we weren't entirely convinced we were both there. But tonight, we were finally free. We'd turned in our grades, and we were both officially done for the semester.

She had plans to cook us a special dinner, and we were going to exchange gifts, even though it was only the twenty-first. It was a little early, but I wanted to savor her these next three days before she went to visit her grandparents in Italy. I could tell by how she talked about it, and about them, that she was thrilled to go. I was glad for her, but I felt a little frantic knowing she'd be leaving soon. I was simply happy we'd have some time for just the two of us with no work. I knew by now I couldn't live without her.

I knocked on her door. "Come in!"

My hands were a little full, but I managed it with the key she'd given me the night we made up. I tried not to let on, but I really like having a key to her place.

I'd expected to see her rushing around in the kitchen, but she wasn't. When I shut the door, I saw her standing in the hallway to the bedroom wearing a robe. As our eyes met, she dropped it.

My mouth nearly hit the floor, and I almost lost hold of the items in my hands. She stood there in a dark red push-up bra with a small bow on it, red panties, and black high heels. She turned around with a jingle—her underwear was a red thong with a big red bow and a small bell on the back.

"Do you want to come unwrap your present?" she asked me from over her shoulder, running a hand over the red bow.

Do I ever.

"Yes," I managed to get out as she turned around.

God, she was sexy. I rushed to put her present down and stalked toward her. I ran my hands over her hips as I leaned in to kiss her. Her skin was satin under my hands.

Her fingers moved to my chest, and she broke our kiss by pushing me onto the bed. She followed, straddling me, and worked on the buttons of my shirt, kissing and nibbling my chest with each new part of skin she exposed. When my shirt was off, I tried to grab her, but she shook her head. She'd taken the belt off her robe and now was wrapping it around my hands. I groaned as she pushed me back onto the bed.

She tossed her hair back and said, "This is what's going to happen, Oskar. First, I'm going to kiss you all over until you till you come in my mouth." She held my hands above me with one hand, and rubbed me through my pants with the other. She kissed my jawline and whispered huskily in my ear, "It turns me on so much, hearing you moan and knowing I'm responsible."

Suddenly even harder, I managed to ask, "And then what?"

I liked this side of her. She didn't bring it out often, but I was always happy when she wanted to take charge.

She leaned back and ground against me, using the hand that had been touching my dick to run a finger down her breasts. "Then I'm going to ride you until I can't take it anymore, but before you come inside me, I want you to take me on my knees and pound into me, so I can hear the bell jingle while you thrust."

She flicked the bell on the back of her thong to punctuate her words. I hardened almost painfully at the enticing sound and image she'd conjured.

She rocked forward again and nipped my ear. "How does that sound?"

"Süsse," was all I managed to strangle out as she slipped off me and trailed kisses down my neck, chest, and stomach.

It sounds like the best Christmas present anyone's ever given me.

Her nails trailed down my sides, and I couldn't help the noise that escaped me—something between a groan and a moan. She pulled off my pants and shoes and kissed all the way down to my ankles. I quivered when she worked her way back up with her tongue and nails, slowly teasing me. When she finally got to my cock, it was practically dancing for her. But before she touched it or kissed it, she blew on me.

"Please, Lucia," I begged her. She smiled at me before taking me into her mouth.

She started humming as she trailed her mouth over me, sucking me deeper. My pleasure built between what she was doing with her mouth and hands. When she looked up at me with her hazel eyes, I exploded, saying her name. Finishing with a final lick, she kissed my inner thigh. I trembled under her, my skin now overly sensitive.

"Come here," I ordered.

She looked up but bent down to take off her shoes before she complied. Her lovely ribbon was showing, and I felt myself already starting to respond to her again. I swear to god, she had the most fantastic ass I'd ever seen—that bow only made it better. She inched up, kissing my hypersensitive skin before she straddled me. She was stunning, her glorious hair falling around her shoulders and breasts.

"Untie me," I demanded.

She smirked at me before bending down to do so. Her breasts were right above my face as she unwound my wrists. I kissed her lush mounds and moved her bra to softly bite her nipples while she freed me. As soon as I could, I ran my hands down her sides and past her hips and ass. I fingered the silk bow and jingled the bell, and suddenly I was ready for her again. I couldn't wait to hear that noise as I thrust into her. The anticipation made me stiffen further.

I kissed her inner wrist before I covered her hand with mine and ran it along my dick so she could feel how much I wanted her—what she did to me.

I looked at those beautiful lips and kissed her once, hard and deep, before I asked, "Well, Lucia, what are you going to do now?"

She liked bossing me before, and I was thoroughly enjoying this side of her. She smiled and put some lube on her hand and rubbed it on me. Then she used her fingers to brush her panties to the side as she lifted up and over me.

"Ride you hard," she stated as she slid down fully onto me.

Sounds of ecstasy escaped us both. My hands moved to her hips, tugging her harder and deeper. I wanted to see more of her. I unclasped her bra and pulled her closer.

"God, Lucia," I muttered before I kissed her nipples. I moved my hands back to her hips to thrust deeper into her. The jingle of the little bell was hot as fuck as she rode me. I pulled her down lower on me once more as she came with my name on her lips.

I gave her a moment before I pulled her off me with a soft kiss. Then I stood behind her and moved her onto her hands and knees—like she'd asked for. As I supported her with one hand, I couldn't help but think her red bow was wrapped around the most fantastic package I'd ever seen. I rubbed my finger through her folds once, feeling her dripping from her orgasm before I used one hand to move her panties while the other guided her hips back to my cock. As soon as I was in, we both groaned before I started using both hands, pulling her closer and letting me thrust deeper and deeper.

God, that bell was sending me over the edge, and I couldn't resist the dirty talk we both loved. "Is this what you've been dreaming of? Me this deep inside you while your bell rings?"

I grasped her hard. She gasped, "Oh god, yes."

I drew almost all the way out and held her hips still as she tried to buck back. "Tell me. Tell me what you've been dreaming of."

"Oskar," she whimpered.

I pulled all the way out and reached to tease her clit. "Tell me, Lucia. Tell me, and I'll give it to you." I rubbed myself just along her entrance.

"You fucking me. Hard. Fuck me, Oskar."

Her wish was my command. I thrust into her hilt deep several times as she screamed a shattering release, milking me too. I could barely stand, so I crawled onto the bed, where she'd sprawled on her belly. I cradled her so she was half on my chest and kissed her fingers, her inner wrist, then her eyes. Right now, she was so beautiful—rumpled from the bed play and smiling from her orgasms. I still hadn't told her yet, but I loved everything about her. I'd known since that day in the café with my mom. It'd been clearer every day since then. God, it'd been crystal clear when she left me: I couldn't live without her.

I pulled back and traced my hand along her jaw. She opened those hazel-golden eyes and stared at me.

"Lucia, I love you," I told her in the most serious German form, not the most casual one that lovers sometimes used.

She laughed, looking slightly wary. "You don't have to say that just because I gave you the best sex of your life."

She trailed a finger down my chest, and I caught it and placed it on my heart. "I love you," I repeated. Her eyes widened, as if she might cry. "I realized when I was talking about you with my mom in Austria. Every day since has cemented it. Lucia Farris, I love you."

She smiled her million-dollar, perfect smile and inched up to kiss me. "I love you too. I've loved you since the day at Stone Mountain."

I crushed her back to my chest. "I've loved you since the night of your nightmare. I just didn't know it yet."

We stayed like that a long time, holding each other and gently caressing the other's skin.

When she shivered, we got up and reluctantly dressed. She turned on the oven for the veggie lasagna she'd made. She heated the mulled wine we'd picked out together, and we keep sneaking looks and kisses.

"Let's do our presents," she said, motioning to the tiny tree she had on her coffee table.

"Okay," I agreed as she put the lasagna in for thirty minutes. We each grabbed a cup of spiced wine before we did. It felt warm and cozy—like Christmas. She'd made me feel that way, like this was home.

Like with her, I'm home.

"Me first, though! I want to see if you like your gift," she said with an infectious grin.

She handed me a huge box, but it was light, so I wondered what could possibly be in it. I opened it, and as I did, I found another box, and then another. Inside the third box, there was an I ♥ NYC mug with some papers in it. I lifted an eyebrow, but she just looked nervously at me. I opened it and found two tickets to NYC for the end of February and early March.

"You told me you have no classes on Friday next semester, and your last one ends at noon on Thursday. Well, I have a mini winter break, and I thought about New York City."

Her expression was hesitant as I stared at her, dumbfounded. Finally, I snapped my mouth shut and kissed her. "I've always wanted to go to New York."

I knew it was a good sign when we started planning for our future together, when we were on the same page. I certainly still saw us together in March and beyond. I smiled again, and so did she.

"I know. All Europeans do," she said with a wink. "The hotel's in Chelsea. I know you turn twenty-seven on February eighteenth, and I thought we could pick out Broadway tickets together and see a show on the trip ten days later. My birthday present to you."

I kissed her again because I couldn't help it. "It sounds perfect. We can look at shows later."

"I love New York, so your gift is a gift for me too. I hope you don't mind."

I laughed and assured her I didn't. "It's perfect. We must think alike. Look at yours. Well, there are two things."

I fiddled with my phone before I handed it to her. She looked at Google Maps a moment and then back at me in confusion.

"I know you are going to visit Ru this summer, but you haven't bought the tickets yet. Well, I'm just doing research this summer and have time off too. I want you to meet my family. Take four weeks off. Bea can stay with your parents; you said she's fine there. I'd like to come with you to China. I've also always wanted to go, and next summer I may be starting a new job and won't be able to take four weeks off."

I was anxious she'd tell me, no, but she rushed to say, "I don't mind if you come with us. It'd be great. Ru and Edward aren't my favorite couple to be the third wheel with, anyway."

I laughed, understanding that. Some couples weren't as good about it, and from what she'd told me, they tended to start talking in Mandarin around her, leaving her out. When I stopped laughing, I kissed her and showed her the trip on my phone.

"We can fly from Hong Kong to Munich, then take the bus to Innsbruck. Meet my family. They'll lend us the car, and we can see yours. We can travel there through St. Moritz—I still can't believe you've never been. And we can visit Lake Iseo and Franciacorta, that wine region you love and keep telling me I *have* to see. Then we can do the hike you told me about to the Rifugio Bolzano Al Monte Pez that you've always wanted to do before visiting your grandparents. Tell me you'll do it?"

I gasped a little, realizing I'd been talking fast without breathing, like she often did. She was rubbing off on me. I took her hand and kissed it.

She opened her mouth, but I pressed forward, afraid she'd protest. "I still have money from my year in the civil service. I'll pay for the hotels, just help me with the food, gas, and parking. I went to the website for your insurance company, and they'll release medicine early for travel, you just have to ask. You'll have plenty of medicine. And the multicity flight to include Munich is only two hundred dollars more than a round trip to Shanghai—"

"Okay," she said, interrupting me.

We smiled at each other. This was planning months in the future.

Then she clapped. "Ah, I can't wait!"

Her eyes glittered with excitement, and we both studied the map for a minute. It was the trip of a lifetime, but I'd meant it that we might not have the chance again. She understood that more than most.

I kissed her and then handed her a box. "Well, that was my exciting gift. We can get the tickets on Sunday when we celebrate Christmas with your family and Michael. I already talked to your parents about it. This is your practical gift. I bought it for you when I was in Innsbruck."

She opened it up and laughed. "You love me," she said, leaning over to kiss me.

"Yes," I said, slipping her into the super gloves made with goat fur I bought because of her Raynaud's. I'd seen it flare up often here in Atlanta, and she was going skiing where it was much colder. I knew these gloves would keep her warm. They were rated for negative thirty Celsius, the warmest the store sold.

She clapped her muffled hands in the giant mitts, grinning. "And two pairs of wool ski socks too."

"My practical Austrian lover," she teased. "I love you, Oskar." We started kissing—just little pecks I'd be embarrassed if anyone saw me doing, but I didn't care. I loved her.

The timer dinged. She took off the gloves before heading into the kitchen to get the lasagna out of the oven. She opened a Caesar salad bag and mixed it while the lasagna cooled. I poured us two glasses of water and put napkins on the table. It was cozy and homey, and I'd spent more nights here than my own place.

When we sat down and I looked over at her, I realized I'd never been as happy or as excited about my future as I was in this moment.

Thirty-eight

January 14
LUCIA

I woke with a cough tearing through me. I sat up, drenched in sweat and shivering. My body heaved with the force of my hacking, and I was glad I'd sent Oskar home yesterday afternoon. I'd been concerned with all the coughing I'd done on the plane, and it was always a whirlwind trip visiting my grandparents—skiing, eating till the wee hours of the morning, and socializing with distant family every spare second. This wouldn't be the first time the winter break trip had left me ill.

A painful, wet cough halted all thought for several gasping breaths. I knew the first week back to school, paired with a stressful meeting with my graduate advisor about my master's exams, had made me nervous this was coming. It was shocking I'd been healthy this long. I'd only taken four sick days so far this school year, including my doctor visit day—a record for me.

My lupus was also acting up. Despite wearing goggles and a face buff, the malar rash on my cheeks and nose from the sunny and windy ski slopes was just starting to fade. It usually indicated not just a sun reaction, but lupus activity, which was never good. My knees and elbows ached, which was double not good.

The clock read four o'clock. A terrible hacking tore through me again. Once it subsided, I put the thermometer in my mouth while I dug around for some cough drops and Advil. The thermometer chimed, reading 104.2. I groaned and coughed again before drinking a sip of water. My throat was on fire as the water and pill slid down.

I limped back to bed with cough drops and thermometer in tow. I fiddled on my phone until I got to the call-out-sick app and scheduled a sub for the next two days. I also shot a quick email to Anu with my lesson plan. It was a short email, all I was capable of with my fever-fogged brain, but the lesson plan was clear and the copies of the worksheets I'd created last week were made for the upcoming week. I turned my alarm to nine before curling on my side, barking out a lung.

The next thing I knew, the alarm went off, so between coughing bouts, I must have eventually fallen back asleep. I reached for my phone and work email. A sub had picked up, and Anu had written back; she'd taken care of everything. Thank god.

I took my temperature while reading the messages from Oskar. He'd sent a few, since it was weird for us not to have talked by this time in the day. The thermometer read 103.8, and I was glad the Advil was working—kind of.

I shivered once before I called Dr. Steinberg's office. I could barely speak since my laryngitis was already so bad. Of course, I didn't even need to say my full name before they knew who I was. Yes, I could come in at precisely one thirty when he started clinic in the afternoon.

I took a sip of water and my morning medicine. Pain assaulted me from my inflamed throat. I limped over to my sofa and redid my medicine. I looked at Bea and her happy face and thumping tail. With an exhausted sigh, I petted her and threw my sweat-soaked hair in a bun before gearing her up and pulling on a jacket. It was Atlanta's January, but it was still in the thirties. I thanked the sweet lord when Bea did what I needed her to in about two minutes. I could barely walk or stand. If she'd needed more time, I wasn't sure I could have given it to her.

The cold exacerbated the cough, and I had to brace myself on the wall of the hallway because it was so violent, I couldn't stand. As I stood there, a rough hacking continued, and I felt my rib make a little pop. I winced as I coughed again and again. I struggled for air and was forced to wrap both hands around my torso and hold tight until it stopped. I'd dislocated my ribs more than six times coughing and knew the feeling. I winced as I walked the rest of the way to my place, already feeling my ribs swelling painfully.

I knew I should eat or drink something, but with a combination of exhaustion and throat pain, I couldn't force myself. I took off my shirt, grimacing at the rib movement, and dabbed myself with a wet washcloth. It was worthless, and I was already drenched in sweat before I could put on the new shirt.

My phone beeped again as I limped into bed. *Hey Süsse, I'm worried. Are you okay?*

I messaged back, *I'm sick /:* before calling my mom. As soon as I opened my raspy mouth, she said, "Let me cancel my classes for this afternoon. Do you need anything now?"

"No," I said hoarsely.

"Okay, see you at one."

"Thanks," I managed to get out.

I took another Advil and cough drop before setting my alarm for half past noon. Oskar had texted me again. *Do you need anything? My first classes aren't until one today. I can take you to the doctor?*

I texted: *My mom is taking me, but thanks.* Then I tried to sleep a little.

I woke three times to cough violently before the alarm went off at twelve-thirty. I saw a missed call from Oskar, but I just texted, *I'll text after the doctor's app. I can't talk—sore throat.*

I took my medicine but could barely drink the water because my throat hurt so badly. I stumbled around my apartment until I found a tank with a built-in bra. I pulled a sweatshirt on, then jeans. I chose to sit to brush my hair because I was so weak. I managed to get it in a French braid, but I was sweating profusely and shaking by the time Mom knocked on the door at five to one.

"Oh, carina," Mom said when she saw me. "Let me take Bea, then we can go."

I just nodded and sat there listlessly until she came back. She didn't try to talk to me as we drove there, knowing my throat hurt. I felt dreamlike, my fever was so high. Adults didn't usually get temperatures this high, but I did. When we got to the waiting room, Mom flipped open her laptop to work, and I was taken back almost immediately. I frowned when they took my blood pressure: 80/50.

I sighed, knowing what that meant: IV fluids. Dr. Steinberg would never send me home with my pressure so low. My fever read 104.3 now. Sweat ran down my temples, back, and breasts, even as I shivered.

I was led quickly to the room and had barely sat down on the table before Dr. Steinberg entered. "Hi, Lucia. Can you tell me what's going on?"

I strained to smile, but it might have looked like a wince. "The usual—coughing, sore throat, fever, chills, body aches. Oh, and my ribs hurt."

He nodded before feeling the painful lymph nodes swollen on my neck. I stuck out my tongue, and he swabbed my throat. "I think you know what I'm going to say, but I'll say it anyway. IV fluids today with blood work. We will start you on the antibiotic and reevaluate tomorrow. Did you eat or drink anything today?" When I didn't reply, he asked, "Is your mom here?"

I nodded.

"Okay, I'll have her get you some Gatorade and soup before you go home. We are doing the fluid, but if your blood pressure is low again tomorrow, I'll have to admit you."

"Thanks," I croaked.

"Of course, Lucia. Advil every six hours, or Aleve every twelve. I'll see you tomorrow. I'm writing you a doctor's note for at least the end of the week. Please call your school. We will see from there."

I nodded again as I walked over to the IV room, and the phlebotomist smiled at me. "Lucia, I heard your blood pressure is low. Do you mind if we do the wrist splint?"

I nodded, and she got me geared up. My veins were shitty. I had extra small veins because of the PAH, and I was dehydrated. Not to mention, years of going every one to three months for blood work at the rheumatology office had taken its toll on them. I had one good vein in my left wrist, but it wasn't perfect and needed a brace to keep from rolling. If my blood pressure was low, the chances were that would be the only one that would take.

First came the blood draws, then the fluid. It was room temperature, which was nice, so it didn't sting with cold like Vanco. I napped until my mom brought me in a cup of veggie soup and a red Gatorade, my favorite. Dr. Steinberg must have told her about my blood pressure.

Pain tore through my throat, but I ate and drank because I didn't want to be admitted to the hospital. Before we left, we confirmed my appointment for tomorrow at one thirty. Mom stopped at a Publix to buy me Gatorade and soup. Then we went to CVS to fill my prescriptions and buy more cough drops. This had all taken a while, and it was almost six by the time we made it home. I was already ready for bed.

Oskar had texted me repeatedly and called me twice. I'd been avoiding responding. Even after months of dating and *I love you*s, he hadn't seen me like this. When Mom took out Bea, I rang him back, dreading it. I hated this. I abhorred this part of me—chronically ill.

"Hi," I whispered.

"God, Lucia. What's going on? Did you just get back from the doctor?"

It was hard for me to talk, so I continued to whisper. "I have a high fever and low blood pressure, so I needed some blood work and IV fluids. No big deal. I'll go back tomorrow at one thirty."

"I'll take you," he said immediately.

"No," I said just as quickly, my heart speeding up.

I didn't want him to see me like this. Despite everything, I still thought about Ali cheating and Frank leaving me.

I was fighting tears as I said, "My mom can take me. I'm sick. I don't want you to get it."

"Lucia," he said with an edge to his voice. "I'm your boyfriend."

"I'm disgusting," I whispered, and a few tears slipped down my face. I'd been sweating all day, and my hair was a rat's nest. Even as sick as I was, I didn't want to get back in my bed with stale sweat on the sheets. "I don't want you to see me like this."

God, didn't he get it? He would see this part of me and run for the hills. My insides froze with fear. He would leave me.

"I love you," he said in an angry tone he'd never used with me. "I'm going to take you, and I'm still going to fucking love you if you have a fever and look like hell."

I broke down and cried then, and I knew he could hear it. The illness and fever made me more emotional. I felt like crap on a stick.

"Oskar, I really don't want you to see me like this," I finally got out, repeating myself.

His voice turned gentle. "Süsse, I don't love my dad any less when he gets sick from diabetes. This doesn't change how I feel, but it hurts you don't trust me to be there for you. I'll get you at twelve forty-five tomorrow so I can take Bea out, okay?"

"Thank you," I whispered, wiping my eyes. "I love you."

His voice was still soft as he said, "I love you too. Call or text me if you need *anything*, and I'll be there. If you can't walk Bea tomorrow morning, I can."

We hung up, and I told mom about Oskar when she came

back. She looked relieved he cared enough to take me to the doctor. With one last pat for Bea, she let herself out, and I fell right asleep.

The intense coughing had me sitting up several times during the night. At nine, a pounding on the door, then texting, drove me to open the door for Michael, who'd come to walk Bea at my mom's request. I grimaced but forced myself to drink some Gatorade while he did. He told me to let him know if I needed help again. He said he should have helped me yesterday.

With a "don't touch me, but I love you," he left.

When he was gone, I managed to shower, semi-blow-dry my hair, and put it in a French braid before collapsing back in bed for a few hours. At noon, I got back up and managed to dress myself. I forced myself to at least eat some soup and drink more Gatorade. My stomach somersaulted, and my heart skipped. Soon Oskar would see me like this.

My anxiety spiked when I heard a knock before Oskar's key turned in the door.

Thirty-nine

January 15
OSKAR

I stepped inside, my eyes immediately searching for Lucia. She sat on the loveseat. Her cheeks were flushed with fever and what she'd told me was a lupus rash. She also had dark circles under her eyes. She looked worn and weak.

Something painful tightened inside me as I took her in. I immediately wanted to pull her to me and hold her, but as if reading my thoughts, she lifted her knees and wrapped her arms around them, a definite "do not touch" sign. She was shivering, so I hurried inside.

"I'm sorry you aren't feeling well, Süsse. Let me take Bea, okay?"

She nodded and said in a raspy voice, "Thanks for coming."

I looked into those hazel eyes that saw me as no one else ever had. "I love you."

She nodded with her fever-bright eyes as I picked up the little fluff.

"Hi, Bea. Ready to go outside?"

She licked me in response, and I hurried to get her in her harness. I glanced back at Lucia, who tried to smile at me, but she looked terrible and like it was all too much for her.

On the walk, Bea was a good dog, as though she knew Lucia was sick. She did what she needed to super quickly and turned back to the house. Lucia was a little obsessed with this fluffy, yappy thing, but she'd told me how much the dog had meant to her when she had no one else. She whispered to me one night that little Bea had been what she needed when she was slowly recovering. That there had been nights she'd felt overwhelmed, and just petting and snuggling her little Fluffy got her through. For that, I'd always have a soft spot for the dog.

When I opened the door, Lucia was sitting on the loveseat with her eyes closed. My chest tightened further, and I realized I loved her so much I'd do anything to make her well. I hated seeing her like this.

"Ready, Lucia?"

She nodded, and we left after she verified that I had something to do in the hospital because she warned it could take hours.

When we got there, Lucia and the nurse let me come back with her. Her blood pressure was low again, the nurse told us.

Dr. Steinberg was a short man whose eyes widened when he saw me, but after a quick nod from Lucia, he introduced himself and started talking. "Well, Lucia, I'm a little worried about you. Your fever is still over one hundred and three, your blood pressure is still low, and your platelets came back at eighty thousand. I know you frequently run low, but that's almost half of what's the lowest side of normal. I will not have your lupus indicators back until tomorrow. I don't know if I should admit you or not."

Admit her? I sat up straighter. How sick was she?

"No, please," she begged. "I rest better at home."

Concern marred his face. "I'm worried about you being alone. Maybe if you agreed to stay with your parents?"

"I'll stay with her," I said, and they both looked at me with surprise.

"Oskar, no." She shook her head.

"Lucia," I said in an exasperated tone before switching to German. "I can stay on the futon. I want to take care of you. Please. I was so worried about you I couldn't sleep last night." I willed her to see the concern in my gaze.

"I cough a lot during the night, and you won't sleep well," she argued. She coughed and turned to the wall, clutching her rib as she did, as if to underscore her words. Her whole body heaved. She flinched in pain every time she coughed.

"I'll sleep better there than if you're at the hospital," I countered.

We held each other's gaze for a moment, and I wondered how you could love someone so much and want to smack her stubborn head at the same time. No one else had ever made me feel this frustrated. I knew it was because I cared for her so fucking much.

Finally, she nodded slightly and turned to the doctor. "Okay," she said in English.

He looked relieved and said to keep the same routine as yesterday. He told me to make sure she drank three entire bottles—1.5 liters—of Gatorade tonight. Then he led us to the IV room he called the infusion center, which had three lounge chairs. Lucia settled into one, looking like this was the thousandth time she's done this. From what I knew, it might have been.

I had to admit, my mom had been right. It was fucking hard to watch Lucia being poked and an IV strapped to her. But my mom was also right that it didn't make me love her any less. In fact, it made me love her a whole hell of a lot more. She was a fighter, and she smiled through it all.

As the IV ran, the phlebotomist joked with Lucia that they had been missing her this year, and she was glad she'd been so healthy. It slipped out that Lucia used to be in here almost every month, sometimes more, but since dating me, she'd only been in here once—just for that infection after we went tubing.

Fevered, Lucia looked at me and whispered, "It's because of Oskar. He helps me relax, so I don't get sick as much. He's the yin to my yang." Then she closed her eyes and her breathing slowed. I thought she might have fallen asleep.

Her fluids ran slowly, and the phlebotomist cleaned up the IV kit. She turned to me and said softly, so as not to disturb Lucia, "It's true, you know."

It was disconcerting for me to think Lucia had to go through something like this almost every time she was ill. And it also disturbed me she was sick enough she could fall asleep in this bright room with an IV in her. I wanted to speak to her doctor while she was sleeping, so a nurse led me to his office.

"Thank you for seeing me," I said a little nervously when Dr. Steinberg entered. "I was just wondering, if it's just strep, why is this necessary?"

A warm look entered his eyes. "Oskar, it is challenging to fight any type of infection in autoimmune patients," he said calmly. "We can't predict how the body will react. Sometimes, the body might not help fight at all or maybe even too much." He coughed and held my gaze. "Do you realize that rash Lucia has on her face indicates an active lupus flare?"

Sheepishly, I nodded.

Then he looked at me sternly and clarified, "You do know that Lucia has had heart and lung failure before due to a lupus flare, correct?"

I nodded again, suddenly feeling like there was ice in my belly. *I can't lose her.*

In a calm voice, he also described the impact of the immunosuppressants, which I knew she took but hadn't realized how strong they were. He said her immune system was basically powered off and it could take days or even weeks before her body started working with the antibiotics. And there was rheumatic fever to consider; barely a worry in the developed world, it could be deadly to someone like Lucia with her past heart history.

Even if she stopped taking her medicines today, they took a minimum of six weeks to clear her system. Even on antibiotics, she was at risk, so he needed to monitor her closely and try to help her body, like with the fluids, so it could rebuild its platelets, fight the infection, and basically just do its job.

I must have looked worried because he said with a gentle pat on my shoulder, "I've treated Lucia a long time. I'll take good care of her. I have patients in here with HIV, chemo use, organ transplants, and other autoimmune diseases. I have thirty years of experience with this. If you and Lucia listen to me, hopefully, she'll be feeling like herself again in a few weeks."

I thanked him for his time, thinking of everyone else waiting to see him, and went back to Lucia. It was at least two hours later when we got back to the car.

She was quiet, and I didn't press her to talk with how bad her laryngitis was. On the drive home, I kept thinking how the drugs that helped her also hurt her, and I thought about her and her parents' concern about her moving. She had a team of professionals here: Dr. Steinberg, her infectious disease specialist, Dr. Zheng, her rheumatologist, and Dr. Manson, her pulmonologist. She'd already switched rheumatologists once. She'd said she wasn't happy with her last one, and the wait was eight months to get in as a new patient. I'd looked up lupus in Europe, and the current immunosuppressant she took wasn't even approved for lupus there. I couldn't help but feel a little helpless. In the back of my mind was the nagging thought that she was right—she shouldn't move back overseas.

When we walked into the apartment, Lucia finally broke me out of my thoughts. "I can't stand to get in my sweaty sheets again. If I put them in the washer, will you help me make the bed?"

"Of course," I told her, relieved she was letting me help with something.

After she stripped the bed, I remade it for her. Then I forced her to eat before letting her go to sleep. The doctor's conversation kept playing in my head that we needed to help her body any way we could. She was supposed to drink three Gatorades, but she only drank half of one. Her eyes welled up, and she said her throat hurt when I pressed her to drink more.

Finally, Monday came. She'd been sick a week—an entire week. Days had passed, and she didn't get better. In fact, she seemed worse. She was so exhausted she could barely eat. I'd taken her to the doctor on Wednesday and Friday. On Friday, she'd still had low platelets, blood pressure, and potassium. We'd been in the office four hours so she could get the extra slow potassium drip. Her doctor reminded us she needed to drink Gatorade, not the tea I'd been letting her drink.

She'd also lost ten pounds. I knew because they weighed her at the doctor's office. Her fever was persistent. She mainly just wanted to sleep. Only her horrible cough told me how often she woke. I'd crept into her bedroom, and it was frightening to see her face so still and know I couldn't do anything for her, except help her with the dog and make sure she ate. My mom was right: this was hard. Really, really hard.

This morning she'd promised she felt well enough to drive herself to the doctor, so I didn't need to miss class. I wasn't happy about it because she still had a fever. But it was 100.5, not 103, so reluctantly, I'd agreed. It looked like it was a damn herculean effort to make a glass of Gatorade, let alone drive to the doctor, but I did need to go to class. It was frustrating, to say the least, watching her day in and day out, knowing I couldn't do anything. She hadn't even wanted to watch a movie with me. She'd only slept.

On my way back from class, I called my mom to distract myself from worrying about Lucia. "Mom, Lucia is still sick. She still has a fever. She—" I heard the cracking in my voice.

"I know."

"You know what?"

She sighed. "You feel like you should be doing something, but there is nothing to do. It's the worst part of being with someone who's chronically ill. There is nothing you can do but wait. But hope it'll pass."

"It's hard. Mom, it's so fucking hard."

Her voice dropped even lower. "It will only get harder, but it doesn't mean it isn't worth fighting for."

I gritted my teeth, and I couldn't help but agree. God, I'd give my scholarship just to make this never happen again. But she'd warned me. This was what her life was like.

"I know. Thanks, Mom. Tell Dad hello and love you both."

Lucia was home when I got there, which I took as a good sign.

"Hey, sweetie," she said from behind her computer. "Let me just finish updating my sub plans before I forget what I'm doing."

I nodded and poured a glass of water. "How was everything today?" I asked when I saw her hit send.

"Eh, my blood pressure was *almost* normal. Maybe I can go back to work on Wednesday?" She smiled. "Can you do me a huge favor and go to my school tomorrow? I need to start grading, and my principal asked me for my sick note."

"Sure, Lucia. You know I'd help do whatever, but what did Dr. Steinberg say?"

"He said Friday, but I barely have a fever."

"Lucia," I ground out, wondering why she was so stubborn.

"Look, I'm sure it won't turn into rheumatic fever. I'm getting better."

God, she was stubborn. She was getting better, but she still looked like hell on wheels. She needed rest.

"My principal keeps emailing me, asking when I'll be back.

She doesn't like me being out. I need to get back to my kids."

Her eyes were bright with worry, and suddenly I was fucking pissed. No, livid. Mad at her principal and angry she felt like she couldn't take the time to get better. Didn't the woman know what Lucia had been through?

I looked at her and felt a frustration I'd never felt before. "Just get better first," I begged.

She nodded and closed her computer before she leaned back on the sofa. Her skin was almost translucently pale. I hated not being able to fix her. I hated this.

"I need to get out of the house for a minute. I'm going to take Bea on a walk." My voice was hard. I felt so angry and helpless.

Lucia's eyes flashed open, and there were tears in them. She sucked in a ragged breath and shot out, "I knew I shouldn't have let you see me like this."

I stared at her open-mouthed, and my ears pounding as I bit out, "What the fuck?"

She hunched over and said so low I could barely hear her over the ringing in my ears, "Who could love someone like this?"

The room was silent except for her sudden gasping sobs. I stared at her, wondering what had just happened before I rushed to kneel beside her. I tried to take her hand, but she wouldn't let me. She had it wrapped around herself.

"Lucia," I said firmly and slowly. "I am so angry and so frustrated, and so—god, I don't even know right now. It fucking sucks you have been through this. It sucks you are still sick. It sucks your principal is emailing you when you have a valid reason to miss work. And *I hate it*. But I still love you."

Slowly she raised her head, and she looked like a mess. I gently grabbed her forearms.

"I need to get away a moment because I love you so much it hurts. It hurts me to see you sick and not be able to fix you. It hurts me that your stupid principal is emailing you, okay?"

I felt tears in my own eyes, too, and I shook her gently,

holding her gaze.

"I love you so much it hurts," I repeated. "I will never leave you for being sick. But what hurts me the most is that you don't realize how much I love you."

A loud sob escaped her, and I moved to sit beside her. I pulled her against me and rubbed her back and arms.

"I'm sorry," she said, stuttering slightly. "I don't feel good. I can't think. I'm afraid." Her fingers curled into my chest. "I just wonder how anyone can love someone like this."

"It's a lot," I admitted, continuing to caress her back. "It makes me impressed as hell with all you've done. Come on, let me get you to bed." I kissed her temple.

Her fingers tightened on me, and she whispered, "Can I hold you a minute more? I've missed being in your arms so much. I've been so afraid you'd leave me too."

I kissed her temple again and said, "I've missed sleeping beside you." I nervously scratched the back of my neck. "Um, Lucia, can we talk about something?" Her fingers pinched me painfully a moment, and I immediately regretted my choice of words. "What I mean is, I've been staying over here a lot—"

"Oskar, you didn't have to take care of me when I was sick," she interrupted, trying to pull away from my chest.

It was definitely fear I heard in her voice. "Please let me finish. I've wanted to talk to you about this since after Christmas, but you got sick and I wanted to wait."

She stiffened but didn't interrupt again.

"Well, when I signed on with my apartment last year, it was a ten-month lease. When we re-signed, it was also a ten-month lease. Sujit isn't re-signing because he is getting married in May, so he'll be renting his own place with his wife. I was wondering—that is, I was hoping, you'd let me move in here. I'm here almost all the time anyway, and if you need space, I can work in the library or my lab at school. My lease expires the end of February, but we have to let the complex know by January thirty-first—ten days from now."

She pulled back to look at me, and I reluctantly let her go. She was right: I'd missed holding her in my arms. Her eyes were wide. "You want to move in with me?"

"Yes." I threaded our fingers together and asked, "Can I?"

She smiled as it sunk in. Despite her red eyes and nose, she looked radiant. "Yes," she said with a big nod.

We stared at each other a minute, both likely feeling excited and nervous, before I stood. "And now I'm taking you to bed. Get better, because I'm ready to come back to *our* bed."

She let me help her up. "I love you," she said once she was standing.

I kissed her forehead and lead her to her bedroom. I loved her. Her illness showed me as nothing else could—I wanted to be around her, even when she was less than perfect.

Forty

Four and a half months later, June 15
LUCIA

Oskar plopped down beside me as I knelt on the floor, peering into my waterproof North Face duffel backpack like it held the answers to all the world's problems. My heart was racing with anticipation, but there was also a thread of fear.

"You're sure I brought the right clothes for Innsbruck?" I asked.

I said this instead of the words really running through my mind. *Will I have a problem bringing my medicine into China? What if I get sick over there? What if we can't stand each other after four weeks together nonstop?*

The quirk of his smile showed Oskar seemed to know this. He leaned over and kissed me, and I shivered as he traced my jaw with a finger. I was still addicted to him almost a year later, now more than ever.

"Yes, you just need a sweater and jeans, plus all those hiking clothes," he said. "You have one nice dress for China, so that should be fine. We can wash everything at my parents' house."

"Right, then I think I'm done." I zipped up the bag I'd had ready for days, but had just wanted to check one more time. Initially, when I'd been diagnosed with PAH, I thought I might never fly again. I'd flown once domestically with the pump. I could fly, but hadn't been cleared to take such a long trip. I'd had to wait to get my heart pump out to go back to visit my friends from college and my grandparents overseas.

It had been shattering thinking I might never see my motherland again or Paola, my best friend from college. When I'd finally gone, I'd had to go to the bathroom to wipe away my tears as soon as we landed; I was so overcome with emotion.

I looked at my bag one more time and smiled. I thought something like this—a four-week trip across the world—had been forever lost to me. Oskar picked up my bag and set it next to his backpack, which sat fully packed by the front door. I smiled at *our* bags together at *our* front door. Oskar had been officially living here since late January.

My place had been a little tight at times for the three of us. I hadn't liked sharing my closet at all. We'd finally gotten a chair for the desk, and Oskar now used it as it had been intended. Our lives had grown more and more intertwined and inseparable. Now, I would have trouble sleeping if he wasn't beside me, holding me nestled against him. With Michael and me both busy with our respective boyfriends, and Ru in China, Oskar fully wormed himself into the best friend category.

Since he'd taken care of me in January, I hadn't been extremely sick again. When I'd gotten a runny nose after our NYC trip, he didn't let me leave the house for a week except to go to work. He'd bought all the groceries and cooked, saying firmly I needed to take care of myself and get well. He was like a cute protective mother hen.

I had lupus and three other autoimmune diseases. I always would. Some days I'd been tired after work and just wanted to shower and sleep, but he never made me feel guilty about it. That was one of the worst things about being chronically ill—the guilt when you let your friends and family down because you were too tired or sick to do something. Oskar had never made me feel bad for it, and maybe that was why I loved him so much. I'd even let him meet my rheumatologist and Dr. Manson. I'd been doing so well with my lupus blood panel that he'd agreed to let me take one immunosuppressant a day, which hopefully would help me get well sooner if I got sick again. It also gave me a tingling of hope that if I did well, I could stop them completely. If so, I would be more comfortable overseas, and maybe, just maybe, I could visit the large chunk of the world that fell into the yellow fever zone. Or even live in Europe again.

I pushed away those thoughts and focused on my carryon bag. Oskar kept giving me an amused expression, like he knew about my quirky anxiety right now, but didn't say anything when I sat on the loveseat and double-checked my carryon bag for what felt like the hundredth time—medicine, check; passport, check; wallet, check; etc. I let out a breath.

Oskar walked over to the loveseat and held out a hand for me. "Ready, Süsse?"

I nodded, letting him help me up and kiss me softly before we both put on our backpacks. Oskar locked up, and we knocked on Michael's door. Even though the walk to the MARTA train would have been short, it was June in Atlanta. Plus, it was pouring in true Georgia summer style. Hopefully our flight wouldn't be delayed and it was just a popup thunderstorm. Michael had offered to drive us so we didn't have to start our sixteen-hour flight to Shanghai covered in sweat. Oskar, even though he lived with me now, had stayed respectful of my personal space. Michael and I still took long walks alone a few times a week, and I was grateful for that time, just the two of us. We also did plenty of double dates with him and Patrick. He'd been my friend when I needed him most, and I'd always love Mikey in a special way.

"Look at you two! God, I'm so jelly. Take tons of pictures," Michael told us as we walked to his truck, huddling under our umbrellas.

He asked us questions about what we would be doing. Luckily, Ru and Edward had taken some time off work, so we could travel together. They'd booked the hotels, which were moderately priced but up to Ru's standards. Edward had taken care of the travel plans. It made things much more manageable.

The drive to the airport was short, and when we got there, Michael gave me a big hug. "Take care," he said before getting back in his truck.

In the new international terminal, the lines were short; it was a relief to check our heavy backpacks. We cleared security quickly and sat looking over our itinerary as we waited for the plane to board. The rain had luckily stopped, and it was blue skies for days again with steam coming off the asphalt outside.

"I still can't believe we get to go on this trip," I admitted to Oskar.

"I know, me too," he agreed.

I think we both knew that without friends and family abroad, the cost would have been much higher. I thought he understood from my stories just how much getting to travel to new, unfamiliar places again meant to me.

"I feel so lucky to do this trip, and especially to do it with you," I whispered.

It still didn't feel real sometimes, Oskar sitting beside me, my new M.A. degree, and now this trip. I was glad everyone had pushed me to do it. If there was one thing I'd learned being sick, it was to travel and enjoy life when you could—it could all change in an instant.

Oskar wrapped his arm around my shoulder and kissed my temple. "We are lucky, and we both deserve some time off and time together."

Right, as he so often was. Even though living with him had been great, he was in a demanding Ph.D. program, and I'd been working fulltime and writing my thesis, plus preparing for my master's exams. I was just relieved it was all over. We'd worked so hard and been so busy this last semester that it had been "a holiday" if we had a glass of wine or beer at dinner.

Our flight boarded, and despite my awed excitement, I slept fine. Ru was right: the sixteen-hour straight flight wasn't too bad.

The days in Shanghai flew past. Ru and Edward gave us good suggestions for the day while they worked, and we all stuffed our faces with incredible food at breakfast and dinner. I must admit I'd always been partial to the dumpling breakfast, but after day one, I passed on the cold bean soup.

Shanghai was a vibrant city, but it was nice to leave the crowd for the calmer southern countryside. And the Li River blew away every expectation I'd had. Oskar carried my sunscreen with him everywhere we went, reminding me to use it. We got "lucky" the day we did the bike ride—it was pouring rain—so I didn't need to worry about the tropical summer sun. With our raincoats, it actually wasn't bad, and it saved me the risk of getting a sun flare. Biking through the mountains and rice patties felt like a fairytale, the mist clinging dramatically to the jagged limestone peaks.

When we did the village hike in Longsheng, in what they referred to as the Dragon's Backbone, I could tell everyone was as impressed as I was with the layer after layer of narrow rice terraces dotted with dark wooden villages, seemingly unchanged by time. Ru was a little bit of a diva, but Edward spoiled her and catered to her every whim. She enjoyed hiking and biking as much as the rest of us, as long as the room and shower were clean at night. Despite how they acted sometimes, I could tell they cared deeply for each other. I thought wedding bells were in their future, or at least red envelopes. Edward's parents had already given her a dark jade necklace—jewelry, a typical bridal gift.

Oskar was the most wonderful person I'd ever traveled with and never complained about the heat, bugs, or squat toilets as we traveled around China. Every day we found more things to see, eat, and get excited about as we shared the joy of the adventure. I realized I wanted to travel with him forever. Even over here on the far side of the world, I had no fear—not with Oskar there. With him, I was fearless.

Forty-one

Present day, June 29
OSKAR

I glanced over at Lucia and could tell she was anxious by the way she repeatedly crossed and uncrossed her legs. Or maybe it was the coffee. Our flight landed at five in the morning from Hong Kong, and luckily, we cleared customs quickly, managing to catch the seven twenty bus to Innsbruck. But before we did, we'd both drank three coffees to cope with the jetlag.

When she crossed her legs again, I couldn't help saying, "They have a bathroom if you need to pee, Lucia."

She opened her mouth, and I thought she was going to say she didn't need to go, but dug through her purse for a brush and nodded instead. She came back looking calmer, with her hair in the French braid she favored.

"You look nice," I said. "It's not like they haven't met you. We Skype with my family all the time. They'll love you nearly as much as I do."

We lived together, so she'd been there often for our

conversations, and from what I'd told my parents, they really liked her. She had also gotten to talk with my best friend Gunter in Munich, and Josef, my oldest friend and neighbor. I'd, in turn, spoken with Ru numerous times before our trip, and her Italian best friend, Paola, who'd lived with her when she attended La Sapienza. Well, we said a few things, since Paola didn't speak English or German.

She nodded again but didn't say anything. I took her hand and started describing the hike I'd planned for us tomorrow, hoping to distract her. It worked, and she seemed more relaxed by the time the bus stopped and I saw my parents waiting for us.

"Ready?"

"Yes," she answered as we grabbed our bags.

She motioned for me to go first. With a shake of my head, I did. Luckily, it was Saturday, so both my parents could be there. My mom gave me a huge hug as soon as I stepped out of the way of the other offloading passengers. She quickly let me go and hugged Lucia.

"Lucia, I feel like I already know you so well. Come, you both must want a shower," my mom told her with a laugh.

I hugged my dad, and he also hugged Lucia before we filed into their car and drove home. Mom peppered us with questions about our trip the whole time, and we laughed as we told her about it. Neither of us could wait to unveil the treasures we'd bought everyone. I'd only done the short trip with Lucia to NYC before this one, but she'd been as easy to travel with as she was to live with. China had been beyond spectacular. I hadn't admitted it to her, but I had been a little nervous about traveling with her in China. What if something had happened to her?

It had been for nothing. I should have known after living with her that unless she was having a bad day with her lupus, she had a remarkable amount of energy. Usually, she'd been the one dragging me to see everything. Every day we'd both been eager to try everything from food to new places, to having the locals laugh at her few words of Mandarin. If I hadn't already known

Lucia was the girl I wanted to be with, the trip had proven it.

The day passed quickly between showers, clothes-washing, stories with my family, and copious amounts of coffee to beat the jetlag. I slipped into my mom's room as Lucia was getting ready for bed. It was only eight, but with the travel and our early hike in the morning, we both couldn't wait to crawl under the covers.

Plus, even though I didn't tell her, I worried about her sometimes, and after a big day like today, I wanted to be sure she got plenty of rest. With her in my arms, no matter the hour, I would fall asleep quickly.

My mom smiled when she saw me enter. "Well, Oskar?" she whispered.

"I haven't changed my mind," I said in an equally soft voice.

Her smile grew and her eyes watered as she handed me my grandmother's emerald and diamond ring. Set in a yellow-gold, art deco style, it would look stunning on Lucia with her hazel eyes. My pulse raced as I took it, and I kissed my mom goodnight on the cheek. I hurried back to my room and slipped the ring into the bag we were taking tomorrow—right before Lucia walked in, yawning.

"Oh, my goodness. I'm so tired," she said as she headed toward me. "Oh, I forgot water."

She turned to go toward the door, but I stopped her. "I'll get it. I know right where the glasses are."

She kissed me and whispered against my lips, "How'd I get so lucky?"

I laughed. Nervousness still pulsed through me, but her words and actions lessened it. By the time I was back, she was already in bed. I gave her the water, and she took her medicine. I swore we both passed out in a minute because when the alarm went off in the morning, we jumped. I didn't even remember falling asleep.

I kissed her shoulder, suddenly feeling adrenaline coursing through me. "Good morning, Süsse."

She pulled my hand from around her waist and kissed it.

"Come, we have a big hike." I leaned over her and kissed her cheek, laughing at the sleepy look she gave me. "You work on your medicine. I'll start the coffee and meet you downstairs."

I put on my hiking clothes and took my backpack down to the kitchen. About fifteen minutes later, Lucia came down, ready for the day. We had a quick breakfast before my mom took us to the cable car station. From the top, we planned to complete the Pfeis Hut trail, which provided great views of Innsbruck. My mom had made our lunches and kept smiling at us both with a twinkle in her eye. Lucia had no clue this was anything more than one of our usual hikes. Despite having PAH and needing to make more stops going up inclines, hiking was still one of her favorite things. Perhaps that was what I loved most about her: her ability to keep moving forward no matter the obstacle. And her extreme joy for the things she still could do.

The day was perfect, and I was glad for the sunshine and views of the stunning snow-covered Alps and wildflower meadows. We stopped several times as we wound our way up, down, and around the mountain toward the hut. Her heavy breathing and frequent stops didn't worry me like they once had—that was who she was. She was still here hiking, and sometimes it was nice to stop and enjoy the view.

I started getting tense as we got closer and closer. What if she thought it was too soon?

I could barely speak by the time we reached the hut. Lucia was gushing over the beauty of the sheer cliffs before us. I led her a little bit away from the other people at the endpoint, and we found a rock to sit on and eat our lunch. I took a big sip of water and threaded Lucia's fingers through mine.

She grinned, her eyes twinkling green in the sunlight. "Thanks for taking me here. You're right, I love it."

"Lucia, I know we haven't been together that long," I started, "but I think you know how much you mean to me."

"It'll be a year next month. It's not no time, either," she said with a laugh.

"You're right. And in that time, I've seen you sick and healthy and loved you both ways," I continued earnestly. "I've seen you at work and traveling. I've lived with you. Lucia, I don't care where we end up living—I want to wake up every day beside you."

She looked at me like she was wondering where this was going. I kept talking. "Lucia, you told me you haven't had your nightmare since September about the vampires chasing you. Whatever it is, it'll always be inside you lurking, but it doesn't scare me. No matter what monsters come, I want to be there fighting beside you." I sucked in a breath. "Lucia, will you marry me?"

Her jaw dropped, and she said in a hushed voice, "Seriously?"

I took out my grandmother's ring and nodded.

She looked at it and then back to me and again at the ring. Tears started running down her face. She reached forward to kiss me. "Yes. Yes, yes! Of course I will."

I slid the ring on her finger, and relief coursed through me— it fit like I thought it would. I sucked in another breath—here was the second thing. "I have heard you mention a few times that you don't want a big wedding."

She'd joked about this with Ru before when I'd been in earshot. Ru wanted a huge ceremony, apparently. She looked at me nervously, and I knew anxiety made her lupus flare.

"I really don't," she admitted. "But I would be okay with one if you do."

I kissed her knuckle right below the ring. "Here in Austria, weddings aren't official unless they are civically done. Most are small, intimate things. If you want," I looked her in the eye, "and *only* if you want, we can get married here next week when we come back in ten days. I already spoke to your mom and dad about it before the trip. I have the documents we need to file for marriage. We can go to the office tomorrow before we head to Switzerland. If you aren't sure, I don't mind waiting as long as you want to be engaged—a year, two years, whatever you want.

I love you and want to be with you. But we are both practical people."

I turned and grabbed the papers out of my bag and handed them to her—information on applications for economics Ph.D. programs at American, George Washington, George Mason, Georgetown, and Johns Hopkins. She looked at them and raised an eyebrow at me.

"There are a lot of job opportunities for me in DC. I've already spoken to a few recruiters there. All these programs are within an hour and a half from DC. If we are married, you'll be covered under my health insurance. I don't want you to give up your dream of the IMF. If you do a Ph.D. near DC, you can apply for an internship in economics with them. If it fails, you can be a professor or government advisor, or still teach. But you'll know you tried. I know how important it is for you to at least have tried. I can help support us both while you do the Ph.D. We both live frugally already. I want you to try. *This is your dream.*"

Her eyes were bright and beautiful as I continued giving her the reasons we shouldn't wait.

"Also, it'll be easier for me to get a job in America as a green card holder married to an American, not on a visa application. Süsse, we've always been honest with each other, and that's the truth. Maybe that sounds unromantic, but I love you, Lucia. I want to spend the rest of my life with you, and if we are married, it's easier for that to happen. I can't bear to be parted from you and I know, at least for now, you don't want to live here."

I looked at her after my long speech and held my breath. Tears started falling on the papers in her hands, and she looked up at me.

"You would support me so I could pursue this? You would give up Austria to be a permanent U.S. resident?"

"Yes. I think you would be amazing working for the IMF, or if not, as a professor. That way, if we ever decide to move to Europe, it'll be easier for you to get a job. But we never have to move back here. That's why I want to get married—so they can't force me away from you. I swear to you if we do move here, if you ever get sick and prefer American medicine, I'll get a job back over there so you'll have insurance and take you back in a minute. Where you want to be is where I want to be."

She smiled, nearly blinding me with her exuberant expression. "Let's do it." She looked at me with love and excitement in her gaze. "Let's file it tomorrow, and don't be stupid—wanting to stay in America with me is romantic. There is nothing more romantic than that."

I leaned forward and captured her mouth with mine. I brushed her tears away with my thumb, and I only broke away because I knew we weren't alone up here. If we were, there would have been no way in hell I would have stopped. I would have shown her with my body as well as my words how much I adored everything about her.

I leaned back, both of us grinning like children on Christmas.

"So, we'll do things backwards: first the honeymoon and then the marriage."

"I don't care," she said, threading our fingers again. "I've always been special and will always be that two in a million girl." She winked at her PAH joke, before continuing seriously, "I've known for a long time you are the only person I want to spend the rest of my life with."

Finally, we put the papers back away and ate our lunch, grinning stupidly at each other the whole time. Buoyancy filled me as we walked back, and neither of us could resist sneaking kisses when the trail was deserted. When we got to the cable car, I messaged my mom we were heading down, and that Lucia had said yes.

Leaving the station at the bottom, my mom ran up to us and threw her arms around us. At the house, we called her parents on video chat, and her mom started crying. She said she'd bought Lucia a dress, "just in case." They'd already planned to be visiting her grandparents when we were, only two hours away, so they'd be here for the wedding. We laughed at that and told them we would see them in just a few days in Alta Badia.

When we got off the phone, we showered, and Mom had Prosecco waiting for us when we came back down. At dinner, I kept looking at Lucia and the ring on her finger, knowing I was the luckiest guy in the world.

Epilogue

Almost one year later, June 14
LUCIA

Oskar walked inside with Bea as I compulsively opened the closets and drawers, checking everything just one more time.

"We should probably hit the road. It's an almost ten-hour drive to DC," he said gently. I'd always been an anxious person, and he knew that when he married me. Correction, he knew that *before* he married me.

"I'm so excited, but nervous too," I admitted as I wrapped my arms around him, and he held me close.

I'd never tire of his Dax Wax scent or this feeling when our chests touched. Really, I never tired of anything Oskar. Sure, we were human—we got in disagreements occasionally—but I was astounded that I loved him more today than when he'd asked me to be his wife a year ago in a small civil service office with just our parents and his siblings.

"You're going to do great," he said in my ear before pulling away. "Come on, Süsse."

He took my hand and led me to the door. I picked up Bea and glanced back at the apartment. *This is it.* I hated goodbyes, but every goodbye provided a new opportunity, I reminded myself. As we closed the door and I heard the click, I looked at Oskar and he looked at me. Two breaths exhaled, and then we headed to my car and the U-Haul he'd be driving.

I got in with Bea and tried to not cry, even though I was excited. I'd said my goodbyes to both Michael and my parents last night. Patrick had moved in with Michael, and they seemed like they were as happy as ever. I'd miss them both.

I'd gotten my acceptance letter from The George Washington University within days of Oskar securing a job just outside DC. He'd be working with a medical equipment company, pending his graduation. It was no surprise he'd successfully completed his Ph.D. I had thought this dream of working for the IMF and getting an economics Ph.D. had long passed when I'd gotten sick and the brutal months recovering that followed, but Oskar had revived it. It was scary to move and scarier to rekindle dreams you thought long gone, but exhilarating, too. Maybe it would come alive, and perhaps it wouldn't. I knew I had Oskar's support to pursue it either way.

And here we were, about to move together to another city where Oskar would be starting his job in just one week. Our new insurance was already lined up. I'd already scheduled an appointment with a new rheumatologist there months ago, so I could see her two months after moving to DC. If I wasn't happy, I'd fly back here to see my old one, or go to Hopkins, one of the best lupus hospitals in the nation.

I was going to be fine.

Some of my long-held fears had melted under Oskar's love. We hadn't decided about adoption yet, but we both thought it might be in our future, one day. Now, we were moving to a tiny apartment in DC. For a while, it'd just be the three of us with our first wedding anniversary approaching.

Oskar had sold his car, and we would be using the Fiat.

I'd be walking to school. I was anxious, yet hopeful. In this last year, I hadn't had any bad episodes. I still took my medicine, but my lupus was finally considered in remission. Maybe because I wasn't so scared anymore. When I needed rest, Oskar respected that. If I got sick, I would deal with it. If the vampire inside me reared its ugly head, I knew Oskar would be there battling it beside me. And that knowledge gave me the calm that had been critical in keeping my lupus and other issues in check.

Oskar had become my rock, and I never regretted our simple ceremony in the civil service office. I never regretted our backwards honeymoon and traveling when we could.

The trip had been amazing, and we may never have four weeks of travel again. I smiled as he pulled out in front with the U-Haul, and moved to follow him in my tiny car after turning on my audiobook. I'd always be me, vampires and all, and finally, that was okay.

I sighed and petted Bea as I drove down my oak-lined street for the last time towards a new adventure.

About the Author

Liz Hsu has a deep love of traveling, the people of the world and their dynamic histories, and reading and writing. She holds a B.A. from John Cabot University, Rome, in addition to a Master's in Teaching Secondary Social Studies and World History from Georgia State University. She taught world social studies for five years in Atlanta, her hometown. She now lives in Michigan with her Chinese-American husband, daughter, and adorable Pomeranian. Liz tries to write inclusive romance, because we are all capable of love and being loved in return.

For more information about the conditions discussed, the author, and upcoming books please visit www.lizhsubooks.com.

Please consider leaving an honest review on Amazon & Goodreads — It is so appreciated!

Acknowledgments

To my readers, thank you for choosing my book! I hope you enjoyed reading it as much as I did drafting it on the ten year anniversary of my SLE diagnosis. Please consider writing a quick review—it is so appreciated.

It is estimated there are 30 million American women with an autoimmune disease. Lupus is the #10 killer in all women 15-24. I wanted our voices to be heard. I hope it inspires you to remember the end is yet unwritten and the sun will always come up tomorrow (Lupies grab the SPF). We all have the ability to become the hero in our own stories.

For my parents, I know you have always believed in me, loved me, and supported me. Thank you. To my best friends, Kate (Paola), Matt (Michael), and Ashton (Ru) you are my support system through thick and thin. Vi voglio bene. And above all to my husband, Eugene, the most wonderful and special person in my life, who gives me strength and CALM every day. While you can do anything alone, friends, family, and love are what make life worth living and fighting for.

Big thank you to my writing village, GDRWA. You inspired and embraced me. You told me I could do it. You made me laugh about corndogs, silver foxes, and so much more. Also shout out to both the Troy Library and Oakland County Writers' groups. Phil Skiff and Sarah LoCascio, you helped me get my awards for my two #ownvoices books with your encouragement, tears, and critiques. So many thanks.

To the editors—it took a team, because you guys are just too successful! Thank you for fitting me in while you still took clients. My beta reader, Katherine Locke, thank you for all the help in making this MUCH better, clearer, and a more exciting story. And for recommending Gwen Hayes—she, and *Romancing the Beat*—beat this into shape. Rachel Lynn Solomon it was a great pleasure to have you edit this work. I always appreciate your insight and love your positivity. Thank you. C.K. Brooke you caught those pesky last faults and smoothed the edges. Thanks a million.